JOSHUA

HADASSAH POMEROY

ABOUT THE AUTHOR

Hadassah Pomeroy was born in Tel-Aviv in Israel and is married with three children.

She served with the Israeli Air Force for two years. Hadassah speaks five languages.

Hadassah resided in Singapore working as a freelance interpreter and translator, and found Singapore to be an exhilarating place to live. Amongst her other activities she also taught Hebrew and English.

Accompanied by an anthropologist-doctor and a cameraman, she navigated up the mighty river Amazon in an old tug boat. This was a once in a lifetime experience, involving extensive contacts and meetings with the South American Indians.

Some time was spent with the four foot pygmies in the Ituri Forest of the Belgian Congo. She hunted with them, but hunting there was for survival not for sport. They were a thrilling people.

In addition she had an exciting time living with the Bushmen of the Kalahari desert.

In Australia she composed ballads and a light operetta. She has also written two musicals, several short stories and a play (Unpublished). At present she is working on other music.

- -

"I am deeply indebted to Robert Thomas and would like to extend my very sincere thanks to him for helping me, especially with his knowledge of old wooden ships and 16th/17th century sloops, and the use of nautical terms and practices, but most of all for his patience, perseverance and loyalty."

- -

First published in Australia 2011
This edition published 2011
Copyright © Hadassah Pomeroy 2011
Cover design, typesetting: Chameleon Print Design

The right of Hadassah Pomeroy to be identified as the Author of the Work has been asserted in accordance with the Copyright, Designs and Patents Act 1988.

Pomeroy, Hadassah
Joshua
EAN13: 978-0-646-56533-0
pp334

FOREWORD

If every oak beam of the old slaver could talk – if rope and sail could comfort the stolen children of Africa – if masts, crossbeams and rigging could whisper – if crosstrees on high and spars could hear the frightened young in the dark holds – if bower anchor, bulwarks, bilges and scuppers could expel the venom of the ship then every part of it would lament the plaintive cries of the bereft little ones.

Page 95

CHAPTER 1

The rain beat upon the three hundred and forty wretched slaves, who painfully shuffled their feet. They were chained neck to neck in iron collars and the men separated from the women and children. The long file of males led the way in one coffle, followed by the second consisting of the women and children, all making their tortuous way through the dense rainforest. Every so often one could hear the swish of the cat o' nine tails. The beautiful and majestic mahoganies almost two hundred feet high towered over all the other trees. The tinge of yellows and reddish browns mingled with copper was a breathtaking phantasmagoria of colours. Many of the trees had buttresses at the base of their trunks with deep recesses where forest animals took shelter. Among the raffia and rotten plants a female Mono monkey was cleaning her young. The weird dirge of giant frogs was heard on the decaying floor. Many villages were deserted as slave traders pursued their prey, hunting for black cargo. Forked lightning lacerated the sky, followed by roaring crashes of thunder. The rain came down harder and harder lashing upon their naked bodies.

The Cameroons is a mountainous country. From its north-west loom chains of rugged mountains and plateaus; from the south-west, the forests.

Nagamba shivered, clutching her infant to her bosom. The iron collar round her slender neck began to chaff her skin, forming small blisters. The drops of rain ran down her back in pursuit of each other, trickled to her buttocks and then descended her thighs and feet, ending in little puddles. On her right ankle she had a snake-shaped copper bangle. Her face was hidden, and she held her two-month old son with fear. He was wailing with all the strength of his lungs, anguished cries of hunger and discomfort. The baby was wrapped in tattered rags, saturated and cold.

The rain stopped and for a few seconds silence reigned, except for the rattling of chains and the squelching of bare feet dragging on the soggy ground. The route to Benin, the chief slave market, was a merciless one, five hundred miles away.

Encumbered by heavy loads, they trekked their way through tangled masses of gigantic ferns, thorny vines, and hanging, looping lianas choked with parasitic plants. The roof of the forest was speckled with exquisitely colourful orchids, caressed by the sun shining through the trees. A group of mandrills screeched, swinging from branch to branch. A pair of Cameroon Picathaites chirped.

From afar, the wild trumpets of bull elephants were heard. Several of the male slaves carried heavy ivory tusks on their shoulders. They were of the finest ivory; some exceeding two hundred pounds in weight. Endless herds of elephants were pursued and killed during the rutting season, their tusks sold to European slavers on the coast bound for Europe, the West Indies and the New World.

The female slaves carried calabashes filled with kola nuts, ground nuts, palm oil and millet. From their mothers' swaying hips hung babies with beady eyes propped up from their slings. The very young cried and whimpered; others sucked or toyed with the colourful tassels. The older children trudged behind. Nagamba looked around in utter despair.

She remembered the Fang tribe raiding their village,

while she was having an evening meal with her husband Kumbo. It happened so swiftly and a new terror swept across the rainforests. The Fang came in like swarms of bees, attacking from all directions, hunting for slaves. The old and sick they dismembered. Like vampires, with the sharp points of filed incisor teeth, they went berserk at the scent of blood. They tore out the hearts and sliced open the testicles and ate them, coagulate and pendulous spermatic cords hanging from their lips. The feast culminated in a macabre dance, blood dripping over the tribeman's distended stomachs and semi-erect sexual organs. The rest of the slaves were chained and marched away in two coffles.

Nagamba trembled. For a moment she thought she saw Kumbo, but the long column soon disappeared in the dense bush.

'Move on, move on,' shouted Eboua, the chief Fang slave trader, as his whip lashed near Nagamba's feet. She stooped and whimpered.

'Be quiet woman.' He ground his teeth in a vice-like grip, his eyes filled with lust. He had a large mole on the tip of his nose and part of his ear was lopped off. He was grotesque. She looked at her son. His tiny nose was buried in the curve of her breast and his little hand cupped her warmth as he sucked. Suddenly he wailed. She squeezed her dark nipples. Only a few drops trickled. There was no milk in her breasts. Alarmed she broke into a cold sweat. She touched his feet; they were clammy and cold. He had not been fed for several hours. His face had turned to ashen grey.

Towards evening they reached a small clearing at the edge of the forest, and her son lay on the ground lifeless. Her body was numb, and she felt utterly alone as she lifted him, clutching the infant to her bosom, to generate some of her warmth into his small body. It was a forlorn hope. The infant was dead and Nagamba wished for death herself. Her husband and child were now gone from her.

'He wouldn't have survived,' whispered her friend Alimba. 'We better bury him now.' Nagamba knelt on her aching knees. Clawing in quick succession she ripped a hole, removing more earth. Blood oozed from under her broken nails. The pregnant Alimba bent and helped. Nagamba mumbled and muttered incoherent words. She placed her son down gently, covering him first with stones, then with earth that felt warm and moist.

She ached and wished to reach out and hold her little one, buried alone in the large forest. Her mind shrunk with horror at the thought of how dark it must be for the child with only the worms for company. Nagamba laid her wrecked body upon the tiny grave until the first light of dawn. For the first time in her life she froze with fear, and hatred for the evil ones who had brought tragedy upon her.

CHAPTER 2

For three hundred years the anguished African cry of slavery was unheeded. The Europeans snatched her black children. Bloody hands tore her womb open like a diseased festering wound. Throughout the shores of West Africa, thousands of slaves were sold and shipped across the Atlantic to the New World, the West Indies and Brazil. African chiefs, kings and slave traders bartered with the white men in exchange for muskets, gunpowder, tools, rum, gin, salt, tobacco, and trinkets for their women: perfumes, cotton, mirrors and endless other goods. The prices of slaves fetched twice as much in Benin than in any other neighbouring slave markets.

The two coffles of slaves walked for many days. The heavy mist hung like a shroud. The forest sang with incessant insects, the dirge of frogs and other strange noises of the night.

Nagamba lay at the far end of the batch of female slaves. It was dark. Eboua approached, his wild features peering down. She was terrified. He unlocked the large padlock with his key, slipped the chain through and undid the neck manacles dragging her firmly by the waist into the bushes.

Eboua grunted.

'No! No!' Nagamba struggled to free herself, and felt his hot breath. Eboua sneered, his nose twitched, dripping with sweat as he spreadeagled her on the ground. He then ripped off her scanty waist garment, pulled off his loin cloth and threw it aside, standing stark naked, his legs slightly apart. She was petrified; overpowered with numbness. His powerful body towered over Nagamba. Eboua pounced and launched himself with full force. Saliva drooled from his mouth and she felt his protruding mole with revulsion. He forced her thighs open; his clumsy hands cupped her firm round breasts. Then, with a tremendous stroke he penetrated. She whimpered with pain; his thrusts were getting stronger and faster until he climaxed. She remained limp, feeling abused and raw inside. For a few seconds he covered her; then, with a sudden jerk he rose, spat and looked for his rags. Nagamba was faint and dizzy; a vile odour emanated from him. Sweat, mingled with semen, trickled down her thighs. She felt nauseated and vomited, filled with loathing for this disgusting animal. Consumed with hatred, she abhorred the abomination of slavery, and needed Kumbo, her husband, who was with the other gang of slaves.

'Get up.' Eboua kicked and pushed her towards the sleepy coffle and replaced the neck manacles.

At dawn, shafts of light filtered through the trees and screeching monkeys leaped from branch to branch. The hippopotamus whip whistled across the air.

'We move now,' yelled the guard and spat thick phlegm.

During long marches the slaves were given kola nuts. They sustained energy levels. Nagamba opened her small leather pouch and took out two wrinkled green ones. She tore at the dry skin, pulled six white nuts and started to chew.

༄

'Have you seen my wife and children, Ebouko and Marufa?' Bundere uttered an anguished cry.

'Yes, I saw Mahadana walking in front with them,' said Gashaka. He was Nagamba's brother.

The heat was almost unbearable. Many of the children had contracted dysentery. Nagamba kept looking ahead to see if Kumbo was there in the male coffle.

In the afternoon, they camped near a gallery of mahogany trees. The sky was crimson, streaked with orange and yellows. It rapidly sank and the ball of fire became smaller and smaller to a mere speck and vanished. Darkness fell over the land after sunset, the way it had always been in Africa.

The slaves in the male coffle spoke in whispers.

'Every group of twelve is guarded by one caboceer,' Kumbo whispered to Gashaka, Bundere and Moshebere, chained to each other with iron collars.

'Each gang has a padlock with a key. They use the same key for all the padlocks.' Gashaka added. 'It's the same one for the women. Eboua the sadistic one is in charge of all the gangs.'

'We must grab a key,' Kumbo muttered. 'Most of the guards sit around the fires at night, and fill themselves with rum. Eventually they fall asleep drunk, except one who spends a few hours walking between the rows of slaves, til the next one arrives for his watch.'

Gashaka took a long deep breath. 'Somehow, we've got to trick and lure him towards us. In order to do that we must work together and overpower the guard.'

'I have an idea,' said Kumbo. 'To attract the attention of the guard, we can talk about the subject of gold we hid, and pretend we're unaware of him listening so close by, but we have to be convincing.'

'Tricky but it might work,' nodded Gashaka. 'We'll plan it for tomorrow night. Alert all the others. Be careful, the caboceer's approaching.' They huddled on the ground and feigned sleep.

＊

The following morning the slaves shuffled through a stretch of grassy plains when they came across two small brackish water holes. A pair of marabou storks feasted on giant frogs, honking and tooting. They tore and pulled ferociously with their enormous yellow bills, their bare necks and heads totally covered, in between their slate wings. Several water hogs wallowed and rolled in the mud sending whiffs of dust over their greyish hairless hides with their curved tusks. A lonely bateleur eagle rode the wind with superb aerial acrobatics gliding through the warm air currents. It hovered over the sparse bush for a long time. Suddenly the bird arched its powerful magnificent chest, flapped its black wings, and disappeared over the horizon. Something caught at Nagamba's throat. She desperately wanted to cry, and fought back her tears.

'If anything should happen to me,' Kumbo murmured with a tremor. 'Take care of Nagamba.' The wretched and miserable slaves continued marching towards the giant trees. Evening braced her cloak once more over the looming forests. The guards and caboceers, inebriated with liquor, snored around the glowing fires. Their muskets, machetes and swords lay beside them.

'The guard is approaching our file,' Kumbo said in a sibilant tone. 'I'll start whispering about the treasure when he's near.'

The man came closer.

'Our chest of gold is well-hidden in the rocks,' said Kumbo

in a staged whisper. 'No one will ever find it. If we get out of this situation, although that is doubtful, we'll be rich for the rest of our lives, but should they sell us in the slave market, the gold will be locked away for ever. Such a treasure ...'

The guard halted. Kumbo lifted his head, as the guard stepped forward.

'Gold?' the guard queried. Kumbo hesitated for a few seconds. The guard repeated, 'You have gold?'

There was silence.

'I could lead you back to your familiar territory and you lead me to the treasure and you'll be free. Then we shall split the gold in half.' He bent over and stumbled in the dark.

Kumbo pounced and looped the chain around the guard's neck while Gashaka pulled from the other side, tightening and breaking the guard's neck. It snapped like a twig. Gashaka snatched the key from the dead man and unlocked the chaffing padlock around Kumbo.

Gashaka grabbed the guard's musket, a knife from his belt, and gave the key to Kumbo. One by one the slaves slid the length of chain through the rings. Kumbo, silent as a grave, methodically prized open several padlocks. Gashaka followed him when suddenly the guard on watch appeared. They all froze. The hush was nerve-racking,. They lay in wait. Once the guard passed the unshackled slaves Kumbo dived for his legs, bringing him down. Gashaka pierced the base of the guard's skull with the point of his knife, ground it upwards and it entered his brain. The guard let out a final breath.

To their horror, the clanking chains and the scuffle had woken Eboua. He kicked and yelled at the guards sprawled around the fires. Confused, they trampled and moved in all directions. Gashaka, lurking with Kumbo behind a tree, pressed the trigger of his musket and launched his deadly strike at the staggering guard.

'Let's go and free the women,' Kumbo said. Eboua spotted them and gave chase. 'You go to the right; I'll distract him and run in the opposite direction.' To elude capture, Kumbo, with the agility of a young buck, spurted through the thick undergrowth. Eboua blindly pursued his tracks, panting.

'They are coming fast.' Moshebere grabbed Alimba by the hand in desperation and kissed her. Kumbo, on eagles' wings, reached Nagamba. She rushed and clung to her man. He was out of breath.

'Where's Bundere?' Moshebere whispered. Like an arrow Bundere appeared from behind a clump of bushes and clasped his wife and children. The slaves' collar was hinged on one side with a padlocked hasp. Moshebere and Bundere, using a communal key, released and opened the fifty collars of the escaped slaves.

'I must go and find Gashaka, run, run to the north immediately,' urged Kumbo. Bewildered, he looked around at Nagamba. 'Where's the baby?'

'I had no milk. The little one lived for only a few hours. I buried him beside a tree.' She looked at her husband. 'I'm not leaving you,' she pleaded.

Immediately, Moshebere, Bundere, their wives and two children fled in panic with other slaves. Nagamba and Kumbo slouched behind the tall reeds. A guard crept near them.

'I can smell the vermin'. Within seconds Kumbo hurled himself like a leopard, twisted the man's jaw and dug the sword into his ribs.

The cacophony of guards and slaves set the teeth on edge. Kumbo knew that Gashaka was hiding near. With the eyes of a lynx and ears of a hare, both waited and listened. Eboua was on their trail. Long ago in the Cameroons, Kumbo remembered that when hunting wild game with his brother they would imitate a certain night owl. Gashaka smiled. With mincing steps he crawled towards the welcome sound.

'They are all around,' said Kumbo in a plaintive muffle. 'Take Nagamba to the North, I'll zigzag and confuse them. I have wings on my feet.' He melted away, but Eboua's raucous growl was heard at a distance; they dared not move. Nagamba shook like an aspen leaf. Eboua came closer,

'Let's split,' he bellowed. Within an hour the faint streaks of dawn brushed the canopy of the forest. Eboua approached the tall bush and prodded his musket. It hit Nagamba's shoulder painfully but she managed to remain still and quiet. He struck the butt of his gun again and lunged blindly near Gashaka's groin. With searing pains Gashaka clutched his abdomen. Eboua peered inside the tall reeds and uttered a terrifying shrill. Nagamba gaped at Gashaka with terror in her eyes.

Eboua shouted to the guards. 'Chain them to the other slaves. Now I have to find someone else; he couldn't have fled very far.' He lashed the whip across Gashaka's legs. Eboua was an expert tracker. A swollen vein twitched on his temples; he could detect a broken twig, a bent leaf, a crushed insect. His sense of smell was acute, but primarily he used his keen perception and sharpness of eyes and ears. He was determined to catch Kumbo.

Eboua was furious. Traces of ground nuts were spread around with peeled kola nuts and strips of tangled hair on parasitic plants. He ran faster and faster.

The undulations and slithering movement of the black mamba were camouflaged by the thick undergrowth. Eboua stepped on it with his full bulky weight. Instantly the snake inflated its neck, hissed and struck just above his ankle. It was eight feet in length with various shades of grey. Eboua felt the searing bite and instinctively tried to kick it. Being provoked, the snake attacked Eboua's right thigh with lightning speed, again injecting venom from its long fangs. It then slithered away and disappeared into a hole of a rotten stump.

Eboua leaned against a tree, took out his small knife in his leather sheath and quickly cut open around the two fang punctures, letting the blood flow for a few seconds. Within minutes he felt a terrible itching and burning sensation. Eboua knew how fatal the bite of the black mamba was. He felt faint and looked up at the trees. Dizziness overcame him. Perched on a branch above, a pair of bulbuls preened themselves, scattered their tiny feathers and droppings around him. Nausea and weakness seized his body. He got up, took a few paces forward, spat violently, saliva flowing from his mouth. His ears started to drum painfully; he covered them with his hands screaming, running wildly. The eyes and base of his tongue became numb. He had difficulty in blinking. Paralysis spread over his chin, lips, and down to his throat. He fell to his knees, convulsing, and slumped on his back. All sensations of toes and fingers ceased. He gasped, stretching his blank wide open eyes, the irises floating in white pools. The tremors became fewer. Within an hour Eboua was dead.

CHAPTER 3

I can't go on, I can't,' Alimba panted, leaning on Moshebere. 'I must sit down.' She slumped near a bed of giant toadstools, clutching her hands beneath her lower pelvis.

'Let me feel, the child is kicking and strong,' Moshebere smiled. The band of fugitives crouched beneath the umbrella trees discussing where to head.

'We should steer inland away from the coast,' Bundere murmured. 'Meanwhile we will converge near the river'. A steamy shroud hung over the bronze water. Towards noon the heavy mist dispersed. Across the muddy bank crocodiles basked motionless, protecting their clutches of eggs, ready to hatch. A herd of hippopotami swam with their young.

'There's good game here.' Moshebere turned to the men. 'Let's cut thick saplings.' With fast nimble fingers they hacked and shaved fine six-foot tapered spears. Bundere stayed behind watching the women and children paddling in the cool water.

'Don't wander too far,' he called out. The air was filled with giggling and laughter of the young. Bundere watched his wife bathing. He approached and led Mahadana to the bulrushes and in a moment of passion he took her. Moshebere, further up the river spotted a few finfoots.

The men stalked some finfoots behind a straggling fig tree and thrust their long spears with deadly accuracy into their necks. The others fled. Their elongated bodies and necks spattered on the water to the other side of the river and took cover among the tall reeds. The five birds they had caught were tied together with thick vines, swinging and dangling on their shoulders. Several Mono monkeys leaped from tree to tree and Moshebere impaled one.

'It's getting late,' he said.

Towards evening they sat around a small fire. The women roasted the birds and monkeys brains.

At the break of dawn they maintained a northerly course. There was a gibbous moon when the first labour pains started. Moshebere sat beside his wife.

'I'll rub your back, it will help somewhat.' He looked grave and concerned.

Through the night Alimba wrestled with the pangs of giving birth. Contractions became stronger and more frequent. The uterus began to contract; she uttered little whimpers, and was drenched with perspiration. Moshebere sponged her forehead with water. She bit her fingers and flung her head backwards.

'Bundere, come and help me.' Several other slaves rushed in with him.

Alimba shrieked.

'Hold her hands and legs,' cried Moshebere. The women prepared hot water and strips of swaddling hanging on two staves.

'Fight for the little one,' Moshebere pleaded and brushed his lips upon her flushed cheeks.

'Moshebere,' she groaned, in the throes of agonising cramps. The women all stared at the miraculous sight before them. The amnion burst with a gush. With each strong muscular contraction of the uterus the cervix gradually dilated revealing a small tuft of hair on the infant's head as he was finally expelled into the world.

Moshebere held the child and took the small bush knife from the heated earthen vessel, cooled it for a few seconds, and then cut the umbilical cord, tying a neat small knot. One of the women swabbed the baby's body with oil and laid him on Alimba's breast. Moshebere put his hands on her soft belly and felt the distinct small feeble movements of the second baby. Alimba was exhausted. He feared for her life. Moshebere had delivered a variety of animals in his village and he was fully aware of the fatal dangers involving a breech birth, both for mother and child.

'If I don't turn the child to the right position, and quick, there is danger. Alimba is very weak. I must act now.'

With his long tapered fingers he felt the baby's buttocks struggling. He tried to turn the infant into the head-down position but realised the chances were slim. Without hesitation he grabbed for the baby's bunched legs and with extreme caution pulled them straight, sliding the whole body through the narrow passage. With a gush of fluid Moshebere held the infant by its feet, waiting for his first cry. The combined mewl of the twin boys at Alimba's breast shivered on the lofty pillars of the forest.

Kumbo ran for several hours, bruised and lacerated. He kept going til dawn; exhausted, ravenous and thirsty. Finally he rested under an umbrella tree; his feet were bleeding. A small lizard scurried near his big toe. He grabbed and tore it in half and started chewing. Drowsiness overcame him; his eyelids were heavy with sleep. He curled into a ball and was carried into a world with blurred shapes and forms.

'I want ten men in search of Eboua and the slaves who escaped,' the caboceer ordered.

The guards scouted in a semi-circle. 'There are fresh footprints a few hours old I would say,' said the first and followed a narrow trail with excrement.

'One of them passed here, it could have been Eboua,' shouted the second man.

They found Eboua a mile away, his right leg turned bluish-black and bloated. His nostrils, eyeballs and open mouth crawled with maggots. A foul stench exuded from the putrid corpse.

'Look at the leg; mamba. Those snakes are very quick.' The caboceer inched forward. The guards covered the bloody corpse with twigs and leaves and set off.

'There are dry blood stains on these ferns,' one of them hissed. 'Hurry'.

<hr>

Kumbo was fast asleep. His dreams were startled by shooting pains from above his kidneys where the cat o' nine tails flayed him. Kumbo's eyes flew open. He looked at the guard in defiance and spat in his face. The man with daggers snarled.

'Line all the slaves to watch!'

They tied Kumbo to a gnarled wide stump. The guard smirked, prodding his long stick at the safari ants. They gave off an offensive smell.

He threw the branch on the black quivering jelly. Nagamba guessed his evil mind. She tried to wrench herself but the collar was tight and the chains were fastened to the other slaves. The harder she tried, more blisters formed on her neck. At the top of her terrified voice she shrieked.

'Savage murderers!'

Kumbo watched her; he wanted to live, but knew his life would soon end. He loved his wife.

'Never forget this day,' the caboceer sniggered. Kumbo remembered when the safari ants were on the rampage years ago. They advanced by the millions across the two hills. Kumbo faced the cloudless sky; the ants crawled in his ears, nostrils, mouth and eyes. Within minutes they gouged the eyeballs revealing two sockets to which they tunnelled themselves in. Their long jaws, like pincers, were tearing and clawing at his testicles. He tried to scream but couldn't. His throat was filled with ants. They flayed his skin and bore into his flesh. Nagamba fainted. In the throes of death, Kumbo envisioned the avenue of hibiscus and grand lobelias. A light shone and Nagamba emerged. He tried to grasp her but she faded away. Then, total darkness.

'I shall avenge this day,' Gashaka vowed.

During the following weeks the train of slaves trudged towards Calabar. Nagamba looked with breathless stupor at the vast expanse of blue-green sea. She had never seen the ocean. The surf was bursting and pounding white spin-drift against the rocks. A Brigantine and a Cutter ran down the coast. The sky was attired in her pink gown. What lay beyond the stretch of water, Nagamba wondered. Where was Mahadana, Alimba and the rest? The ants boring at Kumbo's tongue ... She covered her face with her hands.

In the afternoon the slaves sat under the coconut trees. A lonely fisherman pulled his boat on to the beach and spread his nets to dry. Screeching noddies flew above. The caboceer snarled at them, scratching his filthy lice-ridden hair.

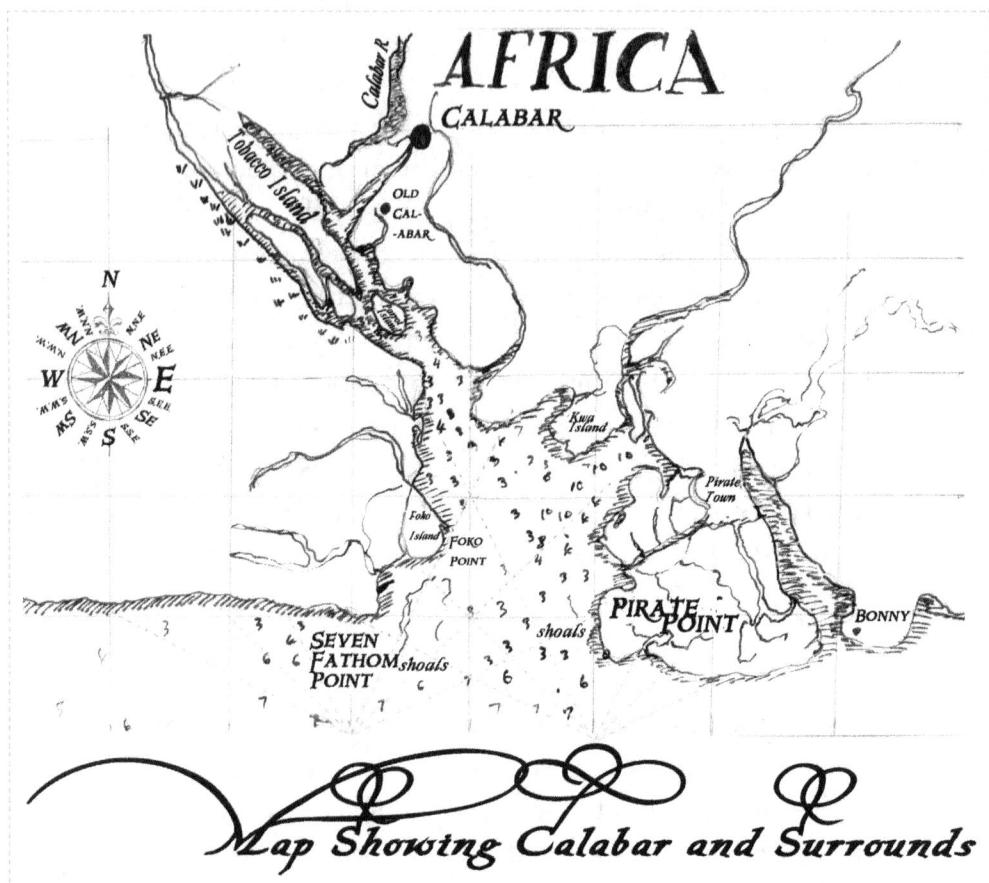

Map Showing Calabar and Surrounds

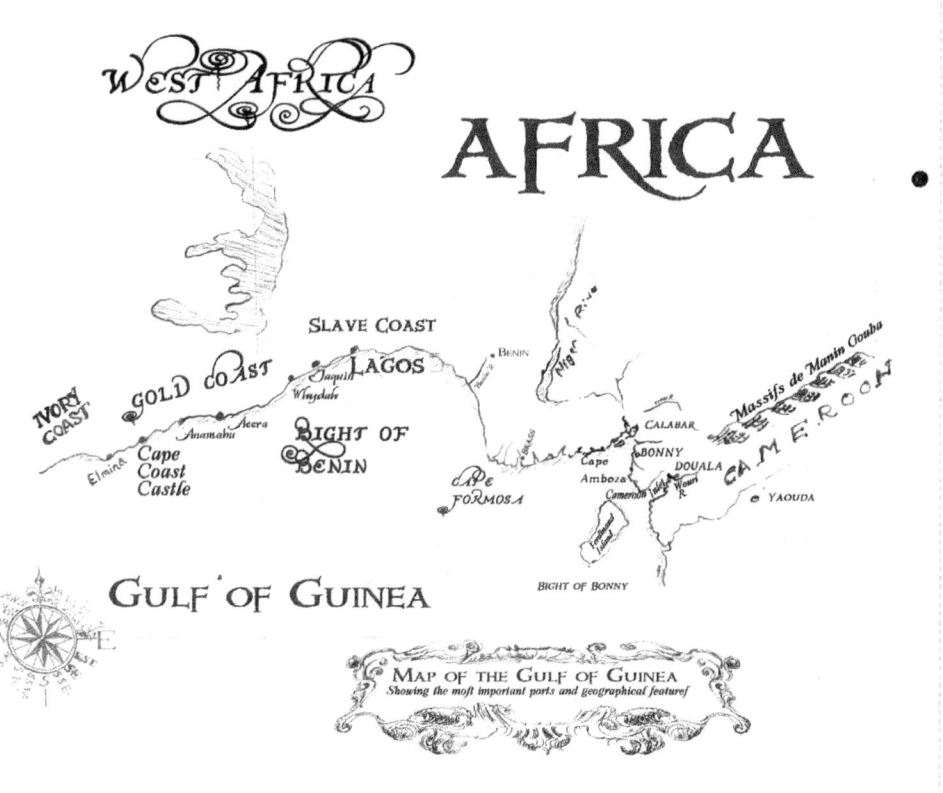

MAP OF THE GULF OF GUINEA
Showing the moft important ports and geographical featuref

CHAPTER 4

'Fire the guns, three times for the old buzzard,' smiled Captain Joshua Quaile to his first mate. 'We'll anchor for a few days.'

'Yes, sir.' Saluting with great confidence, the mate swung round to face the gunnery officer across the deck. 'Three for Chief Atakanga.'

The four hundred and fifty ton brigantine 'Hurricane' opened fire with her thirty-six guns.

'Now, that's what I call a real salute,' the mate chuckled as the Royal African Company's flag was hoisted up on the foretop-gallant mast. With a tremendous splash the bower anchor dropped into sixty feet of water. It was a breezy day, scudding clouds chasing each other. The chorus of gulls and terns was deafening as they flew around the Hurricane to feast on scraps thrown overboard. Gannets dived a hundred feet, hitting the surface with tremendous force, catching a variety of fish. Several hungry sharks circled the vessel to partake in the hunt.

There were five other vessels, one a brig under full sail. Cape Coast Castle was clearly visible in the distance when the first puff of smoke signals rose in the sky.

'I am going ashore to stay for a few nights in the fort,' said Captain Quaile. 'Looks like they've some merchandise for us. I must see the old buzzard; he promised me a good supply of slaves from the interior. It's imperative; our last consignment was a great loss. Remember how many perished from the dreaded flux?'

Smoke Trading was the most convenient way of palavers between the natives and European slavers who anchored offshore. The turbulent Atlantic swell, treacherous currents and perpetual foaming white surf made it impossible to anchor near the shore of the Gold Coast: firing of salutes by gunfire, answered by smoke signals, meant trade.

'Here is the list of goods.' The first mate unrolled the long sheet of paper, handing it to the captain.

He scrutinised with great diligence the items listed. 'Fifty casks of rum, fifty barrels of brandy, cutlasses, tallow, muskets, gunpowder, knives, axes, pewter bowls, cotton, linen, beads, mirrors, five crates of nails, handkerchiefs, perfumes, tobacco, iron bars, copper bars …' The captain paused, smoothed his red bushy beard; the silence seemed endless as he finished perusing the contents. He then addressed his first mate.

'I'll speak to the chief; see what he requires, the sly one. We must reserve some of our goods for other forts and slave markets.'

Within half an hour two native canoes came along her starboard side. They were broad-beamed and round-bottomed, built for the conditions prevailing on the shores of the west coast of Africa.

'By God, how they take the swell, what precision in carving, don't you agree?' Captain Quaile turned to face the first mate leaning against the bulwarks. 'Those Krumen natives are wonderful oarsmen. Look at their superb physiques.'

Captain Quaile, his first mate and bosun descended a wide rope ladder. They sat at the rear of the canoe as the naked Krumen rowed back to the beach. The Krumen tribes were fishermen along the Gold Coast, ebony tall figures. They were the most vital means of transporting slaves from the beaches to the vessels anchored offshore.

The golden shores were fringed with palm trees swaying in the breeze. Slender-built, sooty-coloured noddies soared above the surf and a coffle of slaves entered the fort just as the canoe reached the shore. Cape Coast Castle was originally built by Swedish traders and later taken forcibly by the British who extended it into a massive stone construction, built by the English for the slave trade and as an administrative centre for the Gold Coast. The impregnable walls of the castle jutting out to sea like the face of a great steep rock were very high, constantly pounded by the restless Atlantic swell, riding white horses. From the top of the walls several large guns pointed over the bay. High from the bastion the English flag flew.

'Smell them musky niggers, a heap of jumping baboons,' exclaimed the first mate. 'They're brainless, and belong to the tribe of Ham.'

Ever since Captain Quaile was involved in the Triangular Trade between England, the West Indies and Africa, his sole concern was to ship and sell slaves. He had been doing this successfully for the last ten years, since 1686 when he assumed command of the Hurricane.

'From the days of Noah they were cursed,' the first mate lashed out vindictively.

'Bloody fool,' mumbled Captain Quaile to himself. He did not feel any particular hatred towards them; they were his quick means for prosperity. He had shipped thousands and thousands of slaves to the West Indies, Bahama Islands, Jamaica, St Kitts, Nevis, Barbados and Monserrat.

Two European factors from the Royal African Company,

one caboceer and three African traders greeted them as they reached the shore. The caboceer and one of the traders went over to the boat for a ride to the Hurricane to inspect the goods Captain Quaile had brought to trade.

'Captain Quaile, how does England fare these days? It seems an eternity since I came to this god-forsaken, rotten dirty hole.' The factor grimaced. 'Forgive this outburst. Chief Atakanga wishes to see you in the central hall.' The sallow, wizened-looking factor scratched his scabby face.

'What does he have to offer us this time?' Captain Quaile asked, walking at a slow pace towards the pristine fort, followed by his first mate and the bosun.

'A good supply he has from Ashanti, also some Fanti from Kumasi and from Fort Commenda, Mandingos, I believe,' the factor replied.

With the shifting breeze Captain Quaile could smell the factor's foul, vile breath; his front teeth were tarnished and stained from tobacco and years of neglect.

'You should see those wenches and young bucks, by golly. They are strong and can endure long working hours on sugar plantations, There's also a great demand for Fanti and Ashanti, reputed to be magnificent field hands.'

'Also prone to be leaders of insurrection,' butted in Quaile. 'We had to watch them like hawks on our previous voyage, and had to chain them for six weeks in the stinking bilges til we reached the Indies. Now take the Mandingos; good-tempered and make excellent metalworkers and coopers … have one on my ship, very reliable, helps the cooper. Good breeders as well.' He smiled.

Chiefs, kings, factors, traders, middlemen, merchants, caboceers and slaving captains disputed, jostled, and haggled over prices, arguing and inspecting their human cargo. Eight hundred and ninety slaves stood in the scorching sun, bewildered and frightened. A sickening smell of burning flesh and sweaty bodies hung in the air.

'What a bloody stench, I shall never get used to this, no matter how many times I witness such scenes,' spat the mate with revolting green phlegm.

In the far corner of the courtyard, traders and caboceers had started branding the slaves that had been sold with red-hot irons. Women and children screamed. Men were branded on their chests and women on their buttocks with the Royal African Company's trading initials 'DY' (Duke of York).

In 1663 King Charles II chartered the Company of Royal Adventurers Trading to Africa, under the patronage of James, Duke of York, later King James II. That company collapsed five years later with great losses and was replaced in 1672 by the Royal African Company, chartered using the same brand of DY in this year of our Lord 1687.

'Look at those angry ghastly weals and filthy flies crawling all over them; they would heal much quicker with the silver brands than with those wretched hot irons. I must speak to the general agent about this, the fool.' Captain Quaile was furious

'I believe he is now with Chief Atakanga,' exclaimed one of the factors.

'Let's get into the cool.' Quaile peered at the long flight of stairs, jerked his head and ran all the way to the lovely arcaded balcony. He entered the sumptuous hall.

There were several heavy damask-upholstered chairs and sofas around the room and from the tall windows hung gaudy pink velvet curtains that were brought from England by passing ships.

Four captains, one factor, merchants, middlemen and two chiefs were busy negotiating and disputing over slaves, ivory and gold dust. Here palavers and treaties were agreed upon and signed between the presiding governor-general and the local African potentates.

'I say, Captain Quaile, your brigantine looks a splendid ship in the offing,' said Benjamin Doncaster, a factor of the Royal African Company. 'I hear you're sailing to Jamaica. I'm going there as well on the Salome. I'm responsible for ship inspections.' He sipped some rum punch and wiped his long moustache with his embroidered silk handkerchief.

Quaile lit his pipe and said, 'The old ship might be a splendid sight, but she's sprung bad leaks in the after hold quite recently. The carpenter is demanding extra pay because the first mate keeps waking him up, sometimes several times a night, to cork the leaks. Some copper sheets are missing after we hit a rock near Port Royal on our last trip, and that's giving us problems.'

'Is it that bad?' asked Doncaster.

'Yes, in fact, the carpenter is going to install more shelves in the other holds because I am not going to put any slaves down there; we'll lose too many. It's making the whole operation less profitable for the Company.'

'I think that's the same complaint I hear from so many captains who want to transport more slaves of their own, and put profit into their own pocket. They make silly excuses for why they can't transport a reasonable number of slaves for the Company. I'll see you in Port Royal and if you don't have enough profit on your books, I'll make sure your operation is handed over to someone else.'

Captain Quaile grumbled to himself, *Weasely little mongrel;*

a petty little bureaucrat who thinks he's a bull with horns. He then addressed the factor.

'I do hope she'll survive the journey. I still have to sail to Benin, and then on to Jamaica. I believe the Hurricane's days are numbered.' Quaile took a deep breath, then pointed at the factor and said, 'I'm documenting everything, you know. The ship's carpenter has marked every defect, and the mate has witnessed it with his signature. If anything happens, you won't have a bloody leg to stand on.' The factor frowned and walked off to join several of the other captains.

Quaile turned to the first mate. 'Make sure you put it all in writing.'

Chief Atakanga strode into the room and smiled at Captain Quaile. The two men faced each other, faintly smiling. They were from two different worlds, yet drawn together: the tall blue-eyed bushy red-bearded captain from Bristol and the muscular black beady-eyed kinky-haired king from steamy Ashanti. The mate stood alongside Captain Quaile. The general agent, Sir Mortimer Jordan walked into the room and sat down behind them.

Miserable sly fox, thought Quaile as greetings were exchanged between him and Chief Atakanga in the most obsequious manner.

Chief Atakanga wore a magnificent leopard skin that fell over his right shoulder and across his well-defined ebony physique. His head was crowned with beautiful ostrich feathers, a porcupine quill pierced his left nostril, and anklets of boar tusks and cowries added to his décor. He controlled and was responsible for marching hundreds and hundreds of slaves through Ashanti country to the Assin Manso slave depot, thirty miles from Cape Coast Castle. From there, he sold them to different slave markets along the coast.

'Chief Atakanga, you look well and prosperous. Have the gods been good to you since our last meeting?'

'I am well, Red One. I now have fifteen sons and many daughters; very fat and very strong. They could please many men. Have you sired any in your far-away cold country?'

Captain Quaile laughed. 'Our women aren't as beautiful and fertile.'

'A man as strong as you? Oh! Red One, I must bring you one of our favourite women from my tribe. Imagine how big her breasts would be, great rolls of fat hanging from behind. She would envelope you in her magnificent huge arms and legs like a hippopotamus, squeezing that last moment of pleasure out of your shaking loins.'

Suddenly the two men burst into hilarity. Captain Quaile stroked his beard and turned to the general agent, nodding his head.

'Greetings, Sir Mortimer. I see you have a full house today.'

Sir Mortimer was a stocky heavyset man, and bald but for a few scanty hairs hanging behind his large ears. His upper lip was concealed under a thick moustache. He had a rather longish, pointed nose. He was a most arrogant man. The Royal African Company sent him four years ago to replace Sir Percival McDougall-Fayrsham, the previous comptroller of Cape Coast Castle and general agent, who died of malaria. Quaile despised Sir Mortimer even more than the last general agent.

'Captain Quaile, my compliments upon your speedy voyage; you made good timing. I have heard you complaining about the state of your ship. I hope you spoke to Doncaster as he is most efficient. Now, have you the list of trade goods from Headquarters?'

The first mate rummaged in his coat and handed the long list to Sir Mortimer.

'By the way, I believe we spoke about the silver and iron brands last time. Do you recall?'

Quaile frowned and said, 'And you can see for yourself the damaging results. Damn it, I personally delivered your last order to Headquarters in London. I presume the goods arrived? Headquarters told me the silver brands would be included in the order.'

'I suppose the silver brands were not in stock at the time,' said Sir Mortimer, pulling his hairy earlobe.

A terrible anger churned Quaile's insides; he wanted to tell him, *You lying, vain, pompous ass!* But he held his tongue.

'Captain Quaile, if I may be so presumptuous: the iron brands are cheaper to manufacture in Sheffield and Liverpool; far more economical from that point of view. However, I will be happy to give you a personal letter and you could take it up with London next time you're there. You know you have my full support in this. The health of the slaves is my primary concern.'

'I'm sailing to Benin.' Quaile turned away from him, took his pipe from his waistcoat, filled it and looked at his fob watch.

The three African traders left the room to indulge in their drams of rum punch and brandy. Quaile, Sir Mortimer and Chief Atakanga reclined on the sofa. The first mate, the bosun and the Company's factor sat opposite them on a soft leather pouffe. Quaile was quick to perceive the ugly ulcer on the factor's hand as he tried to conceal it with his soiled long sleeve. It was just above the left wrist, angry and red. Two flies pitched on it; the factor gave a quick swipe with his right hand and squashed a large repulsive fly, swearing loudly.

Filthy, yaws probably, wondered Quaile, blowing his nose with disgust.

In the centre of the room was a solid round oak table displaying a variety of drinks: Madeira, French wine, rum, palm wine, and punch. There was also a number of African delicacies: baked and boiled kenki made into little buns and rolls, shea butter from the shea tree resembling a pear, fufu with vegetables, okro sauce and meat, roasted locusts, kola nuts, ground nuts, salted meat, gammon, fowls, pickles, tongue and fish. The air was heavy with the pungent odour of tobacco, alcohol and spices. Six oil lamps hung on the wall. There were several leopard and cheetah skins covering the floor.

Two slave negresses approached the table: They carried large calabash bowls on their heads filled with roasted plantain soaked in palm oil. A twelve-yard, white-and-blue traditional Kente cloth was draped around their slender bodies, fasted over their right shoulders, exposing their round firm left breasts.

'What a perfect elegant gait they have you must admit; the way they sway those hips.' Quaile turned to his first mate, smiling. 'Women in England ought to learn to walk this way.'

'The trouble with our wenches is that they are concealed under such a paraphernalia of ridiculous garments,' the first mate grinned.

Chief Atakanga scrutinised both men, his eyes wandering from left to right with amusement. Conversations usually took place with an interpreter from the Company's factors, who lived on the coast and spoke several of the tribal dialects, though Captain Quaile was quite fluent in Bantu and Ashanti.

'I hear you have a large supply from the interior,' said Quaile, 'How many slaves do you think I could have? I promise you a fair deal.'

'You are a shrewd man Red One. I can supply you with Fanti slaves, Ashanti, some Mandingos, and other merchandise.'

Quaile nodded, puffing on his long pipe.

'There's a good demand for scented Guarea and mahogany in England,' interrupted Sir Mortimer. 'Beautiful; finest wood on this coast.'

'What about something for your women?' smiled the Chief. 'Lovely Kente—my slaves brought these from Bonwire up north.'

Quaile laughed, revealing a set of sparkling white even teeth. 'What a sensation they caused in England.'

'My father was a former captain on a brigantine, retired now. I remember the stories he told me about the exquisite cloth when it was introduced to the court of Charles II.' Quaile trimmed his pipe. 'The Merry Monarch, a man of great tastes and talents.' The first mate yawned and stretched his legs.

'The first weaving was practised in Ashanti at Salaga,' continued Quaile. 'There were various designs and patterns; one of them is the 'Abawere', a small local bird. The most exclusive ones must be first shown to the King of Ashanti and are worn only by Queen mothers, princes and princesses from the Oyoko royal family.'

Quaile's eyes followed the slender negress as she bent to offer him some plantain; her body, shiny with palm oil, was very close to him. It had been many weeks since he left England. He vaguely remembered the hot-tempered and lewd hussy he bedded in a Bristol inn. How alluring that negress was.

'You can have her tonight for two barrels of brandy.' The chief clapped his hands. 'How's that for a bargain?'

Quaile gave an embarrassed guffaw as the others laughed at him.

'Send her to me tonight. Now where was I? The Abawere Kente has a black background with bands of white, yellow, crimson and green or blue: truly a perfect gift for any beautiful woman.' He looked at Chief Atakanga. 'I shall want several lengths.' The captain was excited at the prospect of bedding a black woman for the first time in his life.

Sir Mortimer stood up, strutting towards the open window overlooking the bay. He scratched his bald head and in his suave manner turned to face the captain.

'Well, I think we ought to go down to the dungeons and see the slaves, our prime concern. Then we will proceed to the storerooms and show you the abundant supplies.' He paused. 'How long do you think it will take you to reach Jamaica?'

'From Benin with good weather conditions and favourable winds, we should reach our destination within six weeks. Last voyage we ran into foul weather. God spare us such an ordeal again.'

Chief Atakanga started to fidget with the porcupine quill that pierced his nostril. He was getting bored with the white entourage.

The group stepped towards the open doors. They emerged into the white-washed cool arcaded balcony. Six sentries strutted up and down the courtyard near the main gate. The chief, his caboceers and the rest of the men descended the long staircase to the court. The dungeons were situated on the west wing of the castle facing the Atlantic.

'I don't believe there could be a worse hell than what you are going to witness,' said Quaile to the bosun, who had not been on a slaver before. 'This is the black pit of Cape Coast Castle.'

The heavy door opened with a tremendous thud as they proceeded along a dark corridor dimly lit by oil lamps. The walls were damp and a fetid smell emanated from within. It seemed a long time before they reached the end of the lengthy passage leading to the slave dungeons. There were almost nine hundred slaves caged in a maze of hollowed-out caverns and tunnels hewn from the solid rock that jutted out to sea. Cape Coast Castle was a formidable fortress. At the top of the walls there were several small, barred openings allowing for ventilation. Joshua could hear the waves crashing against the outer ramparts; he felt nervous walking beside the chief.

A Fulani slave peered up at the dim light. 'I can smell the sea,' he said in Bantu to the Mandingo standing beside him.

The Mandingo replied, 'Our own black people sell us to the white man. They have no shame. Africa is cursed and doomed. I understand some of their language and heard the factor saying that they would brand us like cattle, before we sail on the ship.'

'I shall not leave these shores,' said the Fulani slave. 'They cannot kill me for I am Africa.' The Fulani crouched and huddled in the corner.

The tall Mandingo pined for his wife who had been transported to Benin. The hope of seeing her again one day kept him alive.

'I'll show you first the women slaves; they are on the other side,' said Chief Atakanga.

The foul stench of human excrement, urine and vomit hit them as they approached the pens. Quaile pulled out his handkerchief and pretended to blow his nose. There were eighty slaves crammed in one small cell behind thick bars.

'Here are some Ashanti, Fanti and Mandingos,' said Chief

Atakanga as he scrutinised the slaves. 'All young and in their prime; your white planters across the sea should be pleased with this lot. My sources in the Bahamas tell me prices have gone up so for every male, I want ten iron bars now, not nine, but I want twenty copper bars for Mandingos.'

'Twenty?' Quaile spluttered. 'Seventeen copper bars were an exorbitant price and now you are asking for three more?'

'Come now, Captain Quaile, you know as well as I do that traders in Calabar are asking for more than forty. I also need more muskets, gun powder and tools.' He asked one of the sentries to bring an Ashanti slave.

'Let me show you a real good buck.' The slave was tall, lean and naked. He trembled. The chief pirouetted around him, praising his shoulders and back: Then, gripping his short whip with one hand, he inspected the slave's firm buttocks and strong legs.

'See his wide chest, and strong handsome body with no scars.' His whip descended slowly to the slave's abdomen and genitals. Chief Atakanga's perversion was demonstrated by taking pleasure in displaying his victim in the most humiliating and degrading way. He knew that Captain Quaile was tactful and would watch as he did on other occasions. Chief Atakanga stood in front of the Ashanti taking his sharp knife and placing the blade beneath the slave's penis, lifting it upright. He raised the firm testicles, exclaiming, 'Strongest male buck you'll ever see; good for work, excellent for mating.'

The bosun laughed and said, 'Quite right, quite right.' The slave stared at the knife, and gave a sigh of relief when it was removed. Quaile watched the man and saw utter despair in his eyes.

On the extreme right of the dungeons the women and children huddled together, penned in like sheep.

'Those wenches and children should sell as cooks or good field hands.' Quaile looked at Chief Atakanga and nodded. Hundreds of slaves peered at them from behind thick bars, in morbid trauma. Quaile began to sweat thinking of the woman who was coming to his room tonight.

A group of Fanti slaves clutched their breasts in plaintive dirges when a distant baritone rose high above their voices, moving through the dark walls of the dungeon to a crescendo. At this point the Mandingo alone continued to sing. Only his voice was heard amid the world of slaves and slavers, of rats and bats: he was celebrating going home to the forests. The song ended in a bursting finale.

'Shall we proceed to the storerooms?' asked Sir Mortimer hastily. Quaile sighed with relief at the suggestion. He wanted to get out, away from those condemning eyes.

At last they came to the end of the passage into the bright glaring hot African sun.

The storerooms were situated just above the dungeons.

'Here are the treasure rooms,' Sir Mortimer demonstrated. 'Truly such magnificent gifts that only Africa can offer. Let me show you the finest rare timbers.' The strong sweet scent of wood permeated the air.

The second store had a display of skins and glorious plumage of African birds.

'Absolutely breathtaking,' muttered Quaile.

The last storerooms were filled with ivory tusks, rhinoceros and buffalo horns, thirty-five hundredweights of capsicum, chilli pepper and, then, the gold: two hundred pounds of pure yellow gold.

'Excellent!' exclaimed Quaile.

Sir Mortimer took out his ivory snuff box, inhaled a

pinch of the brownish powder through each nostril and then sneezed. 'Wonderful stuff, clears the head. Care for some?'

'Disgusting habits you English have,' Chief Atakanga commented, fiddling with his porcupine quill.

'Habits die hard. I shall settle for my pipe and tobacco. I prefer to stick my pipe in my mouth, rather than put some foreign substance in my nose,' said Quaile.

The whole group returned to the central hall. Chief Atakanga's caboceer had just returned from the Hurricane with the African trader.

'I think the English goods are a reasonable exchange for the slaves.' The captain suddenly thought he might have undervalued his cargo because usually the caboceer raised a few quibbles.

'Trust is important in our palaver,' Quaile said to Chief Atakanga.

Sir Mortimer presided over the final agreement between Chief Atakanga and the captain, who in turn had to pay his port dues in golden guineas. The European factor read the long document with the list of trade goods and slaves pertaining to both parties in Ashanti and English. Sir Mortimer stamped the papers with the Royal African Company's seal and Chief Atakanga with his thumb.

'Your six hundred slaves will be branded early tomorrow morning,' Sir Mortimer addressed Quaile. 'After receipt of your goods they will board your ship so we won't have any confusion.'

'Quite so, quite so. I think I shall retire.' Quaile nodded to the chief and the governor. Chief Atakanga whispered in his ear.

'I'll send the girl up to you at once.'

CHAPTER 5

Bundere gazed at the peaceful sunset as the women settled the children for the night. The coals of the fire glowed red. The cicadas sang. The bats began to squeak, but all of a sudden it became quiet: the forest seemed to hold its breath. Bundere began to feel that something was wrong. A luminous glow circled the moon. Bundere crept to a clump of bushes. He heard faint rustling and crackling of leaves.

'Danger,' he muttered. He kicked the drowsy Moshebere on the ground. The slave traders from the east were raiding the camp. Bundere aimed his musket at the face of the oncoming slaver. He brought the butt of it down hard upon the man's eyeball, causing it to splatter and hang limply from its socket. The trader ran in circles and dropped. It was hard to discern who fought whom. A slave held his hanging intestines. Both sides attacked with blows of pangas and muskets but Bundere's men were outnumbered. Four were killed and the forty-six escapees were chained with the other slaves in the coffle and marched to Douala.

It started drizzling. Tears were shed for the innocent, the endless slaughter and life of bondage. From the coast they veered down to the north bank of the Wouri River surrounded by the tenebrous morass of the swamps. They had been walking now for several weeks.

Mahadana said to Bundere, 'We're going to have another child.'

He tenderly touched his wife's belly. 'In years to come will the child be a slave?' With a sinking heart he added, 'Our people the Bakoko settled here several generations ago, until the accursed Douala drove them out'.

᪈

Monneba a Mulabe, the headman and leader of the Douala people, lived on the north bank of the Wouri River. He was revered and feared, as much for the sake of his famous grandfather, Mulabe a Ewale, who was the first Douala leader to barter with the Dutch, many years before. The Europeans who came there to trade called the village Monneba's village: not after him, but after his ancestor Mulabe.

When he passed among the people, they averted their eyes and did not look directly at him until he walked away. He was a just chief to his people, and cruel to everybody else.

Slavery wasn't the Doualas' only source of sustenance—they did farming, fishing and hunting for their daily needs—but it did earn them wealth. A Dutch ship was moored about four miles up the river.

The weary slaves stumbled into Monneba's village utterly exhausted and frightened.

'Sit by the big tree,' the caboceer barked. They slumped near the wattle. A vendor slouched under a skimpy palm awning with large calabashes filled with shrimps. Shrimps were abundant in and around the Wouri estuary. Slavers along the coastline passing through Douala territory purchased them in great quantities.

Captain Van Den Hoosten, with his first mate and factor, approached Monneba's hut as he emerged. Monneba was tall and spindle-legged. His penis was covered with a gourd a size larger than the other men's and strapped with a leather thong around his waist, to protect it against insect bites. Around his neck hung crocodile and hippopotamus teeth. On his ankles and wrists dangled baboon teeth and on his head was a dusty top hat. He looked so bizarre and comical that the officer had to suppress his laughter.

The Douala people were Bantu, and Captain Van Den Hoosten spoke to them in their tongue. He had sailed the Cameroon coast for years and dealt directly with them.

'A beautiful morning, my friend Monneba.' Captain Van Den Hoosten took off his hat. Monneba nodded his head, trying not to laugh himself because of the captain's poor pronunciation. Monneba scanned all the slaves around with his piercing cold eyes.

'You specifically requested more slaves, and the hurricane season is starting up soon in the West Indies,' said Monneba. 'Not many ships will be coming this way for months.'

'They won't last long on my ship,' said Captain Van Den Hoosten. 'The flux will soon do away with them. Where do they come from?'

'Below the Massifs de Manin Gouba,' snarled the caboceer

'A long way,' uttered Monneba. 'How many slaves have we got altogether?'

'One hundred and forty-six,' said the second caboceer, his voice raised.

'De-lice them,' said Captain Van Hoosten.

Monneba flicked and rattled the profusion of baboon teeth on his wrists and ankles.

'Now, Monneba, since I must leave soon I wish to buy some ivory.' They walked over to the shed. Twenty tusks lay on the floor.

'Call them large?' said the captain.

Monneba feigned astonishment. 'At least ten of them are.' He stared at the captain. 'Five tusks, no more.' Monneba was adamant.

'In exchange for one hundred and forty-six slaves I can supply and offer to you the following: one thousand pounds of lead, twenty hogsheads of brandy, three hundred pewter tankards, seven hundred basins, five hundred and fifty yards of linen, one hundred knives, and a hundred brass bells.' They haggled and came to a compromise.

'I accept,' said Van Den Hoosten. Monneba signed with his thumb.

Moshebere, Alimba, the twins, Bundere, Mahadana, their two children, and the other slaves were herded on to long-boats to be transported downriver to the ship.

A wide horizontal plank was lowered down by means of the block and tackle attached to the davits—two curved wooden bars that swung out over the side of the sloop enabling the plank to be raised and lowered, while still remaining on a horizontal plane. There were ropes underneath to keep it level which went into the gunwhale through holes. The slaves were made to step out of the boat and on to the plank which was then raised, and the slaves stepped on to the deck.

The elders eyed the hogsheads of brandy, wishing to open them as soon as possible. Monneba and the captain stood by the side of the river. The first mate and the bosun were in the rowboat, ready to go back and board the ship.

Captain Van Den Hoosten said, 'It will be quite some time before I return. God be with you until then, my friend.'

Monneba replied, 'May the Miengu give you a safe journey, and may your Jengu not sink your ship, good friend. I hope the Miengu speaks well of you to your god also.' He lifted his hat as the Dutchman returned to his ship.

Captain Van Den Hoosten sailed out that evening.

The water from the earthenware vessel was cool and refreshing and Joshua washed himself down to his waist, then lifted the pitcher and poured the rest on his head, shaking his hair. Quaile had broad shoulders, his chest and back covered with a fuzz of fine hair, his skin a rich auburn. He had bushy eyebrows with a droopy right eyelid, at times giving the impression of a sad face. He was six feet and two inches tall, with a muscular neck, protruding jawline shaped by a bushy red beard, and a crop of red hair crowning his strong sunburnt features. His dauntless, sagacious veneer belied his youthful twenty-one years; his gait was that of a man of radiating strength and exuberance.

Quaile splashed the water again over his face, then dried himself and walked towards the small verandah overlooking the open sea. His lofty room was cool and spacious. Facing the window stood a large iron bed with four brass posters covered by a light-blue mosquito net. There were two straw mats on the stone floor and a basket in the corner of the room. One clay jar filled with cold water was placed on a bamboo rack. To the right of the bed was a mahogany table, a calabash on top filled with coconuts, plantain and fruit, and beside the bed a small cask with rum and a pewter tankard. The white shutters were semi-closed to keep the room cool.

The sky was a mixture of crimson, orange and yellow. Gulls and terns skimmed above the water. Joshua stood on the balcony watching the Hurricane swaying with the evening breeze. Soon the red glow vanished and darkness fell. He could hardly perceive the dim light from her night lamps hanging on the cross-trees and the other above the cutwater on her stern. He took a deep breath. African sunsets captivated him; it was as if God's finger left His imprint.

Other men had wives; he had his brigantine. He had been master of the Hurricane for just over one year. She was built in Bristol, famous for its oldest industry: shipbuilding. He knew every single part of her, every nook; each solid oak timber so well carved. She was a fast sailor and never ceased to fascinate him; her dazzling white sails filled with the wind and the gilded Neptune figurehead on her bow was a marvellous sight to behold on the water.

His thoughts of all his tomorrows seemed to be swallowed in an endless maze leading nowhere; he felt quite empty and tried to cast his morbidness away by remembering the slave girl. He bit his lip. A terrible restlessness overcame him, thinking of the negress as he paced the room, pouring himself some rum in the tankard, gulping it hastily, and returning to the balcony.His whole body ached.

The sweet smell of frangipani filled the air. From the courtyard below he could hear the obscene language of the drunken redcoats as they plunged into their nightly orgies. Often ten soldiers shared three black wenches. After so many years in the slave trade he thought he might be accustomed to witnessing such acts of bestiality, but it left him only with revulsion. He was nervous and irritable, and swung back to see if the slave girl had arrived. He filled his pipe and inhaled.

Joshua listened to the pounding surf and looked across the Atlantic. Beyond, thousands of miles away lay England and his birthplace, Bristol. His mother, long dead, and his father who still lived in the cottage where he spent his childhood. A terrible nostalgia overcame him. Where did all those years go? He remembered as a boy when his father used to take him by coach to Avonmouth. It all happened so long ago. He loved to watch the tall ships sail in from the Bristol Channel, through the Severn and into the harbour—a breathtaking sight.

Suddenly he sensed that he was being watched and he turned his head to see the Fulani slave leaning against the white slats. Her large sparkling eyes, shadowed by malachite, beckoned him. With a half-smile he approached her. She was very young and slender with a scanty leopard skin wrapped around her waist. On her right ankle she wore two brass bangles.

The full moon beamed on her face; a tinge of red ochre adorned her cheeks and she had one beauty spot on each nostril. His eyes fixed on her lovely voluptuous figure. He pressed his body against her, raising one hand to cup a firm round breast, caressing it gently. How strange that he did not feel that she was a slave. Her nipples became erect and her whole body trembled. He could feel his blood rushing and throbbing in his head, pulsating through his veins. A strange tingling and wondrous sensation overcame him, shooting from his neck to his loins. The way she moved in a sensuous rhythm was not like a white woman. He crouched, kneeling on his knees, resting his head against her soft warm abdomen while his lips caressed the inner part of her thighs. His beard tickled her and she laughed. The laugh turned into a whimper and then a cry. He caressed her naked body and thrust strongly into her. Finally jerked his head and with a sudden vigorous stroke he climaxed. Joshua lit his pipe and sat on the side of the bed.

'Where do you come from?' he asked.

'Ashanti.'

'Where is your family?'

'My parents and brother were snatched.' She kept gazing at the window.

'Would you like some cold water?'

'Yes.' She turned around and looked at the room. 'It's cool in here.'

He poured water from a jug and a few drops spilled on her dark breasts.

She said, 'Atakanga has a large palace between here and Manso. When he leaves Cape Coast Castle six slaves carry him on a wide bamboo chair attached to four poles. The other porter slaves cart all the goods from the ships. Several women and myself follow behind.' She paused to sip more water.

'There are many slaves who work in Atakanga's palace and around the high baked-mud walls. We were caught in the Ashanti interior not far from where I lived.' Her lips trembled and her eyes blazed with condemnation. She stood up and walked to the window.

'I love the smell of the sea; it is so clean,' she said. Joshua approached and stood behind her.

'There is my ship; the one on the left.'

'You are a free man, like the birds,' she said. 'You will sail the blue waters and come and go as you please. I envy your freedom.' She turned to face him.

He drifted into a deep sleep thinking of his friend, Moustapha Daoud. Tomorrow he would sail to the slave market of Benin and see him.

At dawn she slipped out of his room.

CHAPTER 6

'The slaves are panicking,' the factor yelled. 'Fulanis are prone to suicide. Let's get on with the trade.'

As soon as the branding started, the Fulani walked behind the Mandingo in the yard. The giant Mandingo smelled the burning flesh and retched. To him this was an abomination. The Fulani looked beyond the light-blue sky meeting the dark-blue waters of the ocean. The fresh sea air filled his lungs. He made a fiery headlong dash across the compound, sprinted over the wall, his arms spread-eagled, and plunged into the foaming swell of the Atlantic. The Mandingo watched in horror.

The Fulani was free at last.

❦

Before noon Joshua returned to the Hurricane. He conversed with the ship's carpenter on the quarterdeck.

'I had better go below and see about the extra bulkheads I put in,' the carpenter said. 'I will have to build more shelves and partitions.' He scratched his head and sneezed.

'Captain, I thought you wanted to see the cooper.'

'Thank you, yes, here he comes.'

'I'll be on my way then.' He blew his nose and off he went.

'It is imperative we take more water this time,' emphasised

Joshua to the cooper. 'Last time there was a leak in the large vat. Let's go to the cooperage and check on all the casks.'

An hour later dozens of canoes came alongside the Hurricane. The bosun shouted at the top of his voice, giving orders. The timbers were hoisted up and placed near the bulwarks. Gold in bronze containers, skins, feathers, ivory tusks and several hundredweights of capsicum, chilli and pepper were stored below.

Joshua walked in quick strides. 'Bosun, are the women and children in the centre and aft section?' he asked.

'Yes, sir.' Joshua watched the frightened slaves staring at him through the gratings. He felt uneasy; his throat was dry. He turned round and called the carpenter.

'Make sure you batten the hatches before we get into foul weather. Too often the slaves' hatches are neglected.'

'Yes, sir,' nodded the carpenter. He continued to inspect the gratings for ventilation above the holds. These were usually covered with solid hatches to protect the cargo on the northbound return voyage from the West Indies to England. At noon, a moderate westerly wind arose. Joshua stood on the poop humming to himself.

'Ahoy, ahoy, heave on the capstan, weigh anchor.' His proud voice echoed across the Hurricane. He watched with almost childish delight as, one by one, the sails were set. The guns saluted twice and bade farewell once more to Cape Coast Castle and Chief Atakanga. Joshua glanced anxiously at the slaves beyond the gratings, and thought to himself, *What a dirty business this is.*

The young Ibibio, with his cumbersome musket hanging on his right shoulder, ran towards Captain Lawrence, and Billy Fidelity, the Efik slave trader, sitting on the long porch sipping their Mimbo.

'Plenty slaves come, and ivory,' he shouted at the top of his voice with excitement.

'What in heaven's name?' said Captain Lawrence. 'They look on the brink of death. Must have covered hundreds of miles.'

Billy Fidelity gulped his drink, ran down the flight of creaking stairs, and into the sun. Captain Lawrence watched the long column shuffle up the winding sandy path, and his gaze was drawn to his brig, the Rainbow, moored by cable to the forest trees on the banks of the Calabar River. At midday the heat was intense, and all was still except for the Palm Nut eagle, soaring above Duke Town in Old Calabar.

Billy Fidelity drew out his buffalo horn and blew on it twice. The scattered wattle huts were hidden among the thick foliage and giant trees. Suddenly like a pack of hounds at the call of their master, Efik traders, Ibibios, caboceers, and three white factors swarmed out from all directions.

'Fire the gun,' said Captain Lawrence to Billy. 'Our friend upriver would be interested in this.'

A cutter moored near the ocean, just north of Parrot Island and Seven Fathom Point, acknowledged with her guns. Within half an hour, a canoe with a captain and crew paddled up the Old Calabar River.

The guards gathered all the slaves into a large compound, surrounded by an eight-foot wall of baked mud.

'King Adebayo should be arriving soon.' The Efik trader turned to the guards. 'Line them up,' he yelled. Gashaka, seized with hate towards the white man, clenched his teeth.

They are the cause of all my brothers' deaths and suffering, he thought.

'Well let's get on with it now,' said Captain Lawrence, turning towards the short factor, who coughed up phlegm. He addressed Captain Ramsay.

'Oh, before we start, I should mention that I got raided by the navy again.'

'That's twice you've been raided in the last twelve months apparently. The navy must really dislike you, following you about like a foul smell,' Captain Ramsay snorted, turning purple.

'No need to get enraged,' Captain Lawrence replied. 'I'll absorb the losses this time. Righto, on to business.'

The two captains and the factor approached the coffle of slaves. Nagamba had never set eyes on a white man before seeing Captain Lawrence. He walked up to her. She lowered her head in fear as he gazed upon her. After a few seconds Nagamba lifted her head feeling uneasy as she watched him walk away.

'She is stunning,' Captain Lawrence remarked.

'Yes. She should fetch many gold coins in Jamaica. Unless you intend to keep her,' said Billy Fidelity with a glint in his eye. He turned to the other captain.

'Hope King Adebayo doesn't notice her. His eyes are sharp, take my word. He is a witch, and when he curses people they die. Everybody fears him. Let's go to the other side; I think he's coming now.'

King Adebayo arrived with twenty Efiks. He waved his gold-laced round hat with colourful plumes and placed it on his head. A yellow tunic with black stripes covered half of his lower body. He was tall and slim, with sunken cold prying eyes. Having noticed the factor and captain at the far corner of the compound he beckoned his chief counsellor, Otto Ebro to approach.

'I think I shall raise my price of slaves for my white friends,' said King Adebayo. Otto nodded.

'Ah, Captain Lawrence, I suppose you will be leaving soon.'

'I've been here for four months, am planning to sail to Benin. The fishing, shooting parrots (which actually are delicious) and the palm wine are excellent. I mustn't forget your women. One can become bored with everything else, but not your women. How could one ever forget them?'

'How far downriver did you bring your ship?' asked King Adebayo.

'We're up near Parrot Island,' replied Captain Ramsay.

'You'll have to bring your ship down, or else it will take too long to load and unload,' said the King.

'Er, you see,' said Captain Ramsay. 'I can't be seen to associate with Lawrence; he is an illicit trader. If the Royal Navy or another African Company ship catches us with him, my career will be over.'

'We will keep to our usual plan. Lawrence will load up first, and then after he has left I will come up river,' replied Ramsay.

'What's Lonegan doing this morning?' asked Lawrence.

I bet he is off with a woman; probably with one or two,' said Ramsay. 'He will be away for three or four days. A rumour came to his ears that there are illicit traders landing on the far side of Fernando Po Island.' Lonegan was the company's agent.

'It is strange that such a rumour spread just when we arrived,' said Lawrence.

King Adebayo pulled a long hair from his right cheek. 'We are having a big feast tonight. At least we have slaves here now.'

King Adebayo started his inspection of the slaves. Nagamba stood naked. She felt like a trapped animal and looked at the black king. King Adebayo's tapered fingers touched her slender neck and travelled down to the soft curve of her bosom.

'What is your name?' King Adebayo squeezed her large nipples.

'Nagamba.'

'Nagamba is not for sale,' King Adebayo said, gazing upon Captain Lawrence with a leering smile. 'Otto, take her to my house. Prepare her for me.'

Gashaka was herded with the others, attached by an iron collar around his neck. He saw Nagamba being taken away for King Adebayo. Gashaka was tormented. *Would he ever see her again? Would she stay with Adebayo, enduring sustained abuse?* Gashaka had promised he would be her hero, but now he was shackled and imprisoned. He seethed with anger.

The crews of the numerous pirogues shuttled up and down loading the Rainbow.

Lawrence followed the bat-eating kite. It circled several times, then swooped and disappeared in the thick foliage. From the shore he could hear the drums. Darkness fell. He walked towards the open fire and heard a woman screaming in pain, giving birth in one of the huts.

King Adebayo sat on an ivory stool surrounded by ten Ibibios and a witch doctor. Also present were Captain Ramsay and the crew. At King Adebayo's feet crouched Nagamba, stupefied by drugged palm wine. Lawrence stood in the shadow of a tree watching her for several minutes. His thoughts ran wild trying to find a way to rescue her from that baboon.

King Adebayo called him. 'Come and join us, Captain

Lawrence. Look what we have for you. Anyone you choose will be yours.' He gulped more and more of his drink. The women wore exquisitely coloured tunics from the waist down. Their faces were deeply striped by tribal cuts. One of the tall plump negresses approached Captain Lawrence, pirouetting around him to display her magnificent hair, twisted into a comb one-foot high. Most of the women wore burnished copper rings on their legs and arms. She beckoned him to go into the bush.

'Have her,' King Adebayo said, staggering forward. 'I tried her myself.'

Captain Lawrence replied, 'When the party's over,' and approached Nagamba.

'Now for some entertainment,' King Adebayo said, 'we have our laws, and you Brown-Fow have yours.'

'What does Brown Fow mean?' whispered Captain Ramsay.

'White-faced people,' replied Captain Lawrence. 'Brown-Fow means white-faced people.'

'Ha-ha-ha, I don't believe it; how now Brown Fow,' Captain Ramsay shouted in Lawrence's face, suffocating him with the smell of rum.

'Yes, Brown Fow,' King Adebayo said. 'The great spirits punish those who are bad.'

Suddenly masked dancers appeared and were joined by others on stilts in a bizarre performance, with incredible flights and sprints. Within minutes warriors emerged from the darkness, resembling gruesome puppets hideous in appearance. They bolted in, slashing and hacking the dancers to pieces.

'They were very baddy baddy,' exclaimed King Adebayo. 'The great spirits came and killed them.'

A shiver ran down Captain Ramsay's spine.

King Adebayo shrieked, 'We must respect our laws, Brown Fow.'

In the affray, a hysterical woman ran and screamed after two Efiks, each holding two newborn babies in their arms. Blood streaked between her thighs after having given birth. The witch doctor, sitting on the ground, ripped a vulture's beak and hippopotamus horns from his neck. He circled the twins.

'Put them in the clay pots, alive,' bellowed King Adebayo like a raging bull. 'Then put the lid on. They will soon suffocate.'

The woman flung herself upon the earth, trying to snatch the twins, when the sharp panga decapitated her head.

'Why did you have to kill the mother?' scowled Captain Ramsay. 'She tried to save them.'

King Adebayo said, 'They are evil spirits in two. Only one soul can live in one body.' Ramsey began shaking in anger.

Nagamba trembled.

Billy Fidelity noticed Captain Lawrence open his mouth to speak, and he nudged him to remind him not to pursue the subject. The birth of twins in the Oil River tribes was an unforgiveable calamity.

'I think we have had enough excitement for one night,' Ramsay said.

King Adebayo grabbed Nagamba and walked away. Captain Lawrence's heart went cold as a stone. He noticed that Billy Fidelity was standing beside him.

Billy said, 'You will never be able to come back here if you snatch the woman. For the sake of our friendship I will show you to the hut where he will take her, but don't involve me if things go wrong. I value my own skin.'

Along the muddy river two harrier hawks swooped low among the trees. Billy Fidelity disappeared into the darkness. Lawrence hid behind a thick hedge of rosy oleanders. He could hear several native guards chatting by the big trees.

The faint light of the quarter moon shone through a small window, exposing two bodies entwined together like a pair of eels slimy and shiny. King Adebayo grunted and panted lying on top of Nagamba. After a few minutes he went out the back of the house down to the river to urinate.

Lawrence slipped through the window and clutched Nagamba's wrist saying, 'I came to take you away from him.' Nagamba was confused by his English, understanding only some of his words. She feared what the king would do to her if he found this white man in the room.

Lawrence dragged her to the door, but she emitted a short, sharp scream. King Adebayo's bulk appeared in the doorway. He seized Lawrence by the throat with one hand and began to throttle him. Lawrence drew his cutlass and stuck the sharp blade into the king's breast. Adebayo fell backwards, trying to scream, feeling as if he were being strangled. His mouth filled with blood that spilt down his chin. Captain Lawrence pushed the blade in again, then grabbed Nagamba and ran outside.

Adebayo crawled on his belly, the cutlass still lodged in his ribs. He dragged himself through the door to the porch in searing pain. With great effort he lifted his head. He saw the guards some distance away; they were drunk and laughing.

'King Adebayo's having fun. Don't disturb him. How he made her scream. He wouldn't like us to see him naked.'

Adebayo slumped, coughing, his red tongue lolling from side to side. He murmured, 'Lawrence ... kill him, kill him,' and fell back, dead.

Lawrence rummaged through his navigational charts. He knew it was imperative that he sail before dawn with the tide out to sea. He picked up his sextant and went to rouse the crew to navigate out of the difficult channels of the Calabar River and the Cross River in the early hours of the morning.

The two guards sat below the parasol tree sipping palm wine.

'Do you think we should wake the Chief up now?' asked the short guard.

'We'll wait at least til after sunrise. No wonder we heard all the noises from inside, with a size like hers.' The guard got up to urinate. 'We'll come back later. Let's see what's happening with the slaves.'

Screeching parrots woke Captain Ramsay. He jumped out of his bunk, dressed and went on deck. The first mate was already there.

'I had a terrible dream last night, an ominous premonition,' said Ramsay, buttoning his coat. 'A rumbling volcano erupted; lava flamed across the mountain into the valley. I ran, trying to escape, but it engulfed me, and I awoke drenched in sweat. A nightmare.'

'This is another kind of inferno,' exclaimed the first mate. 'The steamy jungle is infested with mosquitoes, snakes and crocodiles.'

Ramsay went to the bridge to fetch his telescope. He scanned the river, but Lawrence had already sailed, to his astonishment, to Benin. He looked again and saw the tip of the three-sailed sloop appearing just above the tree line.

CHAPTER 7

S everal hours later Lonegan, the Company's agent, arrived. He had a thin moustache jutting from his lips, a goatish beard and bulging frog eyes. He had lived in Old Calabar for years, and exchanged black women as often as he imbibed strong liquor.

'Good morning, Ramsay, haven't seen you for months,' yawned Lonegan. 'You know, I half expected to see that fellow Lawrence here. I always thought you and he had some kind of little plan going, getting around the Company rules by persuading Lawrence to carry your slaves for you; cunning bastard that Lawrence. That's why I came back, but I see I was totally wrong. He must have sailed early. So where have you been?'

'The Arabesque had to undergo some major repairs in Bristol docks,' said Ramsay.

'I don't miss England and will never go back there; I love this wild untamed Africa. Brilliant colours and glorious sunsets.' Lonegan stretched. 'But above all, the rhythm of life; the beating drums and African music. And of course the women, so exciting. Tell me Ramsay, have you ever been with a black woman?'

'No, and I don't intend to. They emit a vile musk odour. You can have them.'

Lonegan walked towards the slave traders and two guards. 'Where's Adebayo?'

'We'll wake him later. It's too early now,' said the tall guard.

'He had a big night,' the short guard replied. 'I don't want to upset him. You never know what he is capable of doing when he's angry.'

After they had finished loading the Arabesque, Ramsay said to the guards,'Well I had better go and say goodbye to Adebayo. I'm going to wake the King. He's had enough sleep by now.' As Ramsay approached the house he saw something just beyond the porch. He thought it might be a dead gazelle, and trod warily through the long grass.

The body was covered with ants. He realised it was King Adebayo. Ramsay panicked. He ran back through the village to the shore, commandeered a boat and rowed himself back to the ship.

He called to the first mate, 'Prepare the ship for sea. Quick! Don't dilly-dally. Our lives could be at stake.' Ramsay then called to the gunner, 'Have the guns loaded on the fo'csle and starboard side ready to fire. This is going to be a bloodbath should they catch up with us. Hoist the mainsail.' Ramsay ordered the rest of the crew, 'Get under way. Luff the ship to the wind. Make haste.'

Fifteen minutes later, Adebayo's son said to the guards, 'I thought Ramsay was going to say goodbye to the king.'

'I assumed Ramsay was still here,' grunted the short guard.

'The Arabesque's sails are up,' shouted the son and started running towards the king's hut, followed by the two guards. They came upon his body. Shocked, the king's son turned and looked at his guards.

'Who did this? The Arabesque.'

'The last time I saw the king he was with that woman,' said the tall guard, shaking like a leaf.

'What woman?'

'It must have been the one with father, when he entertained the Brown Fow.'

'Yes I remember. They didn't like what he did to the twins.'

'Carry my father back to the village. I will find who did this.' They laid Adebayo on a mat. His son covered him with a cheetah hide and blew the buffalo horn.

'The murderers! Kill all the Brown Fows. Eliminate them; slash them, one by one.' Horns and drums sounded all through the village. The Calabaris emerged from every wattle hut dragging war canoes towards the shore.

'You planned to kill my father,' shouted King Adebayo's son to Lonegan in Ashanti. Lonegan panicked and tried to escape, but with a chilling cry and deadly accuracy the panga hissed and penetrated his throat. He fell to the ground, his eyes wide open.

'Black bastards,' he managed to shout, gurgled and became still.

∽

'All is secure. We are ready for action,' said the bosun.

'Well done, carry on,' Captain Ramsay said pacing towards the quarterdeck. There was a favourable wind and the Arabesque's sails were unfurled. Ramsay was ready to scud downriver to the open sea. He knew the river and its hazardous shoals. The breeze ruffled the bronze water. Soon after, the drums of the Calibaris were heard with their frightening war cries. The canoes darted in pursuit of the ship.

'Watch out for mud banks,' cried Ramsay to the seaman at the tiller.

'Aye aye, sir.'

'If we could only have more wind behind us,' Ramsay sighed.

'They are coming fast,' panted the bosun, running towards the officers at the taffrail.

The midshipman on the cross-trees shouted, 'I can see hundreds of them.'

'Once we get to Seven Fathom Point, we should reach the sea.' Ramsay paced nervously up and down the deck.

'Blast the baboons. Number one, run out your guns. Fire! Wipe them from the face of the earth.' The guns fired a larboard broadside.

The mate shouted, 'Number two, blow them to smithereens.' The gunners poured in grape and canister. The four big guns were loaded and primed. With a deafening din they fired at the Calabaris. The canoes and pirogues swarmed from all sides and gained upon the Arabesque. The air was filled with the acrid smell of cordite.

'Look at them.' Ramsay shuddered. The palms of his hands were clammy.

The river turned into a living red hell, heads bobbing in and out of the water. Bodies floating, fragments of timber scattered everywhere. The Calabaris leapt into the water and clambered up the Arabesque's sides.

Below decks a young midshipman was struck with a panga across his hip. He fell, clutching his hand across the deep gash. He faced his enemy. They were both young, the fair sailor and the tall dark Calabari. Then the African brought down the sharp blade again across the midshipman's neck. The head dangled and was held by a thin layer of throat muscles and skin.

'No, no!' screamed the navigator, entering the cabin and

pouncing on the Calabari. More natives swarmed in like hornets, and he too was crushed beneath them.

The sails shivered. The main mast was soon set alight as the fire spread rapidly in the rising wind. Ramsay looked around in despair. The cooper and five sailors lay dead in a pool of blood in the scuppers. The guns were abandoned.

Within minutes the slaves from below stampeded on to the main deck, trampling the women and young to death, diving into the water. Many of the trapped people below deck suffocated.

'Abandon ship!' Ramsay's voice thundered.

The two officers and the bosun on the poop leapt. As soon as they hit the water the arrows ploughed at them. They submerged and then came up to breathe when another discharge of arrows hissed through the air. The bosun caught one in his Adam's apple. He gasped, struggled for a few seconds, and then disappeared.

Ramsay ran through the inferno, his body alight. The main mast and spars tottered and fell upon him. The Calabaris continued firing the flying arrows. The last officer was hit by the sharp darts on his shoulder and lost his grip. He tried to swim when another arrow perforated his skull. Soon the blazing fire consumed her brilliant sails and belched through the oak timbers. The doomed ship drifted to the sandbank, leaving a thin trail of smoke.

⚜

Captain Lawrence entered his cabin. In the dim light he could see Nagamba crouched with fear like a wounded animal. He dumped himself on his bunk and fell into a deep sleep.

It was not long before they crossed the marshy estuary and swung towards the Bight of Benin.

Gashaka knew that Nagamba had been taken to Lawrence's cabin. He sat in the corner of the dark with other slaves. The raw open blister on his right leg was inflamed. There was no space to lie. Gashaka heard the wailing and howling of children and women. He wept. There was no shame in crying; no one listened or cared. Exhausted, he fell asleep on another slave's shoulder. In the eyes of the unknown compassionate slave, whose face was gaunt, stamped with the bond of brotherhood, Gashaka found comfort and a smile emerged ever so slightly.

CHAPTER 8

Moustapha Daoud, the slave trader, watched the Hurricane come in to moor in all her white splendour, her tall spars swaying and sweeping across the blue sky. The Hurricane dropped her bower anchor in eight fathoms of water. Moustapha saw Joshua standing on the fo'csle, waving to him. He smiled and waved back. It was almost eight years ago when they first met in Benin.

His throat felt tight. He looked at his hands and shivered. The index finger of his right hand was a stump. There were numerous dry patches on his face with raised edges. Beads of perspiration accumulated on his high forehead. He longed to cleanse himself from this leprosy, such an ugly sickness. The sun's glare irritated him; he was unable to close his right eyelid completely due to facial nerve damage. Moustapha believed he was being punished for his evil past as a slave trader, and hoped that through redemption by the good spirits he would be granted forgiveness and absolution.

Moustapha was trying to do some good for the sake of black people so that he would be exonerated. Soon Joshua would leave for the West Indies. Moustapha grew in faith that through his meritorious deeds the spirits would also follow Joshua ultimately to fight against slavery. He watched the men furl the sails.

Moustapha Daoud never knew his father. His mother, the Moorish beauty and the most sought-after whore in the slave market of Timbuktu, conceived her son from an unknown Arab slave trader in the seedy world of human corruption. Thus Moustapha was raised and ran the dirty, dusty alleys of Timbuktu. As a young boy, and into his adolescent years, his life was circumscribed by slavery. He worked with the cohorts of despotic slavers who had no compunctions whatsoever about their depredations and crimes. They were truly defined as *Hostis humani generis*: enemies of the human race as stated by the Roman lawyer Cicero.

Despite all, Moustapha was a thinker, a sensitive man endowed with many passions. For years he travelled the caravan routes, across the Sahara by camel, between Ghana and Timbuktu with Arab slave traders and caravan merchants. Koumbi, Ghana's capital had an inexhaustible supply of gold, diamonds, ivory and skins. It was the lure of money that provided the strongest impetus, and Moustapha in his early twenties decided to go to Benin, the largest marketing centre for slaves. There he met Joshua Quaile, and a great friendship began. During all those years Moustapha never failed to see the Hurricane come in. Joshua usually stayed in Benin one or two months. Moustapha dealt with slave traders in the interior, and supplied the Hurricane with slaves who were transported to the West Indies.

Deep emotions welled inside him. The ailing man dreamed of sailing with Joshua to Jamaica. He must face his friend who knew about the disease, but Moustapha's health had deteriorated. His ravaged body was imprisoned in the irremedial scourge. He could no longer move his thumb to hold a quill and leave a message for Joshua. To all intents and purposes Moustapha was illiterate and only managed to write his own name and two or three other words. During the past years when they sat under the palm trees drinking mimbo,

Moustapha was fascinated, listening to Joshua telling him about great scholars and leaders in battle. Morbid thoughts raced and choked him; he longed for death and release from the coiled chain. With a plaintive moan he raised his palms high in exasperation, struggling with mortality. Joshua promised him that one day they would sail to the Indies and build a house on top of a hill facing the ocean.

Moustapha could navigate a caravan route on a camel across the desert sands by following the stars. He was the astronomer of his beloved desert.

Joshua navigated his ship sailing the vast ocean, using his charts and instruments and the stars. He was the astronomer of the seas. Joshua was shocked when he saw Moustapha. 'Moustapha, my friend,' he smiled, extending his hand. Moustapha drew back in trepidation.

'Don't come closer to me. You mustn't catch this disease.'

Joshua instinctively stepped back. 'The months have passed quickly since I last saw you,' said Joshua, trying to avoid looking straight at Moustapha pulling the burnous over the right side of his face.

'Yes, I went up the Rio Niger for a while. The forests seem to agree with me up there. Your hair is still red while mine shows streaks of grey.' Moustapha gazed up at the shrilling grey-crested hornbills flying across. Silence reigned for several seconds.

'Come with me to the West Indies,' pleaded Joshua. 'I'll provide and protect you.'

'What would I do in your white world? I'm dying. I would be a pariah to them. Here I belong in the forests. My body is wasting away. Look at my face, my hands.'

Moustapha flung the burnous off his features. 'Many days I burn with fever; my limbs ache and swell. Eventually lumps will appear on my ears, forehead, chin and cheeks. My throat will be affected. I will struggle to breathe.' He covered his face.

'I know some prominent physicians in Port Royal, renowned in tropical diseases,' said Joshua. 'Please listen to my advice. But now, let's talk about food. We'll go and see big Daboona. Such an excellent cook. Is she still so huge, like a hippopotamus?'

'Fatter,' chuckled Moustapha. The two men rambled up the dusty lane, to where the scent of food permeated from a musty hut. Fat Daboona greeted them with a cry and squeezed and hugged Joshua until he was short of breath. She was a giant of a woman, pendulous breasts hung like heavy bamboo stumps, and arms that could strangle. Her white teeth sparkled and her eyes radiated with laughter and kindness. She grinned at Joshua with mischief in her eyes.

'Josheeya! Me cook for you today, fu-fu and cankee! I knows you likee Josheeya,' she said. 'Daboona has baked and boiled cankee: buns and chicken with okro sauce.'

Joshua smiled.

'Plenty more for Josheeya; yam chops, boiled yams and sweet palm oil, and plenty pepper. Pepper make body hot.' Daboona placed her hands on her hips.

'Daboona smells good,' said Joshua, 'with palm oil.'

'Josheeya, I your woman. I come with you, on ship, faraway. White man's country.'

'White man land not good for Daboona. You stay here in Africa. When I come back I bring you a beautiful dress.'

She clapped her hands and laughed hysterically, rolls of fat swinging side to side. 'Moustapha, many moons, many suns, no see you in Benin. You got bad sickness, so you stay outside, leper. And you, Josheeya, go out. You stay outside with Moustapha. We friends, Moustapha, but I don't want to catch leper.'

Moustapha shuffled and sat on the side of the road ten feet away from the front of the shack. Joshua sat on a large wooden bench in front of Daboona's porch. She followed them and stood in the doorway, adjusting her loose garment over her hanging breasts.

'Where you been?' Daboona asked.

'In jungle,' replied Moustapha.

'See old medicine man, he very good, make good skin. Bad spirits give you leper. Go wash in river, take away sickness.' She shook her head. Moustapha was frustrated.

'No, Daboona, they no help—parrots, beads, crocodile teeth, dog teeth, eggshells, blood and feathers! No good, no good! I get sickness 'cause the spirits punish me. I swear, I no sell my black brothers no more to white man. Spirits very angry with me. I go to forest, talk to good spirits. They take me away, we fly together, all men, one colour, all men good. Medicine man, he know nothing.'

'What you want to eat Moustapha?'

'Plantain with palm oil, black beans and kola nuts—take away horrible taste in my mouth, you good woman.'

'And bring some mimbo,' said Joshua, giving Daboona an affectionate hug.

She pushed him away. 'You bring leper to my house.'

Ten minutes later, Daboona brought out a large steaming calabash with fufu and cankee buns soaked with palm oil, and a cup of mimbo, and gave it to Moustapha on the roadside, with a bowl of kola nuts and black beans. Then she brought out a small bowl of black beans and gave it to Joshua with a cup of mimbo and whispered again, 'You bring leper to my house. No good Josheeya: rotten body, smelly body. I seen it before. When you come in Benin again I give you fufu and cankee, buns and rolls.' She went back inside.

'You will forgive her for making you sit by the side of the road, but she is frightened of your condition,' said Joshua.

'Yes, but I got the fufu, and you didn't get any. Joshua, I heard from two factors that a brig came two days ago from Calabar with slaves. I thought you might be interested to meet the captain.'

'Yes, we'll go and pay him a visit tomorrow morning, after I get a good meal somewhere else, and not black beans. Do you remember the first time we met and we drank mimbo together?'

'Yes, yes, I remember it very well.' He kept rubbing his inflamed right eye. Daboona came out.

'How much?' asked Joshua

'Six coppers.'

'But that's two meals.'

'Yes, you pay for Moustapha. You got plenty money, you have big heart. Maybe he gets better.'

They paid and left.

'I haven't been to Calabar for years.'

'Those accursed Egbo, the Leopard society is strong there. Once a captain is 'blown' his livelihood is over.' Moustapha said. 'They are here in Benin. The Egbo are very elusive, and they could strike any of us, any time. I keep my wealth hidden. The chief Egbo is feared by the natives for his witch-craft and sorcery. Nobody knows his identity. He casts evil spells on those he does not like or favour. The Egbo hate lepers.

The two skirted the outside of the town, with small nilly-nally shacks made of palm.

'We will meet early, near the ship.'

'Til tomorrow.' Joshua watched his friend recede, like a black shroud, out of sight. He returned to the Hurricane, and Moustapha went back to his house in the forest, half a mile from the outskirts of Benin.

CHAPTER 9

Slaving ships that arrived in Benin could often stay for several weeks before being supplied with slaves. The slaves ashore lived in filthy, squalid, crammed huts and pens, before shipment to the West Indies and New England. Women were separated. The caboceers and guards were housed in mud huts a fair distance away. Moustapha was well known among the slave traders having been associated with them for a long time.

Through the years Moustapha became wealthy. Underneath his house, in an ingenious maze, he hid his hoard of gold in small iron chests, covered by stones and earth. Two large mantraps concealed the opening. If someone was caught in them, their hands would be severed.

In the decadent, corrupt world one could see the ravages of diseases, afflicted bodies with yaws, festered boils and suppurating sores. As his condition deteriorated Moustapha isolated himself in the forest. He trapped small animals, fished and survived on fruit, nuts and seeds.

❦

The following day he met up with Joshua.

'Good morning, Moustapha,' Joshua greeted him.

'Last night was oppressive; the mosquitoes are my worst enemies.' Moustapha kept scratching his face.

'Shall we go and see that brig now?' said Joshua.

'Might as well. Perhaps that captain has something interesting to tell.'

Walking to the brig, the people looked with apprehension at Moustapha and, seeing that he was completely covered, gave him and Joshua a wide berth.

At the brig, a factor told Joshua that the ship's captain was called Lawrence, and he had just brought many slaves to the Trunks.

'He will stay for at least three days before setting sail. Would you like me to call the captain down and you can have a word with him?'

The first mate overheard from the gangplank where he was unloading some cargo.

'Captain Lawrence won't be available for half an hour. But I'll tell him, if it's convenient for you, to meet you in the tavern in an hour's time. Your name, sir?'

'Captain Joshua Quaile.' They made their way to the tavern. Joshua said to Moustapha, 'Sit outside that window and I'll be at that table there, and pass a rum punch through to you while I'm waiting for the captain.'

About an hour later a captain walked along the street past Moustapha with a stunning African woman on his arm.

'What a ravishing creature,' Joshua muttered. They entered the tavern; the woman glanced at Joshua for a split second. He was struck by her sad brown eyes.

'Are you Captain Quaile?' said Captain Lawrence.

'Indeed I am. Would you care to join me for a drink? What's your fancy?'

'Mimbo. Not much else is there. Perhaps palm wine if you prefer. Nagamba, sit here,' said Captain Lawrence indicating his lap. His hand ran up and down her thigh.

'She should fetch an excellent price in Jamaica for the

highest bidder. I'll make sure of that,' Lawrence said. He glanced outside. 'Dirty leper. How can he sit there and pollute the atmosphere of this tavern?'

Moustapha heard it. His body shook. His red eye twitched. Tears trickled upon his flaccid lips and cheeks. The insults never ceased to be deplorable to him for there was a time when no one would have dared humiliate him.

Moustapha was a lonely man; Joshua was his only true friend.

There were two other shipmasters sitting across the sweltering room. One cracked a lewd joke: Lawrence watched them both split their sides with laughter, and then said to Joshua, 'I can't stay for very long; have to sort out the water situation with the cooper and the carpenter. Those old tubs need constant corking and repairs. If you need any provisions I have a surplus of yams, black beans and plantains. You could speak to my first mate and I'll give it to you for a very good price.'

'How much per hundredweight?' Joshua retorted. 'I've got extra ivory I could trade. I'll give you two small ivory tusks for five bags of yams, beans and plantains, each weighing one hundredweight.'

'Agreed. Exchange will be in two days. Tomorrow the crew have shore leave. The day after I might not be available; talk to the first mate if I'm indisposed.'

'Since you are sailing to Port Royal I shall in all probability see you there, and we can do more deals,' said Joshua. Lawrence nodded, stood up and walked towards the door. Nagamba followed, and glanced once more at Joshua as she stepped outside. Joshua was startled by the momentary look on her face.

It was a cry for help.

He stood up, captivated by her stunning beauty. She spotted Moustapha crouched beside the open window and smiled at him. Nagamba lanced Moustapha's heart with her expression. Then Lawrence kicked Moustapha.

'You contaminate the air with your foul body.'

The two other captains emerged. One flung some coins near Moustapha's ulcerated feet.

'I'm going to find the first mate now,' said Joshua. 'It's better if you don't follow me. I'll see you tomorrow at your house.'

Moustapha tried to stand up. His breathing was shallow. Meanwhile, Joshua slipped out to the back of the tavern, looking for the busy first mate among the many whores.

Moustapha tried to avoid the crowd and hid amongst the shadows to go home. He wondered whether he should have told Joshua about what he planned to do the following night.

There were several Trunks scattered among the big trees. In each hut, twenty slaves were crammed. It was dark when Moustapha crept between the bushes. Two cabins were situated at the far end of the forest, hidden near the base of the giant trees. Some distance from where Moustapha crouched, three guards sipped rum and chatted. Moustapha approached the small hut, and leaned against the barred window. From within he heard one of the slaves speaking in Bantu.

'Gashaka! You come from the line of the great and brave chiefs of the Bokoko. We trust in your wisdom and judgement. Help us.' There was a complete hush. The dim light of the candle reflected upon the desperate faces of the slaves squatting on the floor.

'I'll give my life for your freedom. The cry of the slaves will be heard one day. If we escape from here, I shall kill that captain of the brig. That white dog has Nagamba my dear sister as a slave.' In this infernal, virulent place, mired in adversity, in the glow of a candle a ray of hope flickered.

Moustapha threw two pebbles inside. Gashaka and the others jumped. They knew it couldn't be the guards. Gashaka approached the window and picked up the stones. Moustapha covered his face with the burnous.

'I'm Moustapha,' he whispered. 'Listen. Tomorrow night I shall come here. Please trust me.' Moustapha suddenly stopped. 'I thought I heard footsteps, I saw a woman slave with this animal captain of the brig. She's Nagamba, your sister. I heard you mentioning her name.'

'She has a snake-shaped bangle on her ankle,' Gashaka whispered, emotion in his voice.

'I hear someone,' said Moustapha and disappeared.

❦

'Don't go near the Trunks tonight. In fact, don't go near the place at all,' said Moustapha. 'There will be lots of trouble.' Joshua eyed him, quite concerned.

'Why, Moustapha? I feel something is wrong. Tell me.'

'I can't, I just can't. You will soon know.'

'The woman who was in the tavern with Lawrence. I'll never forget her eyes: she looked so desolate, almost pleading for help. I heard him call her Nagamba. This business at the Trunks wouldn't have anything to do with her, would it?' Moustapha said nothing; he just stared into the forest.

Joshua took a deep breath and said, 'When I saw her, that look was stamped upon me, as if it were there and then that my fate was sealed. I could strangle that animal Lawrence for gloating that she could fetch a good price from the highest bidder. I have been doing this evil trade for years. Moustapha, do you believe that everything is preordained?'

'Yes, of course,' answered Moustapha. 'Take Nagamba to Jamaica; free her from Lawrence's dirty claws. I have faith in premonitions and visions. Your destiny is with Nagamba. She will stand by your side as a rock, a lamp to light your years.'

Joshua stared at him, clearly startled. 'You never fail to amaze me with your tenacious beliefs and aspirations. Is she perhaps the hidden flame that enkindled the embers of my destiny into a raging, living fire?'

Moustapha rummaged in a drawer. 'I have here in this tiny leather pouch seeds of the Ackee fruit tree. It's a delicious fruit and grows in abundance. When you reach Port Royal, plant them around your garden.' Moustapha approached the window. 'This ravaging disease is eating every part of my body. I'll think of you, when the end comes. Maybe one day our spirits will meet. I shall be free, liberated. I'll miss you Joshua.'

Moustapha stifled his tears.

'All I ask of you is to trust me and protect Nagamba. She'll need your help.'

'Yes. I'm so moved by your words, so moved. I think we'd better go to Daboona.'

They both left the house and reached her small shack. Moustapha sat on the roadside and Joshua on the large bench.

'Daboona, bring plenty mimbo, plenty mimbo for me and Moustapha.'

'My Josheeya, I bring mimbo.' Against her huge breast she held two large clay jars. She went outside and gave them each a drink.

'Ah, Moustapha.' Joshua stretched his legs, sipping mimbo. 'It's Daboona's simplicity and innocence I love most.'

'Yes, yes,' said Moustapha in a sibilant voice.

A young woman walked across the road, her infant strapped on her back, and a few paces behind her, another child with a long leash was pulling an obstinate bleating goat. The mother turned around and clipped the boy's ears. He started to whine. She then took the rope from him and lugged the goat, her son still whimpering, running alongside.

Joshua sipped his mimbo watching the young woman disappear around the corner. The goat was still bleating and the child dragging behind.

Both men were silent. Moustapha picked up a handful of dust and threw it to the wind. A stray dog gnawed at a bone Daboona had thrown to him. Two natives approached, carrying baskets of yams on their heads. Seeing them, the frightened dog bolted with the bone in his mouth.

'Joshua, my friend,' Moustapha began, 'you look too young to be a ship's captain. How old are you now?'

'Old enough to be a captain. I was born in 1666 in Bristol in the west of England. Actually I come from a long line of seafarers. My father was a captain, sailing to India, Africa and China.'

'What about your mother?'

'She died when I was very young. I was looked after by an aunt, who was strict. It was a lonely time for me.'

Moustapha frowned. 'A young child needs a mother and father. They couldn't have been happy days for you.'

'I went to school of course,' replied Joshua. 'I spent most of my spare time daydreaming about the ships that sailed in and out of Bristol. It was better when my father was home. We used to go on long walks around the docks in Avonmouth, greeting the prosperous masters of vessels, and watching the tall ships coming and going in the Bristol Channel. They conjured up names of magical places that I could only dream about.

'I wasn't unhappy, but lonely. When I finished my studies my father, the old distinguished sea dog, arranged for me to ship out on an East Indiaman captained by a friend. I spent two years on that ship before I returned home. I was only sixteen, but had learnt so much in those two years, more than I ever learnt at school.'

'Ah yes, my childhood has been so different from yours: barefoot through the dingy, dusty streets of Timbuktu, I skipped and stole food from the market stalls. We lived in a hovel: men came in and out all day long. When I reached fifteen I decided to join the Arab slavers in the Sahara.'

Joshua smiled. 'I dealt with many people during those two years, and arranged a position as Sailing Master on a merchant ship trading on the Triangular Route—you know, Europe to Africa and then to the Caribbean and back to Europe. I was shocked to discover that the second leg involved me in slave trading, but I kept my concerns to myself.'

'So even then you had moral doubts about the slave trade,' Moustapha said.

'Well, yes, but what could I do? Anyway a couple of years ago I was offered the position as Master of a new ship, called the Hurricane, now anchored out there. Unfortunately on our last voyage we struck a rock near Port Royal and lost some of our copper sheets below the water line. Now she suffers from the depredations of the teredo worms.'

'How bad is that, my friend?' queried Moustapha.

'It's bad—only a question of time before the ship's no longer seaworthy.'

As they were about to leave, Moustapha called out, 'Daboona, I go away, come back no more. I no see you no more.

I go to forest. I die near trees I love. You good woman, good friend. Many years we always friends, our spirits together. Goodbye, Daboona.'

Daboona raised her face to the sky. 'You go with spirits, my friend leper. You good man leper. See you next year in Benin, Josheeya.' Joshua clasped her once more. She returned to the kitchen sobbing.

'Farewell, Moustapha. Godspeed.'

'Farewell, Joshua Quaile. All things must pass. Remember when we sat beneath the palm trees, drinking rum. The intoxicating nights pulsated as the women danced to the rhythm of the African drums.'

'Look, Joshua, the kite has flown in haste. Far out, the storm is brewing with my impending doom. Adieu, adieu.'

'I grieve for you, Moustapha; I depart with sadness. Across the golden shores the winds sigh.'

The two men turned and walked in opposite directions.

CHAPTER 10

Moustapha was an expert in extracting poisons from the seeds of the onaye plant and kept a clay pot of the white powder underneath his house. He also had six small darts in a box, each impregnated with resin from the bark of the same plant on the sharp ends, which would be dipped into the white powder to give them potency. The arrows had a wooden peg for gripping them.

The heat was oppressive. Around the fires sat slave traders and captains, who were all drunk. Some distance away, Moustapha, with caution, crept near the last trunk, where Gashaka was imprisoned with the other slaves. A guard reclined against a tree. Moustapha approached him.

'Warm tonight.'

The man was taken by surprise. 'Want some palm wine?' he yawned.

'Yes please,' Moustapha nodded, clutching the tiny clay pot in his right hand.

'I have two calabash cups, let me find them.' He rummaged in the dark. As he bent over, his shirt was pulled up, showing part of his buttocks. Moustapha rammed the poison dart into the guard's exposed flesh. Within seconds the man's tongue hung from his frothing mouth. The poison had a quick effect on his heart muscles and nervous system. He soon stopped breathing.

Immediately Moustapha groped for the keys of the trunk

from the dead man and raced to Gashaka's hut, unlocking the padlock. Nineteen slaves sped out and vanished into thick scrub. Gashaka and Moustapha approached the next trunk, when they heard voices coming towards them. They hid in the bush and waited.

Two caboceers inspected the second hut. 'I thought I heard something.' They waited for a few moments, and then walked away.

'Come, I'll take you to the brig,' Moustapha whispered. 'We'll get that white dog. Nagamba is with him now. I've a small fishing boat hidden among the reeds, just upriver from the wharf.'

Moustapha and Gashaka crawled on their stomachs through the undergrowth. Moustapha was short of breath.

'It's somewhere around here.' Moustapha fumbled and waded through the reeds and found the boat. It swayed and rocked as Gashaka helped him to board.

A canopy of giant trees covered the riverbank on both sides like parasols. An owl hooted somewhere in the distance. Before long, they could see lights on the side of the river, and they knew they were approaching the wharf in the town. The river opened out and slowed. There were many small vessels, canoes and pirogues scattered about, dipping nets and dropping lines.

'There she is.' Moustapha pointed to the brig. 'At the extreme end of the jetty.' He looked down at his right ankle and saw that the skin had broken and was weeping.

They paddled their way among the multitude of fishing boats, past several jetties and ships, and then drifted behind the dark hull of the Rainbow. An oil lamp was suspended from the side of the ship, illuminating a rope ladder whose ends swished in the dark waters of the bay.

'You go up first,' said Gashaka. 'If you stumble, I will help you. I don't know where the magazine is so you will have to show me.'

'I can't feel the rungs very well; I won't be able to climb. Why don't we sneak up the gangplank?'

'We can't do that. The wharf's too well lit and there are many people. A sailor from the ship is bound to see us. I'll climb up and see if I can find a way to bring you up in the long boat. They've left the davits set up to swing it down.'

'That's absurd, there's no way you could do that on your own.'

'You don't know what I'm capable of Moustapha.'

Gashaka clambered up the rope ladder. He alighted on the quarterdeck at the stern of the ship. Suddenly he stopped, as still as a leopard. He heard snoring and approached the sounds emanating from the shadows and saw two drunken sailors sprawled, one holding a bottle of rum in one hand and a blunderbuss in the other. He carefully prised the pistol out of the sailor's hand. Gashaka checked to make sure that the blunderbuss was loaded and powdered. He primed it, and at the click one man opened a single eye and saw the funnel of the gun in front of his nose.

'Get up.' Gashaka kicked them. The men staggered and stood still. Gashaka grabbed another blunderbuss from the second guard. 'Lower the long boat or you'll have an extra breathing hole.'

'Not bloody likely.'

'I've killed men before. Two more white men mean nothing to me.'

Reconsidering, the men dropped the long boat but the block and tackle squeaked. Gashaka watched to see if anyone was coming, aiming the blunderbusses at the nervous men.

Moustapha elevated himself from the canoe. The two boats rocked to and fro. The extremities of his fingers were numb and bleeding. He lifted one foot at a time and landed in the longboat, puffing. Gashaka then made the sailors raise the longboat. As Moustapha reached the top, Gashaka pulled him over with one hand, his eyes riveted on the two men. Moustapha fell on the deck with a thud. The loud commotion and lewd voices on the wharf wafted over them. Gashaka shot one of the guards in the throat and he fell to the deck, lifeless. The second man started to scream. The discharge from the second blunderbuss ripped his mouth open.

Moustapha climbed to his feet. 'Follow me,' he whispered. They crept down the companion way. Moustapha went to knock on the cabin door.

'Wait!' Gashaka wrenched an axe from the bulkhead a few yards away, and struck at the cabin door. It fell inwards. Lawrence stood there naked. Gashaka pounced.

Nagamba was crouched in the corner. On seeing Gashaka she tried to get to her feet.

'Stay there,' Moustapha warned as Gashaka slashed a vicious blow on Lawrence's right hand. The captain winced in great pain.

'This is for calling us dirty niggers. You will never sell or beat slaves any more.' The two men grappled fiercely. Lawrence tripped over the broken door, trying to escape, and Gashaka brought down the axe on his other hand.

'I can still hear the wailing and crying of women and children crammed in the stinking steerage. Your rotten ship was infested with rats, biting the little ones. From Calabar to Benin it was hell. Hell!'

The gash on Lawrence's hand was deep. Blood spurted all over him. He saw the shiny axe hurling down at him again. He sprang back and with great force swung his right leg upwards and kicked Gashaka in the testicles. Gashaka was disabled for a moment, clutching his groin. Lawrence fled through the corridors on to the main deck pursued by Moustapha, Nagamba and Gashaka. They followed him across the poop deck, past the mizzen and main masts. As the three approached him he babbled insensibly. He had lost a great amount of blood and his head started spinning. He stumbled towards the fo'csle and slipped into the scuppers, almost reaching the bow. Gashaka, with the agility of a young buck, crashed on to Lawrence, his axe swinging. Near the rail, Gashaka thrust the axe upon Lawrence's knee, breaking it with a loud crack, and then lunged once more at his thigh, exposing the bone.

'This is for kicking Moustapha and for defiling Nagamba, my dearest sister. You will never leave this place, never!' Gashaka bellowed.

Gashaka pushed Lawrence between the rails and he fell into the murky water below. For a few seconds Lawrence was submerged, and then floated and dragged himself on to the boardwalk. It was very dark on that side.

'Do you think he's dead?' asked Moustapha.

'If he's not, the sharks or crabs will soon get him,' said Gashaka.

The crabs came out by the hundreds on the muddy banks towards him. His muffled screams were drowned out as the crabs scuttled down his throat, tearing out his tongue, eye sockets, and stripped his entire body of the flesh. His life ebbed away. He looked like a squirming, moving skeleton.

'Let's go to the main magazine,' said Moustapha. The three entered the dry hold where two hundred barrels of gunpowder were stored. There were several small leather cases on the floor. They picked them up and filled them with gunpowder. One by one they emptied their bags, making an unbroken line of gunpowder on the companion way ascending to the main deck and on to the fo'csle, and then set it alight. This gave them time to get to the longboat. Gashaka and Nagamba lowered it down to the water with Moustapha in it, and then dived into the river below. Moustapha started rowing as Nagamba and Gashaka boarded the longboat, took the oars and paddled away from the ship.

Moustapha guided them, familiar with the marshy estuary. They were among the floating reeds when they heard the cacophonous blast, followed by ringing bells, horns and drums. It was safe for them now to drift through the thick morass, and they neared Moustapha's house.

'The Rainbow! The Rainbow's on fire,' yelled the factor from the shore, pointing to the bow. The rumpus thundered across the surface of the swamp. People in confusion darted to and fro on the wharf, milling around and screaming. Joshua came out with the other captains and watched. He knew and understood then what Moustapha had meant when he said, 'There'll be lots of trouble.'

Many hurled buckets of water at the ship. Some tried to form a line, but there was too much confusion. Others jostled and tried to climb up on to the deck, gesturing for people below to pass buckets up to them, but the heat was too intense, and they jumped back into the river. The breeze came in. The fire increased. Along the bulwarks a drunken crewman, his clothes on fire, fled and threw himself overboard. Within a few minutes a tremendous explosion erupted with bursts of fury as the magazine detonated. The whole ship rumbled; shooting flames belched in all directions licking the oak beams and rigging.

'Who would have hated Lawrence so much to do this?' another captain asked.

Joshua said, 'I don't think I'll stay here much longer. It's too dangerous,too risky.'

'I dare say you're right. I wonder what happened to Lawrence? He just vanished.'

Joshua watched the burning inferno and exclaimed, 'I'm going back to my ship. There's nothing more we can do.' He turned and walked away.

The next day a fisherman approached the burnt wreck on the side of the boardwalk.

'Body dead! Body,' he yelled. The crowd stampeded. The crabs still feasted and devoured the rest of the corpse.

'It must be Captain Lawrence,' said the factor.

The skeleton was left to bleach in the scorching sun and a day later the agent ordered the sailors to bury the remains. The crew of the Rainbow stayed in Benin for a week and then joined another slaver.

CHAPTER 11

'Hurry to my house—I wish to give you something—and then you go to the Hurricane. I shall scuttle the longboat and head deep to the forest.' In a maze under the house lay the concealed treasure in small chests.

'I want you to share the gold with Joshua. Tell him to plant the Ackee seeds around his house in the West Indies.' Moustapha gazed at Nagamba's sad eyes and quivering lips. 'Farewell Nagamba, do not weep for me. Your destiny is with Joshua.

'I sank into this wicked life and sold my soul for gold dust. Unforgivable crimes. Gold cannot purge nor purify my corrupt body. My salvation is to die here in the forests alone. Tell Joshua not to grieve for me. This is where I love most.' Moustapha then raised his face. 'Perhaps the spirits will forgive my sins and we'll all meet in the beyond. I love you, Gashaka, my brother. Forgive me.'

The heart of oak and loftiness of spirit touched Gashaka. He hugged the sick Moustapha who was wrestling with death. Gashaka did not fear to touch his leprous friend. He knew that Moustapha would soon be liberated.

Moustapha wept. No one had held him so closely except his mother as a child in Timbuktu. He wore the cadaverous mask of a leper like the mask of a condemned man awaiting the end.

෬ඉ

Nagamba and Gashaka carried the gold chests in two separate canvas bags and trudged through the tangled undergrowth. The air was heavy with the thick smoke from the smouldering brig. There was pandemonium. Captains, caboceers, natives and factors buzzed around watching the calamity. The crew were busy running up and down the gangplank of the Hurricane and did not notice Nagamba and Gashaka going up, just two more black faces among so many others. She wore a loose native garment and headscarf. They knocked on Joshua's door. At once Nagamba recognised him from the tavern.

'I am Gashaka and this is my sister, Nagamba.' They placed the two bags on the deck. 'A gift from Moustapha.' Joshua stared open-mouthed at the gold. Gashaka was biting his lip so hard that blood began to drip down, and Nagamba was trembling. Joshua smiled and poured them some water with lime.

'Please sit down. I am happy that you both made it here safely.' He gazed out the porthole. 'There's a big crowd out there. Remain inside the cabin while I tell the officers that we will sail at dawn.' He smiled again at Nagamba. 'I am glad you're here.' He left the cabin and returned twenty minutes later.

Gashaka said, 'Captain, I must tell you that Captain Lawrence is dead. He will not violate Nagamba again.'

Joshua looked at him in silence for a few moments. 'I shall tell my officers you are Nagamba's brother and speak only Bantu. They must not suspect you of any complicity in Lawrence's death. We must be careful.'

Tears formed in Gashaka's eyes. 'Thank you.'

᪻

'Nagamba, you can sleep in my spare bunk and you, Gashaka, on the deck in the corner next to her.' Joshua watched Nagamba.' You're very quiet. No harm will come to you here.'

No *harm*. Her mind raced back to the tragic events that had occurred since she left her home in Africa. In particular she trembled as she recalled her dead son buried in the forest.

'You will come under my protection as long as you are on this ship. You are among friends now.' She cast her sad eyes upon the large table piled with charts and navigation instruments. Facing her was a young white captain, but still a slaver. The very thought made her shiver and yet his warmth puzzled her.

With a tremor she murmured, 'I would like to believe your words but …' On impulse she stood.

'You are now the master of two runaway slaves; you own us.' She covered her lips with her hand.

'No, I am not your master, he's dead.'

Gashaka wiped his sweaty forehead, watching Joshua sit down.

'Listen to me, both of you. There is great danger if you stay here because of the events of tonight. My ship sails in the morning for Jamaica. I hope you will agree to accompany me.'

'Why can't we just slip ashore and disappear?' said Nagamba. 'We could be miles away by daybreak.'

'If that's what you really want, you are free to go. But consider my urgent suggestion first, I beg of you. As a beautiful woman you would have been seen with Lawrence ashore. You wouldn't get far at all. Someone will recognise you and raise the alarm. Please stay here where you are safe.'

Throughout the night they spoke in whispers. Gashaka told Joshua what happened to Lawrence and the brig. Finally Joshua dimmed the small oil lamp.

'Good night, Nagamba,' he said softly.

༄

It was still semi-dark when Joshua, Gashaka and Nagamba went on deck. The bosun had just stepped out and stretched.

'Good morning, Captain.'

Joshua nodded. 'I bought these two slaves yesterday. They come from the Cameroons. He is her brother. She stays with me, as my woman. Give him the servant's cabin next to mine. He can polish my boots and serve liquor to me. The cabin boy will still clean my cabin. Since Gashaka here is my personal servant, make sure he gets a decent meal. If he has nothing to do, he can help in the manger. She told me in Bantu that he was some kind of animal doctor back in the Cameroons.' Joshua lit his pipe. The bosun nodded and walked way.

'Turn out the crew, set the sails,' said Joshua. 'Let's get out of this hellhole.'

'Aye aye, Captain,' said the first mate

The brigantine sailed out to sea. Her dazzling sails fluttered with the wind. Nagamba, from the deck, watched the receding African coast for the last time. Joshua stood on the quarterdeck pondering the momentous events of the previous night. He could still hear Moustapha's words: *She'll stand by your side as a rock, a lamp to light your years.*

Gashaka walked out of the captain's cabin carrying a servant's tray with a bottle of fine Muscat and a glass. Joshua approached Nagamba, who was silent and reserved in his presence.

Joshua said, 'I hope you will like Jamaica.' He buttoned his coat against the chill of the early morning wind. 'There are stretches of mountains like in the Cameroons on the island.

'Are you going to sell us along with those poor wretches rotting in the hold?'

'No, definitely not. You and Gashaka are not going to be sold as slaves or servants. I will do everything within my power to help you both. Please trust me.'

Joshua was a white man, Nagamba thought. He must want something. What was it? She had now been raped three times and men's lustful behaviour seemed to her the obvious answer. Whatever it was, she felt that it was only a matter of time before he tried something.

CHAPTER 12

Soon after captain Van Den Hoosten arrived in Bonny, near Old Calabar from Douala, the men were separated from the female slaves. Alimba clutched her twins in panic when Moshebere and Bundere were whisked away. The one-eyed Caboceer spotted the older children, Marufa and Ebouko, who sat beneath the straggling trees.

He whispered to the factor, 'We'll take them to Captain Montague of the Nightingale. He pays more than the other slavers.'

Several ships lay anchored not far from the town. Slave traders abducted children for them. Like vultures they snatched the young and innocent who were highly prized in the West Indies. The captains had no compunction whatsoever. They were devoid of compassion and ignored where the children had come from or who their parents were.

Bundere and Moshebere sat below the trees with other slaves, along the extreme right of the riverbank, waiting to board the Primrose.

'My wife is heavy with child, Ebouko my son and my daughter Marufa; what fate awaits them?' Bundere murmured, looking at the misery around them.

'I heard one of the caboceers mention they are shipping us to the West Indies.' Moshebere felt like a caged animal. He needed Alimba, his woman, and the twins. He gazed across the river in the opposite direction where the Nightingale and the Skylark were moored.

The day came and went. Evening fell. Mahadana was shivering, an attack of malaria. She was delirious and eventually fell asleep. Awana, the twin boy, sucked at Alimba's breast and Onana on the other one. She reclined, concealed behind the tree, the caboceer and factor not aware of her presence in the dark. They approached like prowling animals and pounced, gagging Ebouko and Marufa. Alimba screamed.

Mahadana awoke, weak from high temperature. She looked around, but the children were not there. She tried to stand and then fell, rose up again and shuffled a few paces. Her legs gave way. She crawled, lacerating her bleeding knees, and slid on her side, her cumbersome body scraping the ground. Her calls went unheeded. She felt the unborn child kicking.

'I must live for the baby,' she shrieked, demented with grief. She spat at the guard. 'Evil spirits will hunt and kill you!' Blood trickled down the side of her mouth.

He prodded her with the butt of his musket and laughed.

'May your tongue be glued to your mouth. You will never laugh again.'

A canoe waited on the shore. With haste, the slave traders paddled towards the Nightingale. From the deck Captain Montague watched the men hauling Marufa and Ebouko up the plank.

Once on board the captain and bosun led them to the steerage surrounded by rope and sails to muffle their cries. There were sixty other children huddled in the corner. Captain Montague took out a leather pouch containing gold coins and gave half to the factor and half to the caboceer.

'When I return next time, I want more mongrels,' hissed Montague.

'The price will be higher,' replied the factor.

If every oak beam of the old slaver could talk; if rope and sail could comfort the stolen children of Africa; if masts, crossbeams and rigging could whisper; if crosstrees on high and spars could hear the frightened young in the dark holds; if bower anchor, bulwarks, bilges and scuppers could expel the venom from this ship—then every part of it would lament the plaintive cries of the bereft little ones.

The Nightingale, full to capacity, set sail for Port Royal. Among the children were Ebouko and Marufa.

Through the morning the canoes and pirogues paddled towards the Primrose. Moshebere and Bundere climbed into the last canoe which was overcrowded. The boat started to rock and sway, and with a fierce sucking sound, she capsized, throwing everyone into the water. Bundere, Moshebere and the other slaves swam in panic towards the Primrose. Crocodiles lurked nearby. From underneath the brackish water, they leapt with tremendous force, their gaping jaws propelling the slaves upwards. As the slaves crashed into the water, the crocodiles dragged them underneath, shaking them from side to side, lashing their tails.

Captain Shokeby leant over the rails and shouted, 'Who's going to pay for the slaves? It was their men that overloaded the canoes.'

Moshebere and Bundere were hoisted up with other slaves.

'This is a morbid country,' said Shokeby, pacing towards

the fo'csle and watching the main mast. He pulled his fob out and looked at the time.

'Get the longboat ready and ask the bursar to look over the accounts,' he cried out to the first mate. 'We're going ashore to sort this out. We lost twenty slaves and they need to either make good on the number of slaves or pay me back.'

Then the captain saw several palm nut eagle vultures circling above the town. 'This is a bad sign. The stench!' Shokeby wrung his hands. 'It smells of the pox.'

The first case of smallpox was in the market. It flared and spread throughout Bonny. The victims were people of the town, and slaves alike. Corpses lay around covered with weeping pustules. They were left to rot in the scorching sun. Carrion birds feasted on the cadavers. It was like a ghost town, similar to the black plague. Alarmed merchants, guards, vendors and agents vanished deep into the forest.

'Look!' he called out. An eagle extracted and hooked a large hunk of a dead corpse between its talons. 'Unfurl the sails! We must flee at once from this doomed town.' The westerly breeze filled her wide shrouds. She sped close to the wind, racing across the wild swell, leaving behind a trail of white spindrift.

There was a dim light in the hold from a small hanging lamp. The pounding waves broke against the running ship.

'In many years to come we will drive the white men out of Africa.' Moshebere shrugged his shoulders with deep-rooted antipathy. He knew that he and Bundere would never see Africa again. His eyes portrayed depths of sadness and longing for the high mountains in the Cameroons, where he was free without fetters or chains.

The wind picked up and the Primrose sailed out across

the vast ocean and arrived at St Kitts before the hurricane season.

Many of the women and the young were hoisted up and dumped on the deck of the third ship, the Skylark.

'I hear the drums beating,' said Mahadana. 'The sky is dark, covered with vultures and eagles. The white men brought a bad sickness from their land.'

'I wonder why the bells are tolling' said Captain Winter-bottom.

'Listen to the horns,' the bosun rasped.

From the shore a caboceer shouted, 'Smallpox!' Everyone ran in panic, leaving the goods on the riverbank.

'Damn the cargo, we sail at once. The bubonic plague wiped out half of Europe. But the smallpox epidemic is as deadly. Years ago there was an outbreak in Accra, thousands perished.' The captain bit his nails. 'We sail now, let's get out on the open sea.'

'Aye aye, sir,' the bosun saluted. Upon the news spreading the other slavers, half empty, fled to the coast in panic. The epidemic pursued the Skylark. Six cases of smallpox erupted in the lower deck after one day at sea.

'Don't touch the corpses or handle any of their belong-ings,' shouted the doctor. 'Use the pitchfork and throw them overboard. It is imperative to fumigate the entire ship. Put hot shot in buckets of vinegar and spill the stuff everywhere. The fumes will kill anything.'

The next few days no new cases appeared. For the rest of the journey to Nevis in the Indies, the women remained in the hold.

Captain Winterbottom was on the main deck, talking to the officers. He was pleased that all was well, and quoted from the famous African proverb:

'Beware and take care of the Bight of Benin; few come out, though many go in.'

The two families were torn apart. Unaware, they sailed within a few hours of each other on three different ships out of Africa to the West Indies. The tragic irony was the proximity between the slavers while in Bonny: they were less than a quarter of a mile apart.

CHAPTER 13

After one week's sailing Nagamba had relaxed a little and had even talked to Joshua. She still worried about her fate on arrival in Jamaica, but felt some degree of assurance from Joshua's positive words.

'Nagamba, I have your well-being at heart, and will make sure that you are well looked after. Come with me.'

With reluctance she followed him into his cabin, unsure of his motives.

'Look.' He showed her some papers and documents he had been preparing. 'These are papers giving you your freedom. They are called documents of manumission. You will keep these to prove you are not a slave and will never be sold.'

Nagamba looked at him, astonished. 'You would do this for me?'

'And for Gashaka too. Nagamba, I am sick of this immoral trade. Once I get to Jamaica I intend to buy some land and become a plantation owner.'

'Won't that require slaves to do the work?'

'I will not employ slaves. Instead I will pay men to work for me as free men. You and Gashaka could live on my plantation.'

Nagamba was speechless.

'Please, I must go. I feel overwhelmed.' She slipped out of the cabin and went up to the fo'csle, her mind in a whirl. She managed to calm her fluttering heart. She decided to adopt a wait-and-see policy with Joshua. He was displaying kindness and courtesy towards her, but did he have an ulterior motive?

Three weeks passed by. Nagamba stood on the after deck gazing at the sea, her mind brooding on the enigmatic Captain Quaile. During the last three weeks she had steadily warmed to him. Could he be genuine in his desire to help her? What were his feelings towards her?

'Morning, Nagamba, you're looking lovely as ever today.'

Nagamba jumped.

'You took me by surprise, Captain.'

'Pardon me, I didn't mean to scare you. What were you thinking about?'

'Oh, the freedom I lost when I was taken into slavery. I'll never regain it.'

Joshua took hold of her hand. 'Nagamba, listen to me. You are now free. Free to do whatever you wish.'

She sighed mournfully. 'No, Captain, I am not free. I am on a ship on a mighty ocean heading to a strange country. This is not of my choosing. Where is the freedom in that?'

'As soon as we reach Jamaica you can do whatever you want.'

She looked at him with a faint smile. 'No I cannot. I was free in Cameroon but that was taken from me. To dump me ashore in Jamaica and tell me I am free is not freedom. I would not survive in Jamaica on my own.'

'I will be there to look after you. Remember, I intend to purchase a plantation and you and Gashaka can stay there as long as you like.'

'Thank you, Captain.'

'Nagamba, you did not have freedom in Cameroon either. You were subject to tribal raids, attacks by slavers, famine, drought and flooding.'

'That's right, but it was what I chose. And it was forcibly taken from me. Now I have no freedom.'

Joshua smiled. 'You're a most perceptive and engaging person, Nagamba. Alright, I will help you to find the freedom you seek, wherever it is. I'll do whatever is possible. I really want to help you. I am a free man and I'll do all I can to make you feel the same way. The most important aspect is freedom from fear.'

'Thank you, Captain.'

Nagamba was becoming more entranced by Joshua's kindness and chivalry towards her. She decided to test him.

'Captain, may I call you by your name?'

'Yes, of course.'

'Joshua, I would like you to do something important. It concerns the slaves.'

He was somewhat puzzled.

'There are four goats in the hold, two nannies and two billies,' she said.

Joshua laughed heartily. 'Indeed we have four noisy goats.'

'Well,' smiled Nagamba. 'I'd like the children and women to have more goat's milk. It is essential for their health. I remember in the Cameroons we had a herd of fifty. I don't mind milking them myself, or helping Gashaka. My second request is if the slaves could have bigger rations of boiled horse beans and yams, and on occasion, salted meats or fish if there are any in stock, please. After all, Joshua, if the slaves are well fed, I think they'll remember you as a kind captain.'

'You're quite observant and sharp. Of course, I shall attend to it now.'

She smiled and walked around the spacious cabin. He caught and lifted her in mid-air.

'I can foresee a life full of adventure for you, Nagamba. I'll be back shortly.'

'Bosun, your attention please,' said Joshua. 'Have all the slaves brought up for a few hours on the main deck. It's hot down in the holds. Have the portholes and gratings opened for ventilation.'

'Aye aye, sir, right away.' The bosun left. Joshua happily paced the quarterdeck. The young midshipman darted towards the poop.

'Young lad, come here please.'

'Yes, sir.'

'Ask Gashaka who tends the goats in the manger to see me at once.'

The midshipman saluted and ran off.

Joshua greeted Scully the cook. 'Smells nice.'

'Good morning, Captain.' Scully was astonished by this early visit.

'What have we got for lunch today?'

'Ah, well, I thought of dishing out some gammon, tongue and yam chops. You like yam chops don't you?'

'I do. Now show me the list of meals for the slaves.' The cook fumbled around the paraphernalia of kitchen utensils and kegs.

'Here we are, sir.' His greasy, grubby hands smudged the paper. Scully wiped his runny nose with his soiled sleeve.

'Disgusting manners! Wash your hands more often when you handle food and don't wipe your nose again in front of me—repulsive!'

Scully contorted his face.

'Any rats around?'

'They're everywhere,' said Scully.

Gashaka appeared then.

'You're a good tracker and would know where rats hide,' Joshua said to Gashaka. 'Scully will show you where all the traps are. I want you, the cook and cooper to lay them everywhere. Those black furry beasts bite young children. Gashaka, kill those filthy vermin please. I'll check with you later this afternoon.'

Gashaka turned around. He was swift, almost as if he walked on air, leaping from one foot to another with nimbleness.

'Scully, as from today the slaves will be supplemented extra rations of boiled yams and horse beans; also, fish and meat. And don't forget to give more goat's milk to the children. Check with Gashaka.'

'Yes, I've seen this young buck squeeze the goats' teats with such speed,' Scully chuckled.

'Well, I am busy.' Joshua turned and walked away.

'Bloody arrogant man, grumpy,' Scully mumbled to himself and then pressed one finger on each nostril and blew his nose, letting the snot fly with the wind.

'I'll show him disgusting manners,' he growled.

The albatross flew behind the brigantine for many days.

'Look at her large wingspan,' said Joshua. 'How she glides motionless above the water.'

Nagamba stood close to Joshua, wanting to touch him, trembling with anticipated happiness although still with a hint of fear. They had been travelling in close company for nearly six weeks across the ocean. Her feelings towards Joshua had developed from fear to warmth and affection, even love, although she would never admit this.

'Ah, her brilliant white chest,' he exclaimed, leaning against the taffrail. 'Did you know, Nagamba, that albatrosses mate for life? If one dies the other flies to a remote island and pines away. I'll show you one day the isolated places where they breed. There are hundreds of them, breathtaking. 'Will you follow me, Nagamba?' he asked in a serious tone.

With her dark moist eyes in pools of white, she looked at him, startled by his words. Then she whispered, 'Yes, Joshua I will.'

'Come, let's go to my cabin.' Spontaneously he carried her across the deck. The sailors watched with amusement.

'The white slaver and his black slave,' said one man.

'The captain's been a bit dotty since we left Benin,' another chuckled.

⚜

Joshua laid Nagamba on his bunk, covered with cheetah skins, and rested his head between her soft breasts. Her nipples swelled. Wisps of his red beard brushed them. He explored with tenderness her young body. A slight tremor ran through her.

'I shall be your albatross, Joshua Quaile.' She clung to him.

He would never shame or humiliate her and realised with a start that, if she conceived, their child would be a mulatto. This concerned him for he was aware of the intrigues and gossip that would shroud their lives in Jamaica.

Oblivious to Joshua's musings Nagamba sat near the porthole and looked at the endless panorama of the blue sea and sky. Joshua approached from behind and held her tight. He loved Nagamba, and in spite of his past he believed in the sanctity of marriage as his parents had. The bond with Nagamba would never be severed.

❦

There was a fair wind the next day with cirrus woolpack clouds. Nagamba stood near the porthole and looked out at the endless panorama of blue sea and sky. Joshua approached behind and held her tight. She felt safe under Joshua's wings. He was her lighthouse that beamed across the far unknown land to a new beginning. The man was her anchor from yesterday's despair in Africa to the dawn of her tomorrows: to be beside Joshua, that is all she desired.

❦

Joshua strutted noisily towards Samuel Taylor, the carpenter, who was working with his adze.

'My dear fellow, still caulking the old girl?'

'Good morning, Captain.' The carpenter ran his fingers through his thick crop of grey hair. 'She has what I might describe as signs of debilitating old age. Worm eaten, riddled with them, a severe touch of arthritis. She groans and creaks.' Taylor and Joshua burst out laughing. 'Several of the magnificent oak beams are decayed.'

'Well, Captain Quaile, the brigantine served you well for years on the Triangular Trade. When you reach Port Royal, she'll have to undergo a strict and grave inspection. I doubt if she'll be seaworthy again.' The carpenter knitted his brow. 'At present in good weather she holds her head above water, but in rough seas she'll break in two. I dread to think what her condition is like underneath, should we turn the ship on her keel.' The carpenter wiped his hands on a rag.

'In my opinion she'll never sail back to England.'

'I remember when she was built in Bristol though,' said Joshua.

⚜

'There's nothing more beautiful to the ear than the sound of children coming from the lower deck,' said Joshua as they strolled on deck in the cool of the evening.

'You are sad, my Joshua,' Nagamba observed. 'Why?'

'I keep thinking of Moustapha, sick and alone.' He gazed at the night lamp swaying on the cross-trees. He was also sad because he knew his ship would have to be either sunk or scuttled. It would never sail again.

Nagamba was the centre of his life. Joshua remembered the negress in Cape Coast castle standing near the window saying, 'You're a free man' and Moustapha's dying words: 'Farewell, farewell, Joshua Quaile. All things must pass. Far out a storm is brewing for my impending doom.'

Nagamba snuggled against him.

'The Hurricane has been my home for many years. I know the Atlantic in all its moods. It can be rough in bad weather when huge waves charge us like angry bulls. She lifts her bow, crashing on each hurling monster beneath her. For hours she battles and chases the devils.'

'Are there black-winged albatrosses?' Nagamba said suddenly with childlike innocence.

'Not that I know of,' he replied, touching her nose. 'There are black swans and white swans; they mate for life like albatrosses do. There are albatrosses with black brows though.'

⚜

Alimba looked at the twins on the raised earth pallets. Onana was asleep but restless, covered by a coarse mat. Beads of perspiration shone on his forehead. Alimba poured some water from the calabash and wiped his face. Awana sat beside her, playing with a stick. In the middle of the cabin a small fire burned throughout the night to repel mosquitoes. The earth floor crawled with insects. The hut was made of wattle and small branches intertwined and joined between two long upright posts. It was thatched with wide palm leaves. Whiffs of smoke escaped from the small opening in the roof and the narrow door.

Mahadana's sad voice was heard through the wattle cabin. 'Soon the child will be born. The little one is kicking hard. My hands blister and bleed.'

'Put some palm oil on the blisters,' said Alimba, and gave the oil to Mahadana.

With a piercing blast of the conch shell, all the slaves rose at dawn to face another cruel day on the plantation. The first gang of strong male slaves was herded to the cane fields with hoes and bills. They were supervised by a white overseer and a negro driver, holding leather whips. Under the scorching sun they toiled and planted cane shoots in rows, resting their exhausted bodies for only a short period at noon.

The women distributed water from large casks driven by mules. Pregnant women and those with minor infirmities were weeding. The third assemblage consisted of youth employed in manuring by hand and stumping. The slaves were given meagre food: plantains, yams, and on occasion, pickled fish.

Decomposed vegetation and the ashy loam were ideal for growing crops of sugar in the tropical Leeward Islands of St Kitts and Nevis. Both twin islands were separated by a three-mile passage. Nevis is oval and St Kitts's topography shaped like an Indian club. The lofty mountains were mantled with forests. In the 1620s the English began to colonise the Antilles but until 1670 the numbers of slaves were few.

The pains became frequent. Mahadana clutched her distended belly. The heat was intense. A few rats scrambled around her. Within an hour her screaming blasted through the lush green cane stalks. The overseer and driver rushed to the scene.

'Woman, woman, I take out plenty babies before. I take piccaninny out.' He knelt between her wet thighs. It was a quick and easy birth. The excited negro held the infant in the air.

'Hallelujah, Hallelujah little one!' he cried and gave the baby to Mahadana.

The overseer peered at her and curled up his lip. 'Another baboon.' He grunted and turned away, lashing his whip on the dusty ground. The negro driver helped Mahadana shuffle back to the hut. Alimba cleaned and swabbed the infant.

'My instinct never fails me,' she said. 'You'll meet with Ebouko and Marufa. Ships' captains sell kidnapped children to wealthy planters, who employ them as servants and cooks. You have a lovely son, only a few hours old and such a strong grip from his tiny hand. He'll rise with the sun and follow his destiny with heroes.'

A few days later Mahadana was working back in the cane fields with the newborn Yabassi strapped on her back.

The slaves were allotted a small parcel of land near the huts to grow produce. They also kept some goats and chickens. The animals were fattened with cane refuse.

Every Sunday morning the two women went to the

market to sell their small harvest. Upon their shoulders and heads they carried heavy bundles, and the twins dragged behind. Using the money they earned they bought clothes and a variety of goods they required.

The months flew by, the boys romped around and Yabassi sucked at Mahadana's pendulous breast bursting with milk. Life fell into a pattern. Both women longed for their husbands, not knowing that they were on another sugar plantation only three miles away.

CHAPTER 14

The two-masted schooner, Pandora, sailed into Nevis with the setting sun and anchored among the tall ships. Its owner and captain was Pinkus, a Jewish merchant who had sailed his ship for years around the Caribbean. He dealt in merchandise brought by slavers from England and Africa to various ports in the West Indies. It was a lucrative enterprise. He sold his goods to plantation owners and their wives in luxurious mansions as well as to the local people and slaves in the markets who came on Sundays with their own produce.

In every port where Pinkus stayed for a period of time he berthed the schooner on the far side of the quay, near the large warehouses and emporiums where he bargained and purchased his commodities from merchants, agents and captains he knew.

Pinkus, the angel of mercy, was a Spharadic Jew. Years ago his grandfather had fled to the Caribbean from Portugal where Jews were being persecuted. Conscious of his past, Pinkus deeply felt the suffering of the negro slaves.

His two assistants, Ezekiel and Shyloh, half starved, had roamed the wharfs of Barbados seeking work. Sometimes they were lucky, carting and loading heavy bales from the ships to the warehouses. They lived like scavengers, stealing whenever the opportunity arose. Then Pinkus spotted them and took the two under his wing. Ezekiel the musteefino and Shyloh the mulatto started working for Pinkus.

'We'll stay here longer than usual,' said Pinkus. 'The Pandora needs painting before we sail to St Kitts. Tomorrow we will hire a horse and cart as we have done in the past.'

Early the following day they lugged the stock from the schooner to the wharf, loaded it on to the cart, and then threaded the narrow streets to trade. This means of transportation was expedient and cheap.

Sunday was market day. The mule snorted and brayed, flicking the flies with its tail. Pinkus watched the woman with the twins and the other child crawling on all fours with its mother.

Pinkus was a practical and religious man. He often read his family Bible which he carried with him everywhere.

He remembered vividly, with loathing, the notorious candle and scramble auctions he saw in Port Royal. His dislike and bitterness against the white planters churned inside him.

Slaves on the wharf were negotiated with a factor at the candle auction. Those with pustular syphilis, dysentery, blindness and other diseases were thrown to the waiting sharks. The emaciated, the ailing, touched with the wind and other infirmities, were bought by small traders for a pitiful pound each.

The scramble auction was far more ruthless and barbaric. The slaves were herded to a large compound and the gates opened to start the sale. Hordes of purchasers stampeded, swooping down like vultures, clawing and throttling their victims with ferocity. Overseers and drivers hurtled ropes to lassoo, cordon and pluck the terrified slaves. Young babies were savagely abducted from their mothers' breasts, their tender limbs almost torn from their sockets. The white planters impaled and broke their butterflies on the wheel. Pinkus never forgot.

'Hard boiled eggs, goat's cheese, plantains, boiled yams,' Alimba's voice rang with the morning breeze.

'I haven't tasted goat's cheese for ages.' Pinkus looked at Ezekiel and Shyloh. 'Do you like goat's cheese?'

'We do,' they said, and burst out laughing.

Pinkus turned to the two women. 'Good morning, ladies.'

'Good morning, sir,' said Alimba.

Pinkus said, 'We'll take a dozen hard-boiled eggs and some goat's cheese please.'

Alimba handed over the food. She smiled as Pinkus gave her the money.

'Thank you, sir. I am Alimba and she is Mahadana. We grew up together in the Cameroons.'

Shyloh and Ezekiel had never heard of such a place.

Pinkus grinned. 'That's in Africa, up in the mountains.'

'So far away,' Shyloh mumbled.

'I am sure you will be delighted to see our scarves, silk, cotton, linen, and calico to make pants for the boys.'

Ezekiel began unpacking the goods.

Bewildered, Alimba replied, 'All our goods will never be sufficient to repay you.'

Ezekiel smiled. 'We will barter next Sunday.'

Feeling pleased with himself, Ezekiel eyed Pinkus.

Alimba said, 'I would like the colourful, fringed scarf.'

'And you Mahadana?' Pinkus asked.

'I would like the white silk to wear when I see Bundere again.' Her voiced showed signs of despair. 'They took our men and kidnapped my two older children.' There was a tightening in her throat. Yabassi was trying to stand but was unstable. She picked him up.

'He's hungry, I'd better feed him.'

Her words recalled to Pinkus shadows of his people's suffering at the hands of the Spanish Inquisition. He uttered a short prayer, his hands on his Bible stacked in the cart in front of him.

'We sail to Barbados, St Kitts, Nevis and Monserrrat where slaves work on sugar plantations. I have a way of spying or using bribery among thieves and overseers, as well as receiving information from wealthy housewives who employ slaves. It is a merciless game. Now please supply me the names of your husbands and children.'

Pinkus wrote the names down in his big Bible. 'We'll keep a look out for them.'

For the first time Mahadana felt a tiny glimmer of hope.

'Next Sunday after market we'll take you on board for lunch.'

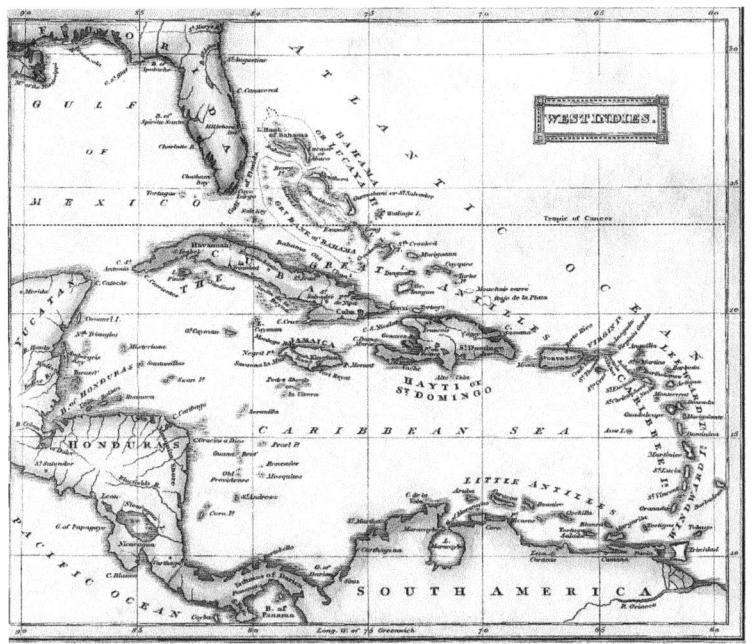

West Indies

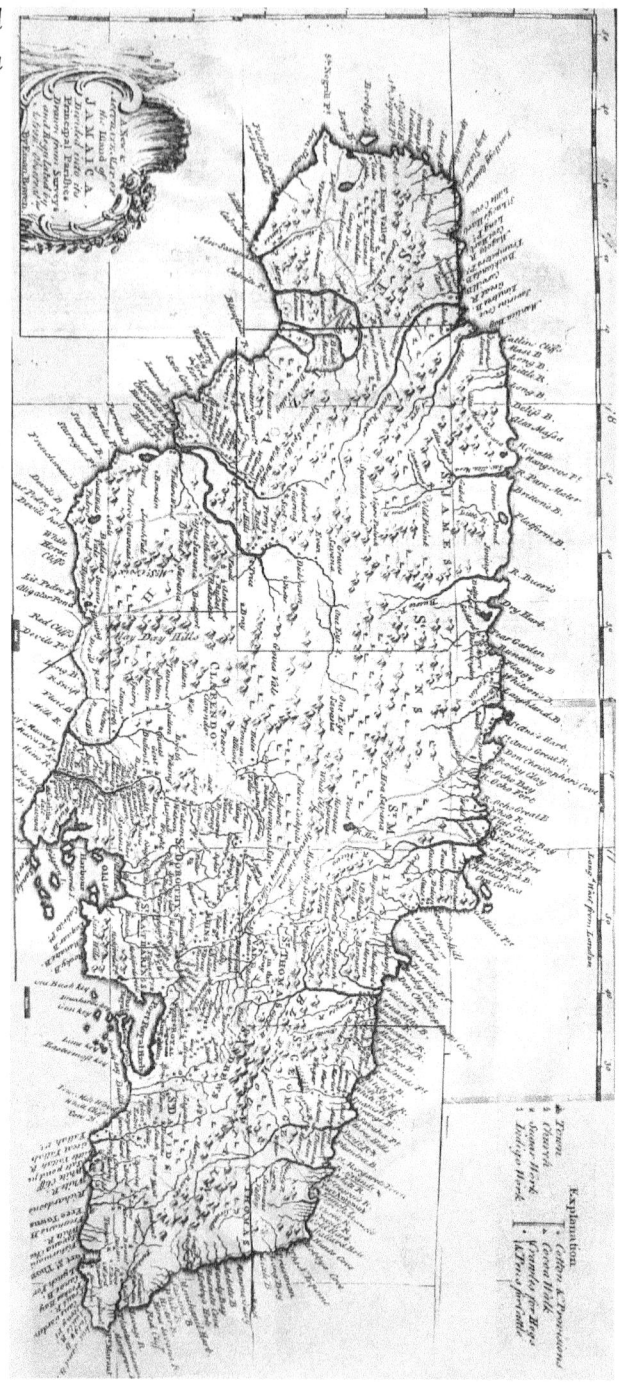

The Island
of Jamaica

CHAPTER 15

The Hurricane slipped into the remains of Port Royal Harbour. Joshua surveyed the ruins of the once beautiful port. The majestic, heaven-kissing Blue Mountains piled in folds at the far horizon, their lofty peaks shrouded in mist.

He placed his arm around Nagamba as they admired the scene.

'Just imagine, Nagamba, five years ago there was a terrible earthquake here in Port Royal. On the 7th June 1692 just before noon, the ground rumbled followed by terrifying tremors. The earth was ripped asunder and caved in with a loud hammering. The first giant quakes shook the fortifications, merchant shops, churches, planters' houses, and uprooted trees which crashed and toppled over. The sea gushed in with a terrifying tidal wave, drowning hundreds of people. The wharfs along the harbour, and a slice of the Palisadoe peninsula and sandspit were swallowed under thirty feet of water. Graves were flung open; floating skeletons and carcasses were sucked into the harbour, mingling with the other dead.

'The impact of the earthquake was catastrophic for everyone. The Jamaican authorities decided to build a new port at Kingston, across the bay from Port Royal. However, many people remained in Port Royal and soon rebuilt part of the town in the ensuing years.'

They both watched as the Hurricane glided smoothly alongside the quay in Kingston.

Lord Francis Gableshaw and his elegant wife conversed on the quay with Sir James Farrel, the London financier, and Benjamin Doncaster, the Royal African Company bureaucrat who Joshua met over two months ago in Cape Coast Castle. Lady Felicia Gableshaw, holding a parasol, chatted to her son. A few feet behind, two piccaninnies, attired in bright red, grinned their little funny faces, and a negro footman stood adjacent to Lord Gableshaw's magnificent carriage with a black horse.

'Ask them to come aboard,' said Joshua to the bosun. 'No scavenging hyenas this time.'

'How do you do, Lady Gableshaw.' Joshua doffed his hat in greeting as she stepped on deck smiling. 'Lord Gableshaw, Mr Doncaster, Sir James.' They entered Joshua's spacious cabin.

'Nice to see you again, Lady Felicia. It's been quite some time since I left this beehive. I missed Port Royal last year, had a large consignment, and sailed from Bristol to West Africa, then direct to Barbados. I love your hat; it matches your eyes.'

'It's the latest fashion in London,' she chuckled.

Joshua observed the young lad beside her. 'Your son, how old is he?'

'Richard is fourteen and rides his filly with remarkable equitation; he's passionate about horses.'

'Marriage, a son—' Joshua paused, '—it appeals to me,'

'Joshua, the knight-errant, with all your past escapades,' she giggled, 'she's somewhere out there riding a black stallion.'

Joshua turned his head. 'Strange you should say that, most strange.'

Felicia was baffled at his unusual remark. The reference to 'black' meant nothing to her.

'Well, here we are again, Mr Doncaster. How was the sailing on the Salome?'

'I must confess, I'm not a good sailor,' Mr Doncaster said, brushing his long moustache.

Joshua faced Lord Gableshaw. 'I presume you received my letter I despatched with Captain Morgan on the same ship. He left Benin before I sailed.'

'Oh yes, I perused it with great interest. We must discuss the subject in detail soon.'

Puffed up swollen peacock, thought Joshua. He disliked the man. Felicia was tense. Joshua fanned the embers by showering her with compliments.

'I must say your exquisite dress is ravishing.'

Felicia's eyes sparkled. Lord Gableshaw only frowned.

All along the wharf stacks of barrels of rum, and casks holding sixteen hundred pounds of molasses were piled. Shipping agents checked large bales of cargo and hogsheads of sugar weighing a thousand pounds.

'Oh, I can see the charming philanthropist, Aaron Pardess, milling among the other merchants,' Joshua noted. 'As always with his extraordinary plumed hat. He has a vast collection of plumes.'

'I met Aaron Pardess on several occasions,' the first mate remarked. 'A most distinguished personality. Not only is he a prominent entrepreneur, but very knowledgeable.'

Joshua butted in. 'His greatest attribute is being a philanthropist for his own Jewish people and others. That quality I hold in high regard. There are two classes of Jewish Cadre Spharadic in Port Royal – the paupers and the prosperous. Jews are brilliant at handling finances. That's why I'm going to ask Aaron for his advice where to invest and purchase land here.'

'He is a pillar of society,' the first mate added.

'Do you know Aaron Pardess?' Joshua asked Lord Gableshaw.

'Oh, I met the jolly Pardess on occasions. Very well known figure here in Port Royal.'

Joshua detected a touch of resentment and jealousy in his voice. He knew Lord Gableshaw did not like Jews; in fact he barely tolerated them. He thought they were the pariahs of Port Royal.

'Aaron's popularity and reputation rides with flying colours in Barbados and throughout the Lesser Antilles,' Joshua replied.

'Indeed, indeed, I often wondered ...' Gableshaw grinned but did not finish his sentence. Joshua took out his repeater with its hanging golden chain from his pocket.

'My apologies, I must go and welcome the others.' Joshua greeted Aaron, the factors, consignee and shipping agents. They all boarded the Hurricane and stepped inside the large cabin.

'Lady Felicia, how do you do?' Aaron took off his plumed hat, bowed and kissed her extended white glove. 'Lovely and young as ever.'

The second compliment in one morning, she thought. 'And you Aaron, always a gentleman and gallant cavalier. How many horses have you at present on your stud farm?' she asked.

'Many thoroughbreds and other splendid mixtures of horses. When Richard turns eighteen I'll present him with a fine specimen.'

Joshua paced outside towards the poop. 'Bosun, please

summon the cooper and carpenter at once with their cata-
logues and notes, as well as all the officers, on the double.'

'Yes, Captain, will do.' The bosun turned. The midshipman, running hastily, nearly bumped into Joshua.

'Young lad, here we are again, at each other's throats,'
Joshua laughed. He liked the eager youngster still in the
flush of youth. 'Go and tell Gashaka I would like to see him.
He might be near my cabin or in the manger. Also ask Scully
to bring drinks and food for our distinguished guests.'

'Yes Captain.' He saluted and sprinted away.

Gashaka arrived soon after and waited near the door.
Joshua tapped him on the shoulder and said, 'I'll tell everyone you're Nagamba's brother and my cabin boy and that you
don't understand English. I'll speak to you only in Bantu.
Now go to Nagamba.'

Everyone was present. Joshua stood and glanced at the
influential entourage.

'May I introduce you to our shipping inspector, Mr. Benjamin Doncaster, and the honourable London financier Sir
James Farrell. They will be staying in Port Royal for a few
weeks.'

A large brass bell hung on the cabin door. Several tables
divided the room. Upon each table were small copper basins
to wash hands; also copper cups and several tiny brass pots
filled with delicacies. In the corner stood an ostentatious
copper chest with a brass padlock, upon which was a collection of gold and brass medals. Also on top were trenchers
of pipes. Joshua's trumpet hung on a wooden peg. He had
owned it since childhood.

'I have a surprise for you,' said Joshua. 'I shall return in a
few minutes.'

Nagamba swayed like a willow. Beside her walked Joshua

followed by Gashaka. She had a long raffia skirt draped seductively around her body that left her breasts exposed. A snake-shaped copper bangle surrounded an ankle. There was a hush in the room. All eyes were transfixed upon her. The air was electrifying. She was alluring and provocative.

'This is Nagamba, and her brother, Gashaka.' Joshua could hear Moustapha's words to him, *Nagamba is your destiny.*

Aaron, of gentle breeding, approached her. 'Nagamba.' He spoke softly as he gazed at those dark pools of triste eyes.

He thought negroes held their heads high with pride and leapt like panthers, whereas his own people had a conspicuous trait: their carriage and gait stooped like a gueebenet, a humpback. They hunched their heads between their shoulders, almost as if they were carrying the sins of the world.

Joshua sat beside Nagamba. Next to him was Gashaka and on Nagamba's left was Aaron. Gableshaw stared at Nagamba with carnal lust. Doncaster and Farrell sat opposite.

'If only London's nobility could see this captivating negress,' Doncaster uttered, ogling her.

'Apropos my plans.' Joshua stood. 'Ladies and gentlemen, and of course Master Gableshaw.' He smiled at the boy and his mother. Joshua squeezed Nagamba's hand. 'I think we shall hear what Mr Taylor the carpenter has to say. Please proceed Taylor.'

Taylor opened the thick file. His pince-nez hung loose on his nose.

'It is my personal conviction, and I am adamant that the Hurricane is not seaworthy any more.' The atmosphere was stark, the man's voice dramatic.

'Which, in your opinion, are the most ravaged parts of the brigantine?' asked Doncaster.

'The old English oak beams are riddled with worms and are warped throughout,' said Taylor. We cannot replace all the timbers; too costly. Might as well build another ship.'

'Quite so, quite so,' Farrell nodded. 'I totally agree with Taylor.'

'Mariners' worst enemies are the dreaded teredo worms,' Taylor continued. 'They do great damage to wooden hulls by excavating burrows with valves on their shells.'

Farrell and Doncaster made notes in their journals.

'I must stress,' said the first mate, 'she is leaking below; patching is useless. She'll spring holes elsewhere. Also, the Norfolk pine mainmast needs replacing.' Taylor wiped his pince-nez and continued. 'It is not a worm, but in fact an elongated clam which can grow up to two feet in length, with the shell being one foot.'

'Fascinating, fascinating,' claimed Felicia. 'I thought they were minute worms.'

'Mmm, Mmm,' Gableshaw mumbled.

'The highest numbers of teredo worms are found in Caribbean waters. They also feed on plankton. Christopher Columbus used copper sheathing for protection,' emphasised Taylor. 'Centuries ago seafarers immersed the timbers with thick layers of tar and hair along the ship.'

'Sulphur and oil were also used for prevention,' added Joshua.

Nagamba watched and listened in silence. She understood little of the conversation. Joshua was her world. She wrapped herself within a gossamer of Joshua's life.

'The Hurricane will never sail in gale-force winds, never; she is a floating disaster. Scuttle her in the swamps,' Taylor stipulated.

Joshua approached the bell. 'I bought it in Bristol the day

before we sailed to Africa.' He watched the solemn faces. 'What steps do we take now?'

'If all of you present agree unanimously,' Doncaster said, tracking Farell with half an eye. 'I shall approve the report and include it in my dossier. And you Captain Quaile?'

'I know every part of the Hurricane like a woman,' Joshua remarked. 'Her furniture made of such splendid timbers, teak, deal, yellow pine and spruce.

'Sir James Farrel and I are sailing back to England soon on the Swallow. We'll inform London upon arrival.'

Aaron said with enthusiasm, 'I suggest early tomorrow we unload all the cargo and store it in the warehouse. It's imperative to have the consignee check the inventory and costs of all stock with the Company's agents.'

Scully and three of his kitchen helpers brought in the laurels of the sea, finest of seafood, turtle baked belly from the Cayman Islands.

The banquet gained momentum with the variety of dishes that followed. On each table a bowl of brandy laced with sugar was placed, also a kill-devil punch rum, mixed with water, nutmeg, lime juice and sugar.

'Marvellous, bloody marvellous, scrumptious,' guffawed Gableshaw. They drank and ate with enthusiasm, washing their fingers in the copper basins.

Aaron said, 'I try hard not to indulge in such epicurean and appetising delights. Must keep my weight down, otherwise I won't be able to mount my black stallion.' Aaron and Joshua split with peals of laughter.

'Goodness gracious me, some more!' exclaimed Lady Felicia.

Fruit arrived in three large baskets: guavas, pawpaws, pineapples, mangoes and two small coconuts. Joshua with a long serrated silver knife ripped a small hole on top of the coconut. He then knelt in front of Nagamba.

'For you, my albatross. I know you love coconut milk.'

'Bless one's stars,' Aaron cheered. 'Such chivalry.' Everyone clapped.

Nagamba tilted the coconut and let the white milk trickle on to her semi-open lips. Some spilled on her breasts. Gableshaw's eyes burned with lust.

Felicia was disgusted. She whispered in his ear, 'This time Joshua beat you, and not with a prostitute.' Gableshaw bridled.

Gashaka was amused. *White people are stupid and ignorant,* he thought to himself; *Covering their entire bodies. Our African women are proud of their breasts to please men and feed their young. There is no shame in nudity.*

'Next on the agenda are the slaves,' Joshua said, puffing on his pipe. 'I have six hundred on my ship, as per the letter I sent. Did you consider my proposal?'

'Of course,' Gableshaw replied. 'In fact, it so happens I purchased five hundred more acres to extend my plantation. Your offer certainly comes at perfect timing. Soon it is time to plant cane shoots in plots on cleared land, and I will need a hundred and fifty very strong niggers.' He laughed then.

'Agreed,' said Joshua, 'you can have a hundred and fifty but on one condition: families are not to be split. Thirty-three pounds for males, thirty for females, twenty for working boys from the age of fourteen, and piccaninnies two pounds. Piccaninnies perform many chores. They cart water in calabashes to the men in the fields, weeding, errands etc., etc. I think the little fellows are frightfully cute. Those are my terms,' Joshua quoted adamantly.

'Indeed, indeed.' Gableshaw grinned with sarcasm.

Joshua clicked his fingers. 'First mate, paper and quill please.'

The officer unfolded paper sheets and handed them to Joshua who signed the transactions and documents of slaves. Gableshaw did the same.

'Now, Aaron, let's talk about land I wish to buy, raising cattle and other stock, and growing various crops.'

'There's a thousand acres of pristine forest, arable land, cocoa walks and indigo for sale at St David's Parish in Dicksons South. My estate is below at Fargar Springs. Nagamba and you will be delighted with the view. I shall investigate the price if you wish.'

Aaron took out his lace silk handkerchief and wiped his sweaty forehead. 'I have several more stables I would like to build, and need to buy fifty slaves from you, to help with the horses, gardens and outbuildings.'

'Splendid, splendid,' Joshua grinned.

'I know Philip Tumbridge, a wealthy plantation magnate from St Andrew's Parish,' said one factor. 'He's at present on the quay. I'm sure he came for one purpose, to buy slaves.'

'Very well, bring him up please'.

Mr Tumbridge walked with rapid giant strides in his ridiculous heavy embroidered blue coat on that sultry Jamaican afternoon. A piccaninny followed him holding an umbrella; heavy clouds gathered. The factor approached him.

'Captain Quaile wishes to invite you aboard the Hurricane and would like to discuss an issue that might be of interest to you. Mr Pardess, whom I believe you know, is also on the ship with other guests.'

'Thank you, most kind of him.'

'Please follow me.'

'How do you do, Mr Tumbridge,' Joshua greeted him.

'Captain.' He took off his coat. 'Rather warm.'

'You know Aaron Pardess?'

'Yes, of course.' Mr Tumbridge glanced around.

'Felicia, again we meet under such unusual circumstances.' Mr Tumbridge doffed his hat and bowed. 'Beautiful as ever.'

To Joshua's astonishment they all knew each other. He realised that most planters met at taverns, brothels or entertained in their ostentatious homes.

'I haven't seen you for months,' Aaron remarked.

'I had to go back to England for business reasons,' Tumbridge said. 'It was good to be home. I enjoyed most of the long walks in the old English lanes.'

'A change from this humid paradise.'

'Have you heard the latest news of the runaway slaves in Barbados?' Gableshaw's eye twitched.

'Yes, the bloodhounds chased them to the swamps. They soon sank in the quicksand.'

Joshua watched Nagamba and Gashaka; he read their minds.

'You're interested in buying slaves the factor told me.'

'Thank you, Captain.' Tumbridge adjusted his light-green ruffled neckerchief. 'My property is beyond the hills in St Andrews, called Berry Hunt, only a short distance above Gableshaw's plantation. I require a hundred slaves to work in the mills, boiling houses and clearing more scrubland.' Tumbridge sneezed several times.

'I do beg your pardon; it's the pollen in the air this time of year. I'm allergic to it. What price do you have in mind?'

'Here they are,' Joshua handed the details to him.

Tumbridge perused the list. He buttoned his waistcoat. 'I'll never get used to the heat.' The sale was complete and sealed by three signatures witnessed by Aaron.

'Please finalise now the agreed sum to Mr Pardess,' said Joshua

'Once this is resolved, I trust you'll attend to all the slaves being transferred to Gableshaw's and Mr Tumbridge's estates. I'll pay your commission as agreed. I shall be at Aaron's house.'

'Of course, Captain Quaile, we'll proceed upon your instructions,' said the tall factor.

'Certainly, it's been a most unique and fascinating day,' smiled Felicia upon leaving. 'We'll meet again Joshua.' She glanced at Nagamba. 'Most extraordinary.' Gableshaw and Tumbridge followed Aaron to the emporium.

Joshua stepped outside on to the stern gallery. Below the quay three bawdy prostitutes were parading. Several mischievous piccaninnies chased each other like butterflies and one of them pulled the knot of the red ribbon sash on the harlot's posterior. It came undone and he started to run but was not fast enough. She grabbed him by his tattered calico pants and clipped his right ear with a thump: he yelled in agony.

'Now get, scram, you little … go to your mamma. I bet you don't have a pappa. If I catch you again I'll clip your other ear. Be gone.' The piccaninny took off, his cherub face turned grey, his eyelashes fluttering with fear. The harlot's body shook with heavy laughter and the two others joined in.

One peered up at Joshua and said, 'You've a gorgeous smile.' He was touched by this warm comical scene of the innocent urchins roaming the streets, and the courtesans tramping the dark allies for a crust of bread. Aaron returned later, his face radiant with smiles.

'It's all paid in gold and secured in bronze chests brought by Gableshaw and Tumbridge in their carriages. We'll take the lot when we head home in my Berlin coach. My place is well guarded. The rest of your slaves can stay at my estate until you settle your affairs.'

'I've great faith in you Aaron. Never trusted anyone except Moustapha; I've known him as long as I have you.'

'Yes I remember.'

'Joshua, tomorrow we will commence unloading your ship of everything, including the furniture, and store it in my warehouse. It'll be safe there until you get established.'

'Aaron, you have my heartfelt gratitude for helping and advising me. I'll address the crew about the decisions that finalise the fate of the Hurricane. I'll pay them generously for all the years they served under my command.'

Within ten days Benjamin Doncaster and Sir James Farrell sailed on the Swallow to England. Some of the crew members were given the choice to go back, others boarded ships bound for New England. The remainder stayed in cosmopolitan Jamaica. They mingled with the wealthy planters and merchants. The young men dreamed of riches in the tropical paradise of the West Indies.

In the far side of the port at Long Point Swamps, the Hurricane sank; her timbers groaned and were crushed under the quagmire of murky slush. She gave her last sigh and vanished.

The sun's orange-red ball dipped beyond the horizon. Joshua held Nagamba close. She brushed his tears away.

'Every dawn and dusk, Joshua, I shall be your albatross.'

CHAPTER 16

Moshebere had dropsy. For a year he had worked with Bundere in the boiling house under appalling conditions. His legs and hands were swollen and he could barely close his fists. His face was puffed and sallow with sunken eyes.

It was the dry season. The sheaves of cane arrived all day long from the fields, transported by oxen and carts to the sugar mills to be crushed between heavy rollers. The gluey, gummy raw sugar was conveyed on a trough to the furnaces.

'I don't feel well.' Moshebere leaned over the suffocating, seething cauldron. Bundere tried to hold him when he fell on the floor, thick with molasses. The overseer ran towards them and slipped in the swilling mess.

'You, nigger!' he shouted to Bundere. 'Take him outside.' He lashed his leather whip across Moshebere's dropsical legs. Moshebere screamed with shooting, grating pain.

'From now on both of you will work in the curing house.'

The heat was intense. Small fires were lit in order to dry the sugar. The driver with the long whip gave orders. Moshebere and Bundere stood for hours with other slaves, filling small pots with sugar. Beneath the vessels the molasses, dark gravy, oozed and drained through holes and then were sent to the distillery to make rum.

With the setting sun the slaves trudged back to the sprawling wattle huts made of sugar trash and small branches.

'My legs, my legs,' Moshebere cried, and fell on to the dirty mat. Bundere poured him some water and mashed black beans and millet in a calabash they shared.

'Mahadana must have given birth in the West Indies, if she sailed,' Bundere said in a muffled voice. 'The smallpox, everyone fled. Ebouko, Marufa,' he stammered, and put his hands above his head.

'The twins are probably running by now,' Moshebere said, and looked at his legs with horror.

꧁

Pinkus, Ezekiel and Shyloh sat on the long dray pulled by the snorting mare towards the plantation compound. They had arrived in St Kitts at first light, and set to work immediately. Soon they could smell the stench of the raw sugar from the boiling house.

'Wait here,' said Pinkus 'I'll talk to the man.' He approached the guard who held a thick hippopotamus whip. 'Can I see the overseer? I've goods for the slaves.'

'He is over there, in the white house.'

Pinkus walked over to the building where the short factor stood. 'Is the overseer here?' 'He's away but I remember you. The months have passed so quick since you've last been to St Kitts.'

'We visit many islands.' Pinkus turned and waved to Ezekiel and Shyloh. 'My helpers in the business,' Pinkus smiled. 'When I last spoke to the overseer he was interested in purchasing bills, hoes, shoes and other items. I've merchandise that's always in great demand. Follow me to the cart please, I'll show you.'

'Shoes are essential at present. February is the driest month of the year when we burn the weeds and leaves between the tall stalks,' the short man remarked. 'At harvest time the cane is cut, the slaves wear out their shoes and the soles fall apart. Their feet blister when they run through the hot ashes.' The factor scratched his bottom. 'We also have a plague of rats. Oh yes, the ugly brutes have sharp teeth.'

He examined the items in the cart. 'Yes, we need bills, hoes, they often break. I see you have axes, machetes, excellent, we use them frequently.' The man kept scratching his posterior. His trousers were grubby and soiled.

'How many do you require?' Pinkus asked.

'I'll take forty hoes, forty bills, thirty axes, and twenty-five machetes.'

'And how many pairs of shoes?'

'Fifty. No, I'll take the lot, it is urgent. This Wednesday we're burning the dry undergrowth beneath the cane rows as we do every year. Timing is perfect.' The factor picked his nose. *Vulgarity and crudeness, dregs of society,* thought Pinkus of the short twit.

※

In Benin when Joshua bade farewell to dying Moustapha, he had asked him whether he believed that everything is preordained.

'Yes I do, most definitely.' Thus the spirit of God shone in His infinite glory, and soared above the plantation on the day Pinkus, Ezekiel and Shyloh arrived.

※

'I'll get some slaves from the curing house,' said the man. Pinkus watched one limp as he emerged with three others, approaching the cart.

'Moshebere, stretch your arms,' said the factor. 'I'll put some bills and hoes on.'

Bundere said, 'Moshebere you won't have to bend if they are heavy. Wait for a few minutes. We'll go together in case you fall.'

Bundere lifted and placed several hoes on Moshebere's painful and swollen hands. Pinkus, standing close, held the bundle of shoes from the cart and was going to hand them to one slave. He dropped them when he heard Moshebere's name. Could this be a miracle? Is it possible that this man is Alimba's husband?

The factor walked back to the shed checking and supervising the piled goods. Two slaves followed him. Pinkus's mind raced like a whirlwind.

'What's your name?' he said to the first slave.

'Bundere.'

Pinkus grabbed his chance. 'Are your wives Alimba and Mahadana?'

Moshebere was faint. His gaunt face turned ashen grey. 'Yes.' Bundere's teeth chattered.

'I'll be brief, your women and children are in Nevis on a plantation, and safe. We just sailed from the island. They mentioned your names. Ezekiel, watch out for the factor.' Pinkus was nervous. He introduced himself.

'Bundere, we must get you both out of here. The man told me that on Wednesday they will burn the trash in the cane fields. On that morning we will hide with the horse and cart on the far edge, right side of the pine forest. Do you know this spot?'

'We do.'

'Once the heavy smoke spreads, seize your chance and run towards us, we'll wait for you.'

'He's coming back,' Shyloh warned.

'Remember, Wednesday,' Pinkus reassured them.

'We shall see you next time in St Kitts, with more shoes,' the factor said flatly.

Wednesday was a scorching day. The temperature soared. The fire swept quickly between the rows of sugar cane. Slaves and two overseers with clubs and machetes watched out for rats as they swarmed in great numbers, threatened by the fierce heat. The men beat, squashed and hacked the vermin to pieces. The rats moved with great speed, scurrying and biting the slaves, crawling on their shoes and up their legs. The slaves hurled the ugly creatures by their tails and flung them into the fires. The wind shifted and the billowing smoke covered the sky.

The devouring flames brought out the Fer-de-Lance from their holes. They emerged darting and slithering, as in a battle. The vipers' poisonous fangs perforated their victims, rats and slaves alike. It was difficult to discern in the melée who chased whom. Slaves ran away from the snakes and rats among other slaves fleeing the fires.

'Moshebere, hold my hand,' Bundere shouted. 'I see Pinkus. We're screened by the smoke, let's escape to the forest.'

They reached Pinkus and hopped on the dray. The mare frisked in panic. Pinkus drove off. It was catastrophic on the plantation where the fields lay in ruins. The tall canes were trampled and crushed by the stampeding slaves, running amok. Charred rats and snakes covered the smouldering ground. Five slaves lay dead, several escaped and one overseer was gasping his last breath.

The five men boarded the Pandora and sailed late in the afternoon.

᠁

They left St Kitts with a heavy fog spreading upon the waters. Navigation was tricky; visibility was poor.

'All hands on deck,' Pinkus shouted. The crew mustered on the deck in front of him. 'Take three reefs in all the sails. We're running blind in this murk. We need to slow her down and heave to.' With practiced efficiency the sailors swarmed into the rigging.

Pinkus despatched one sailor to the fo'csle head with a bell to warn them of any ship sightings.

'I can't see a thing. I'll go on the lee side with a hurricane lamp,' Shyloh shouted across. Bundere and Moshebere came on deck.

'Follow me to the stern.' Ezekiel gave each one a lantern. The five surveyed the scene, their eyes riveted on the waves. The wind rose with battering gusts. Manoeuvring around the small islands was hazardous.

'Ezekiel, watch out for rocks. The surf is high,' Pinkus yelled. 'Last year a schooner was wrecked. Raise your lamps.'

Ezekiel bellowed. 'I'll scan.'

Towards dawn the mist eventually dispersed and the Pandora navigated through the three-mile passage from St Kitts to Nevis.

'We'll have turtle today. I'm an expert in turtle cooking.'

Pinkus observed Moshebere's swollen legs. He filled a small clay cup and gave it to him.

'Drink this tonic, a specialty of mine for various illnesses. I believe in natural herbal potions. I pick specific types of plants and leaves that grow only in certain areas. I dry them, grind them to powder, add some cinnamon, cloves and molasses. This potion helps to relieve joint aches, headaches and gout.

'I loathe wealthy planters, slave traders and captains,' Moshebere said. 'Look at me. It is because of them I have this sickness.' He sighed, breathing like a furnace. He started coughing and became short of breath. Pinkus stood up and laid his hand upon him.

'If I could cut my heart in minute fragments and each particle could free a slave, I would do so willingly. Do you understand?' Pinkus said in a sibilant tone.

'Bundere and Moshebere, you must remain on board for a couple of days. It would be too risky for you to venture ashore. On Sunday, my two trusty assistants and I will visit the market and collect Alimba and Mahadana. We can't take any chances at this stage.'

⚜

Alimba and Mahadana woke early. The goats were milked. The women packed the produce in calabashes and baskets. Sunday was a special outing in the market. Alimba washed the twins and dressed them in calico pants. Mahadana finished breastfeeding Yabassi. Alimba carried a large calabash on her heard filled with eggs and in her right hand one with goat's cheese. The boys skipped behind. Mahadana strapped her infant on her back and harnessed a leather bag with yams and plantains to her shoulder. Alimba sat on the ground cross-legged. The market droned and hummed.

White women browsed in the tropical melting pot. They wore flowered silk and taffeta frocks and skirts, as well as colourful hoods and hats to protect them from the sun. The men had brown and white Holland suits trimmed with scarlet ribbons, coloured waistcoats and broad-rimmed hats.

The native women had magnificent head gear, turbans and bandanas, purled with gold and silver thread. Mahadana brushed the flies off her sleepy child and Alimba watched the passing crowd. She gazed at a narrow lane.

At first she thought it was a mirage rising with the hot dust. The mule came into sight. Alimba jumped, dragging Onana and Awana. Mahadana wrapped Yabassi with a wide braided cotton strip and secured him to her bosom. She rested her head upon Pinkus's shoulders.

'Pinkus,' she murmured. He understood.

'A day to remember.'

Pinkus blew his nose. 'How they've grown.'

'It's all that goat's cheese and milk,' Shyloh grinned. 'We're going now to bring more food from the market to stock the ship. We won't be long.'

They returned in an hour. Shyloh held a small bamboo cage with six cackling hens, one bag of vegetables and one with fruit.

'Come on ladies up on to the cart. Your destiny awaits.' He assisted them in boarding the cart with the children.

Bundere leaned against the main mast, watching the ocean. He heard the approach of the cart as it rattled along the cobblestones, and looking around, was struck numb when he saw his wife limping towards him. He fell to his knees. Mahadana's trembling tapered fingers slipped through his hair and lifted his head. He stared at her as though she were a ghost.

With a cry she put her arms around him. 'My beloved Bundere. This is Yabassi, your son.' He lifted the little one and rubbed his face against the wailing boy. Moshebere staggered towards Alimba and collapsed. The twins, puzzled and frightened, looked at the strange man on the deck. Pinkus rushed and lifted Moshebere to his feet.

'Help me to lay him on the bunk in the cabin.'

Alimba brought some cool water and sponged him. 'He's very ill and wracked with fever. He hasn't been well for a long time.'

'Why is he so swollen?'

'Many hours bending over the furnaces in the boiling house, the fumes; he's in great pain.' Pinkus wrung his hands in frustration.

'When we get to Port Royal I'll ask my friend to take him to a specialised doctor.'

Perplexed and dazed Bundere stammered, 'Port Royal? Where is that, and why are you taking us there?'

Pinkus laughed. 'To Jamaica. St Kitts and Nevis are too small to hide in. There are plenty of places to hide in Jamaica and I have many contacts there. You'll be safe.'

'Where are Ebouko and Marufa?'

'In Bonny two men grabbed them,' said Alimba. 'I was ill with a fever. They sold the children to a captain. The guard hit me with his musket and laughed. I shall never forget his face. He haunts me.'

Bundere watched his son who soon fell asleep.

❦

The following morning everyone sat on deck. On both sides of the schooner, spotted dolphins and flying fish dived and surfaced. Raptorial frigate birds flew towards Jamaica.

Feeling timorous and despondent, Bundere was silent. In the depths of misery he vowed to find that captain. With tenderness he touched Mahadana's face, and then grasped Yabassi's little hand and walked towards the poop. Pinkus knew the only road to Bundere's sanity was to find his children.

'I want to talk to you about a fascinating animal, the turtle.' Pinkus brushed his beard. 'The pistle of the turtle is the sovereign therapeutic medicine for curing the dreadful dry belly ache (dry gripes) and other severe ailments.'

Bundere returned to the group. 'Aren't these old wives' tales?' he said morosely.

'Not at all, Bundere. The English are prodigious drinkers. In the distillery, rum is impregnated and conducted through lead pipes, which is dangerous. I have known a sinister case with this malignant sickness. It started with a cold followed by seizures of severe pains that shot like daggers from the bowels. The intestines became inflamed. The gentleman was on the fringe of death. Two prominent physicians, members of the Royal Society deduced that the cause of several baffling illnesses was lead poisoning.. The patients were given small doses of the pistle potion and recovered.'

Grave-faced, Moshebere asked, 'Would this help me?'

'Possibly,' said Pinkus.

'Incidentally we never catch mature turtles. After all, you don't snuff the life of a sixty or eighty year turtle, such gentle creatures. Most are caught in the Cayman Islands, west of Jamaica.' said Pinkus. 'I must admit, I love turtle meat.'

When the upper encasement of the turtle was prised open everyone gazed in astonishment and held their breath.

'This is the carapace,' Pinkus pointed out with his finger, 'and the lower shell is the plastron. What you see inside are the internal organs of the turtles. Every morsel is used, as small as they may be.'

'We have years of experience with this method,' 'Ezekiel said. 'First, Shyloh and I will flay the plates and fibrous horny protein scales that are part of the turtle's outer skin. These are cooked to make palatable, highly nutritious soup. Through the day we shall strip imbue all the parts with bitter herbs, spices, onions, garlic and cloves, and then top with white wine, water and vinegar, sealing and corkling them in large clay jars.' Gentle Pinkus smiled at his curious audience.

'But how will this help Moshebere?' queried a worried Bundere.

'Do not discount the therapeutic value of the turtle. It has been known in the Caribbean for centuries.'

'Green turtles do not have teeth,' Shyloh remarked. 'The upper and lower jaws have sharp ridges which they use to chew and slice their food. I shall soak the turtle's head in a large clay pot and do the same with the flippers.'

Towards late afternoon all the jars were filled.

'Par excellence,' Pinkus hailed. 'I shall give you bottles of the healing medicine. Have a small quantity each day.'

'Thank you.'

Pinkus ached for the sick Moshebere. He held his Bible against his chest and silently muttered a short prayer.

'Turtles have extraordinary night vision,' said Pinkus. 'Female turtles stimulate mating and encourage copulation. Males patiently wait for the females to initiate intercourse.

This is the primordial habit of the turtle.' Pinkus glanced at Bundere, who laughed for the first time. Mahadana threw her arms around him.

The Pandora sailed for Jamaica.

CHAPTER 17

Joshua bought a thousand acres, and a hundred and fifty more slaves from Lady Sarah Buckley, a widow from Port Royal. She lived there for several years with her husband, Sir Stuart Buckley, who died contracting dry gripes.

'He spent more time in the brothels than with me,' said Lady Buckley, more in sorrow than anger. 'He drank heavily every day; his favourite drink was rum. No wonder the plantation was neglected as you can see for yourself. The state of the fields, crops, the dilapidated buildings and sheds.' Lady Buckley looked across at the forest.

'It was most humiliating when Stuart was brought home one evening from the Punch-House, another place of ill repute. That particular evening he comsumed five and a half quarts of Madeira and collapsed. In our cellar he stocked barrels of rum, brandy and wine. We were childless. I'll be glad to go back to the Cotswolds. I always detested the heat, insects, and his carousing. My husband lost the use of his limbs, had his two legs amputated and died soon after in excruciating pain.'

The north side of the plantation was forested with massive silk cotton trees, blue mahoe, mastic cedar and locust. Some exceeded two hundred feet. Hogs ran wild. Eagles and bald-headed black vultures with a four-foot wingspan flew high above, shrieking. There were already several cocoa groves, indigo, cotton and plantain walks under cultivation. Also, there were a few small fields, cattle in large pens, goats near the tannery and a stable with six horses. Adjacent in a long, extended shed were two drays, four carts, two splendid, polished Berlin coaches and a chariot.

'Good evening, Aaron, thank you for coming so promptly.' Joshua flicked off the stinging gnats and merrywings.

'Here's a box of chocolate for you, Nagamba; I know you love them.'

Nagamba smiled and watched Joshua battling the minute merrywings. One could hardly see them; only their wings droned like a faint bugle.

'They won't be merry any longer when I blast them with my fly swatter.'

'Light smoke fires at night when you eat outside; that will repel them,' said Aaron. Nagamba couldn't resist laughing. Gashaka came in with a calabash full of fresh fruit.

'Here are the planned specifications for the new house I designed,' said Aaron.

'An architect as well,' Joshua chuckled. 'Wise Aaron, heaven-born genius.'

'I helped with the construction of my father's house in Barbados. It still stands in spite of several hurricanes. Once the building is complete, you can use the present dwelling for storage. The new two-storey stone house will have one-foot thick walls, four bedrooms and a garret. The downstairs floors will be tiled, the upper rooms laid with mastic boards, and the roof tiled and shingled. There'll be porches on both sides with louvres or jalousies to trap the breeze moving in the wind's eye.'

Joshua was elated. Nagamba crouched on the floor in front of him and looked up.

'We need spacious long sheds for the slaves,' she said. 'And water's most crucial.'

Aaron replied, 'There's no fresh water in Port Royal, yet it rains most of the year. The waterman on the quay sells a tun, which is a cask, for two shillings.'

'Totally absurd,' Joshua baulked. 'An exorbitant price.'

'I've a brilliant idea,' Aaron remarked. 'Why don't you commission two coopers to make several casks of American Oak, each one made of curved staves and bound together by hoops. They will hold 500 or 1000 gallons of water, six feet in diameter, six feet high. The trapped rain will drain from the pitch of the roof to the gutters and into the open casks. You can have them spread around the slaves' quarters, long sheds, your house and stables.'

'Mastermind,' Joshua exclaimed. 'Absolutely marvellous.' He stood and stretched. Nagamba flexed her curved body against his.

'This is all very exciting,' she whispered in his ear.

Aaron looked across the table at Gashaka. He admired the tall lithe African, walking with his head erect, his muscles rippling.

'English architecture is not geared for this climate, not at all,' Aaron remarked. 'When the Spanish lived here a hundred and fifty years years ago they designed their homes for coolness; not like the English, installing glazed windows which render their houses like a furnace. It's vital that the cool breeze blows through the high wide ceilings of all rooms. 'You must erect wooden shutters to block the scorching afternoon sun.'

'A stone house we shall build,' Joshua declared, hugging Nagamba. 'Aaron, we would like you to accompany us and pay a visit to that sleazy dunghill Gableshaw, regarding the cattle he wishes to sell.'

'How many has he?' asked Nagamba.

'A large number and a hefty bull,' responded Gashaka.

'If we purchase for a reasonable price,' Nagamba said, scrutinising their faces. 'We could sell the beef and goat's meat for local consumption and export their hides. Buy another eighty goats—sixty nannies and twenty billies for reproduction—as well as milk and goat's cheese to be sold on Sundays in the market.'

'Excellent resources and revenues,' Joshua agreed. 'All in all, net profit will accrue from meat, hides, cheese and milk, as well as various crops.' Nagamba snuggled against Joshua and purred with her soft lambent eyes.

'I also recommend you get cane trash from Gableshaw. Mixed with dung it stunts the growth of weeds between crops and makes excellent manure; also, lush sugar cane stalks for the slaves to chew. It gives them energy when they work in the fields,' stipulated Gashaka.

'Well, one of my mares has difficulty in labour; I must dash off.'

Aaron left in haste.

&

The following week Nagamba was puzzled when she saw Gableshaw arrive. He dismounted from his horse and walked towards Joshua who emerged from the large shed. She followed him.

'I would have come sooner but was preoccupied,' said Gableshaw. 'I used to watch Lord Buckley ride his chariot. Do you use it at all?'

Joshua shook his head. 'No, it has been neglected but Gashaka will restore it one day. The men in ancient times, how they raced and fought in those chariots. It must have been a spectacular sight.'

'Do you ever think of selling?'

'Maybe.'

I offered to buy it from Lord Buckley before his illness, but he refused.'

'I understand why,' said Joshua. 'The chariot is singular; why I don't think there's another one like it in the Caribbean.'

'If the opportunity arises, I shall be most eager to purchase it. Let me know. By the way, we soon have to discuss the sale of my cattle.' Gableshaw mounted his horse and rode off.

The house was completed before the hurricane season. The racket from the gaggling chickens, ducks and turkeys vociferated with the bleating goats on the plantation. Crops of peas, sweet potatoes, cloves, palm cabbage, cinnamon, yams, cassava, ginger and pimento were planted. Indigo, pimento and ginger fetched an excellent price for export. Slaves relished cassava bread. They extracted the poison from the roots, and then grated, boiled and baked the cassava flour into cakes.

'I would like to go to the market on Sunday, and buy two barrels of herring and turtle meat for the slaves. It is cheap and nourishing for them.' Nagamba lifted her arms above her head.

'Are you aware that planters spend less than two pounds per annum, to feed and clothe their slaves?' said Joshua.

They break our bones, humiliate us and take away our dignity,' Gashaka murmured with bitterness.

Nagamba approached him. 'Gashaka, my hero, steady on.'

In the fields Gashaka noticed a slave shuffling in pain. He examined and ascertained, by the swelling and colour of the leg, that it was hookworm.

'The parasite has to be drawn out immediately,' Gashaka noted sorrowfully. 'I've seen many Africans with this horrible killer. The hookworm can grow to three feet in length under the skin. Their ugly heads, like suckers, move through the body of the victim.'

'Don't you think we should call Doctor Fairchild?' asked Nagamba.

'Please trust me, Nagamba. Our African methods, though they may seem primitive to the white man, are more effective than their customs and ways.'

Joshua was baffled. They approached the shed where the man was prostrated. Nagamba stroked the slave's gaunt cheeks.

'First, I need a small sharp knife,' spoke Gashaka, 'a copper or steel rod, six inches or so, and tweezers. Put them in boiling water to be cleaned. We shall also give the slave a dram of rum to make him drowsy. I'll do this with minimal pain. The worm has to be extracted, but ever so slowly. You must not pull it out by force. If by accident the worm is cut, it will wriggle, slide and penetrate deeper inside. It's very painful for the slave.'

Joshua and Nagamba's eyes followed Gashaka's nimble fingers.

'I'll make an incision on the thigh where the bulge is and grip the head of the worm with the tweezers, then twist it around the rod with caution, snail-like, inch by inch, to avoid the worm splitting and crawling back inside the leg.'

Nagamba wiped Gashaka's forehead which was saturated with perspiration.

'I'll loop and curl the worm around the rod and continue to pull it a bit more, then make a knot around it with string. This afternoon I shall do the same. Give him now a dose of brandy please. The slave must not be moved.'

'I'll come and check on him frequently and bring some food,' said Nagamba.

The next day Joshua and Nagamba viewed with horror as Gashaka rooted out the repulsive three-foot vermin, still wriggling and slithering.

Gashaka clicked his fingers and called, 'Pour some rum on the open wound and then we shall burn the monster.'

Nagamba covered the man with a blanket.

'The slave must rest for a few days. Thank you, Nagamba, for helping me.'

'I wasn't aware you're a physician as well, Gashaka,' Joshua said, smiling at him. 'Truly exceptional.'

Gashaka was proud of his position as overseer, and he worked on the plantation with energy, zeal and devotion. The slaves slashed their machetes through the overgrown creepers and bracken, making a large clearing. With their curved bills they hoed between the rows of cocoa groves, indigo, cotton and plantain walks.

The piccaninnies manured the young shoots by hand. They ran to and fro, fetching water from the cart driven by an ox to the slaves in the fields. Gashaka was strict but treated the slaves with benevolence, and they respected him.

Nagamba stood by the cedar tree and watched Doctor Fairchild alight from his gig, tethering his horse to the massive lower branch. Above, large-throated pelicans nested. Gashaka fetched a bucket of water and chaff for the gelding.

'Greetings Nagamba! I haven't seen you for a while.' Doctor Fairchild made regular pastoral visits to the plantation and was now a friend of both Joshua and Nagamba.

'We've been busy on the plantation since we bought it. There are several slaves with ulcers on their feet. Please follow me.'

'The chiggers.' He shook his head. 'They're a menace; they dig and burrow under the toenails and fester. I've seen slaves with ulcerated feet. They could hardly walk. The chiggers breed in the soil, and the only solution for the slaves who work in the fields is to wear shoes. More than once I had to remove the nail or amputate the toe because of the gravity of the wounds and crippling inflammation. And you, Nagamba and Gashaka, wear shoes at all times, except indoors.'

'I have never had anything on my feet since the day I was born. I will look like a waddling duck with shoes,' laughed Gashaka. 'If the hookworms did not get me, how would the chiggers? Fancy running with shoes on.'

Doctor Fairchild smiled. 'Watch me, I shall snip the toenail just a fraction and drain the pus out from the ulcer, then cover it with a poultice. I'll leave some medicine that you'll have to administer daily, Nagamba, my new nurse. Those curry-combed bites on the slaves are from those damn, filthy cockroaches. Here are prescriptions for creams and lotions you can obtain from the apothecaries.' Fairchild then glanced at Gashaka.

'I suggest you put several buckets in each shed filled with vinegar. The slaves must bathe the bites often with cotton wool dipped in vinegar. It will soothe and heal the wounds. The fact is that slaves sleep on mats, and squadrons of cockroaches swarm at night. They don't usually clamber on hammocks; they crawl on the ground.'

Joshua ran up towards them and hugged Nagamba. 'I do apologise for not being here earlier. The tanner caught me regarding the goats.'

'I explained to Nagamba and Gashaka the war against cockroaches. It's imperative you provide hammocks for everyone to sleep on instead of mats. I detest cockroaches.' The doctor emitted a deep-throated growl.

'Ants are another scourge,' said Joshua. 'You know of Aaron Pardess?'

'Oh yes, I know him very well.'

'Aaron deals with the black ants in an ingenious way,' Joshua said. 'The legs of his four-poster bed are permanently immersed in small buckets of water so the ants can't creep up and devour him, his clothes and bedding.' Joshua chuckled to himself.

'Remarkable. The only way I struggle to protect and store my food is by hanging shelves with ropes, tarred and pitched, which repels them, though it's very messy. Well I must leave now. I'll see you in two days. Thank you, Gashaka, for taking care of the horse.'

The following day the Ackee seeds were planted.

CHAPTER 18

Aaron loved his early brisk walks along the wharfs. On this day he wore a white shirt, embroidered waistcoat and a flowing cravat. The distant Blue Mountains fringed the magnificent harbour and the Caribbean sea.

He knew several of the merchants who berthed their vessels in Chocolata Hole and watched the porters cart turtle pens from the Cayman Islands. The elegant young man stood watching a sloop sailing, when he heard a loud commotion, and saw two white males chasing what looked like, from a distance, a short man. He soon realised it was a negro dwarf child. The boy ran straight into Aaron, clutching him by his legs. Aaron was six feet, four inches and the youngster just reached above his knees.

'Don't let them take me please, sir, I beg you, don't let them take me.' The little chap was trembling. 'I'll do anything you want—wash, cook, clean the house.' He was clawing and digging, his tiny hands on Aaron's breeches.

'Why do you want to catch him?' Aaron snapped at the men.

'We have our street show with two female dwarfs, two pet monkeys. This nigger is part of the circus.'

'He's tried several times to escape,' the second man muttered.

'They beat me if I don't dance with the monkeys, and

chain me up at night,' the boy cried. 'I'm always hungry. They steal food from the market stalls.'

'What's your name?' Aaron enquired.

'Sambo.' The child wiped his snotty nose on a torn sleeve. Aaron handed him his silk handkerchief.

'How old are you?'

'Eight,' he whimpered.

Aaron put his hand in his pocket. The men watched him in suspense.

'This will free him from your filthy hands,' said Aaron as he took out his purse and tossed some coins on the ground. Aaron unsheathed his blunderbuss and aimed it at them. They froze with fear and then ran away.

'Where's your mother?'

'I don't know. Bad ugly men come and go to the house. They gave her cash and took me away.'

'And your father?'

'I don't know.'

'As from today you will start a new life, a good life. You will never go hungry and no-one will hurt you. I'll name you Jonathan. It means 'God has given, God has delivered'. Would you like that Jonathan?'

'Yes,' he stammered. The boy tried to stifle the tears streaming down his cherubic face.

'We'll go now to a shop, and buy you cakes. Come Jonathan.' They walked together, holding each other's hands. They entered the prestigious store.

'For the lad I'd like half a dozen cheesecakes and four custard tarts topped with cream,' said Aaron to the vendor.

'Certainly.' The man leaned over to see Jonathan.

'I'm sure they are made by your expert pastry cooks, as good as the London recipes. Oh, I mustn't forget some syllabub. Thank you. Here, Jonathan, you hold the small box and I'll carry the large one.' Aaron was whistling, glancing with half an eye at the boy, trying to keep pace with him.

Lady Felicia Gableshaw spotted Aaron as he turned the street corner. She waved.

'How nice to see you again, Felicia; you're always so attractive. Do you drink the nectar of the Gods to keep young?'

'I wish Francis was a gentleman like you.' Felicia's eyes riveted on the boy, 'And what have we got here? A little freak? You do have an assortment of odd friends.'

'This is Jonathan and he is not a freak,' said Aaron, feeling peeved. 'Ah, Felicia, you're endowed with beauty, wealth, a lovely son, slaves running and serving you, but your heart is made of stone. For a brief moment, just study his intelligent face only; forget his miniature physique. There's almost a whimsical look in his large brown eyes and long eyelashes.' Jonathan hid behind Aaron's breeches, afraid of the woman.

'She won't hurt you Jonathan,' said Aaron.

'By the way, I had dinner with Nagamba and Joshua last week. They'd like to come and see Francis, apropos the cattle Joshua wishes to buy. Would it be convenient to schedule for, say, this Wednesday?'

'Yes of course, by all means.'

'I'll walk you to your magnificent coach; see you soon. Let's go home Jonathan.' Aaron lifted the boy on to his curricle.

'Its great fun riding in this,' smiled Aaron. He rubbed his hands together.

'Now you need a good wash and fresh clean clothes. You can borrow the other piccaninnies' calico pants till we go shopping next week. Tonight you will sleep on the soft mat in the corner of my room.'

On arrival they went inside to the master bedroom.

'Here's a flock pillow. I'll buy you a mattress as well. Are you afraid of the dark?'

The child looked at him nervously. 'Yes, sir.'

'I'll keep one oil lamp on the windowsill at night.' Jonathan was bathed, dressed in clean clothing and fed. Aaron laid Jonathan down on the mat.

'Goodnight Jonathan.'

'Goodnight,' the child whispered.

Outside the medley of frogs and cicadas filtered through the tall trees. And then Jonathan shrieked. Aaron sprang from his four-poster bed and ran across the room.

The boy buried his face in Aaron's chest and cried, 'They were hurting me, the horrible bad men.' Jonathan's tiny body shook with violent sobs.

'Hush, hush, you had a bad dream. No-one will beat you again. I'll tuck you in my bed on the soft, feathered mattress, just for tonight. Goodnight, Jonathan.'

The boy snuggled against Aaron's back and fell sound asleep.

꧁꧂

The Berlin coach was spectacular. It had glass windows, a door on each side, comprised four seats and a roof for cover. The inside compartment was V-shaped. It had large wheels curved with metal springs; a precaution against the impact on the rough bumpy roads. The wood on the frame of the coach below the glass window was burnished and guilded with engravings. Gashaka sat above the front wheels holding the reins of the two horses. Nagamba and Joshua sat inside. When they reached the stables, Aaron and Johnathan emerged. The moment Nagamba spotted Jonathan she put her hands to her face.

'This is my new friend, Jonathan,' said Aaron. 'I found him on the quay. He helps me with my horses, cleans the yards, fills water in the troughs, polishes the horses' bits, stirrups, all the stalls and even my saddle—an extraordinary worker. I'll promote him to be my manager.'

'Shall we pay a visit to Gableshaw as planned?' Joshua said. 'I can't stand the man but I'm keen to purchase the cattle; otherwise I wouldn't go there. Poor Felicia, what the devil did she see in that beast?'

Nagamba approached Jonathan and gripped his small hand.

'We'll go for a long ride and you'll sit beside me.'

Gashaka lifted the youngster on to the coach. Jonathan felt safe in Nagamba's presence, unlike Felicia Gableshaw. He squeezed his tiny fingers upon Nagamba's.

'Well, handsome Gashaka, let's depart,' Nagamba said with a smile. Within an hour of leaving, Jonathan reclined his head on Nagamba's shoulder and fell fast asleep. Her heart wrung with compassion for the foundling.

Aaron and Joshua sat opposite. Nagamba was dressed like an Egyptian goddess. Her long slender neck was covered with copper bangles. She wore several ivory and brass armlets. From her bare left shoulder a golden silk wrapping flowed across her body. The horses cantered through the corridors of the giant trees. Gashaka's nostrils filled with the scent of the verdant carpet covering the forest floor. Two raccoons hid behind some bushes.

'Pity I'm not a sculptor, Nagamba,' said Aaron. 'I'd like to mould a masterpiece of you in marble. You're blessed, Joshua, with a ravishing woman.'

As soon as they reached the plantation Jonathan awoke. Aaron unwrapped chocolate and gave it to him. As Felicia was brushing and grooming her two cocker spaniels she heard the arrival of the coach. Around the perimeter of the gravelled driveway was a profusion of begonias, blue lotus and ixora. In the front, near the shed, a blue mahoe spread its branches with greens, blues and yellows.

'Good morning, Joshua.'

'Hello, Felicia.'

'Francis is talking to the overseer in the boiling house. You can smell the stench of the raw sugar. Quite revolting.'

'Fasten the horses over there, below the tree; it's shady for them,' said Felicia to Gashaka.

Gableshaw appeared, stamping out with rage after an argument with his overseer.

'Greetings, Nagamba.' Gableshaw undressed her with his salacious look. 'How do you do, Joshua, Aaron?' He ignored Gashaka and Jonathan. 'I've had a disastrous morning. One has to repeat over and over the simple instructions, but they still can't understand. Their minds are addled by the sun and heat, stultified and sterile.'

'We came to negotiate about the herd, not listen to your complaints,' Joshua snapped, trying to control his temper.

'Of course,' said the patient Felicia and picked up one cocker spaniel.

'Quite so, quite so,' Gableshaw muttered. 'We've mustered the cattle from the far end of the plantation as we were expecting you today. There's Clifton the bull over there, always chasing the young, frisky and on heat. He's a brute when he mounts the heifers, otherwise he's docile.' Gableshaw peered at Nagamba and then turned to Joshua.

'I have two hundred heads of cattle.'

'I noticed your heifers exceed the number of bullocks,' Gashaka stated. 'My guess, they're ten months old.' Gableshaw faced Gashaka with resentment. He held his tongue and asked Joshua to step aside.

'That nigger, what does he know about cattle?' Gableshaw snapped.

'He's brilliant. As my overseer, he's in charge of the whole plantation and livestock, and supervises the work of the slaves. He's quick and smart.'

Gableshaw smirked with a foppish laugh. Gashaka watched him striving to control his rage and fury. He knew how much Joshua detested the man, but the opportunity had arisen to strike a bargain and buy the herd, and they had to snap it up quick.

Nagamba felt a tightening, burning sensation in her throat, observing Gashaka's acrimonious look.

'What age do you sell your steers?' Gashaka asked.

'About two years,' growled Gableshaw.

'I'd do it at eighteen months; once the bullocks are fattened you sell them. They're at their prime for beef. It's best to put the heifers to the bull when they are in season at twelve months. The overall result is constant profitable turnover. Calves, castrated males, fattened steers all sell at eighteen months. Calves are weaned till the cow dries, and then you keep a few in lactation.' Gashaka's voice had assumed a commanding tone. He glanced at Nagamba and Joshua. Aaron was astounded.

'We'd better conclude our transaction.' Joshua was on edge.

They entered an extensive, lavishly furnished room and sat around the beautiful refractory table, tinged with brown and yellow intrusions. Jonathan was swallowed in one of the piccaninnies' cane chairs. Gableshaw scowled at him with revulsion.

'An interesting audience we have here,' he said. Gashaka's eyes blazed with wrath. An uproar broke out as an embarrassed Felicia pretended to peruse the documents and flipped the pages.

'By the way, Joshua, have you considered selling your chariot?'

'Yes, at a price.'

'Pray, do tell me.'

'A hunded golden sovereigns.'

'Absurd, that's preposterous.'

'I don't think the aristocrats and nobility shipped another like it from England to the Caribbean. She is uniqiue. Therefore, that's the price. It's no wonder Lord Buckley did not wish to sell it to you or anyone else. Lady Buckley told me he enjoyed riding the chariot and never wanted to part with it. Remember, Gableshaw, you made your pile from sugar and slavery,' added Joshua with sarcasm. Gableshaw swigged more rum.

'The sum which we agreed was for the herd of cattle, the bull, carts of sugar cane, sugar trash, and thirty casks of molassess, less one hundred pounds in golden sovereigns to pay for the chariot. We'll settle up on Friday when we muster the herd.'

'It will take a week or two for Gashaka to paint, check and adjust the chariot wheels. One wheel is warped. Gashaka has all the tools. Also, the blacksmith has to weld the axle. Once all this is complete, bring your horse to my plantation and ride back on a yellow chariot like a roman centurion.'

There was a moment's silence; only the cooing of the turtle doves were heard above the roof. Jonathan tiptoed and stood behind Aaron. He did not like Gableshaw and his wife. The child was stressed. Aaron patted his head.

'Agreed,' Gableshaw growled. 'Felicia, bring the large leather parchment case and we'll sign the papers.' Gableshaw's goose quill flowed with his signature across the documents and Felicia in return did the same. Joshua attested their signatures. All depositions, certificates and transactions were stamped, sealed, signed, dated and witnessed by Aaron and Nagamba.

'Now to celebrate, we must have a drink,' Gableshaw bellowed. His harsh voice frightened the doves away.

'Only pineapple juice for me,' Aaron said, wiping his forehead. 'It's rather muggy today.'

'Yes, pineapple juice, I'll have some too,' Joshua added.

'It's more comfortable in the armchairs. Shall we?' said Felicia. Jonathan followed Nagamba closely, digging his nails into her palm.

⚜

Gableshaw clapped his hands and Marufa entered, looking pretty. Nagamba spotted her and her blood ran cold.

'Bring pineapple juice for my guests and brandy for myself,' Gableshaw snapped.

Gashaka was stunned; aghast. He looked at Nagamba. Marufa was petrified and poured the drink into Gableshaw's goblet. She then served them the drinks. Gableshaw belched guzzling his liquor.

'Tell me, Aaron, what do you see in this little midget?' His finger was pointed at Jonathan.

'He's a friend.'

Gableshaw gazed across the window feeling mellow and

in a state of intoxication. For a few seconds, to those present, he seemed almost human.

Nagamba placed her finger to her lips as a warning to Marufa not to utter a word. Marufa trembled. That fateful night flashed before her in morbid, stinging detail. To be thrown into the dark, stinking hold together with her brother and the other screaming children. Seeing Nagamba again was a shock that confused her. The fact that Nagamba seemed to be a guest in the house bewildered her. She did not know what to do or who to turn to, but she knew better than to start crying.

Gableshaw was already befuddled with the alcohol. Ebouko rushed in, shaking, with a trencher of pipes and tobacco. The youth prostrated himself before Gableshaw, and stayed kneeling, head bowed, to fill Gableshaw's pipe. He then remained still like a trained dog awaiting his master's instructions.

'Light, light,' Gableshaw scowled. Ebouko raised the candle near his pipe.

'Not like that, you mongrel,' He flung his arm hard against Ebouko's face. 'Get out of my sight!' Ebouko saw Nagamba as he fled from the room. Gashaka dug his nails into his chest, drawing blood. He wanted to scream, and bit his lip. Nagamba clutched her lower abdomen. Joshua was startled. He took her hand and stepped towards the door for some fresh air.

'She's not pregnant?' Gableshaw cried with sarcasm.

Ignoring him, Nagamba whispered to Joshua, 'It's Ebouko and Marufa, they are Mahadana's children. The last time I saw them in Africa we were taken by slavers and separated. They escaped in different directions. Gashaka and myself were caught.'

'We will return home soon,' said Joshua. 'Say nothing about the children. We will try to devise a plan to rescue them.' Joshua put his arm around her waist and took her back inside. Aaron was bewildered at seeing how stressed Nagamba was.

'Do you mind if I go over to the boiling house?' Gashaka asked. 'I have never seen the copper vats.'

'Go ahead, it stinks.'

'I won't be long,' said Gashaka turning to Nagamba.

The tall Coromante overseer with a black patch covering his right eye was surprised by the appearance of Gashaka.

'Joshua owns a plantation in Saint David and came here to conclude negotiations to buy Gableshaw's cattle. He said that I could have a look round here, if you don't mind.'. The coromante was astonished at Gashaka's politeness. He waved a hand and ushered Gashaka inside.

'We have night and day shifts. The furnace burns twenty-four hours. The copper kettles with sugar hang above. Many slaves get sick from exhaustion—the heat and fumes.'

Gashaka felt nauseated and bent over.

'There are four sizes here: 190 gallons, 150, 90 and 50,' said the Coromante. 'The boiler who is in charge and two men, each holding a ladle, scoop out the rising slime, then pour the remaining fluid into the next copper, dredging and removing the grime. After the last evaporation, the third and fourth coppers are boiling molten sugar syrup almost crystallised.' The overseer wiped his forehead above the patch.

'Did you have an accident?' asked Gashaka.

'No, it was that devil Gableshaw, he should be hanged.' Gashaka felt instantly that cemented bond of brotherhood that resulted in Esprit de Corps, though he had known the stranger for only a few moments.

'It happened three years ago. He came in running, bad tempered, drunk as usual, howling and beat one slave with his whip, which he carries on him at all times. Gableshaw slipped on the sticky molasses, raging like a wild bull with a sore head. He took a ladle and threw the scalding sugar at me. I lost the sight of my right eye. Given the chance I would kill him. I am Edoo.'

'I am Gashaka.' They shook hands

'Every single slave on the plantation despises him, most of all the ones in here. Often at night, Gableshaw sneaks to the womens slave quarters. He has a friend, Philip Tumbridge, another planter with his son—an evil man. The three meet at Tumbridge's place, where they bring trollops from the brothels and have orgies.' Edoo gnashed his teeth. Gashaka laid his hands on Edoo's Herculean shoulders. He smiled reassuringly.

'Joshua and myself will be back on Friday to drive the herd back. Could you give us a helping hand with casks of molasses to haul up on to the cart?

Edoo nodded. Gashaka thanked him and returned to the house.

'What do you think of the boiling house?' shouted Gableshaw.

'Hell,' came the reply.

Gableshaw gulped more brandy.

'Aaron, would you like to see cockfights? I am going to one. Or perhaps play shuffle board?'

'No, but I do frequent a tavern on occasion where I meet with other merchants. I like a good Madeira at a cost of one shilling.'

'Preposterous, there is a punch house where they serve my favourites: brandy, rum punch and canary,' hiccuped Gableshaw.

'And no doubt, that's where you pick up the strumpets who sell their favours in the dark alleys,' Felicia shouted. Gableshaw reddened with embarrassment. Felicia loathed her husband. She knew that he treated the slaves with despicable cruelty.

'Is it true when rats are caught in the fields and fed on sugar, planters eat them?' queried Aaron.

'Of course; had a rat for breakfast the other day.'

'What do you do with the fur? Make mittens?' There was tension in the air. Gableshaw turned to Gashaka.

'Don't forget to bring a halter for Clifton the bull.'

'I would have done so anyway, without you telling me. We're not dumb or stupid.' Gableshaw bridled at his remarks. His left eye twitched. For the first time in his life he had been humiliated by a negro. He squirmed in the armchair, very drunk by now.

Riding in the coach Nagamba clasped Jonathan against her bosom.

'I have seen children in Africa kidnapped by slave traders. Gableshaw must have connived with a captain who sails on regular trips to Port Royal, and paid him a handsome price for them.'

'I wonder if there is a way of finding out,' Aaron said. 'Felicia, maybe she knows. I must be cautious. We seem to shop the same way, Friday morning near a certain establishment.'

On Friday morning, Gashaka chained a bronze coffer with gold under the seat of the Berlin coach. Three eagles glided above the forest. He checked the carts driven by oxen with five slaves seated in each one. Joshua sat beside Gashaka and gave the signal to move off. The eagles screeched above the scented rosewood trees. Gashaka followed the soaring birds.

'They are magnificent,' he said.

Upon arrival at the Gableshaw plantation, Joshua handed over the money. Edoo helped to load the carts, and muster the cattle.

'Do you ever see the young woman and her brother around the house? asked Gashaka.

'She's lovely,' said Edoo. 'I wish I could speak to her, but that's impossible. We must be careful when Felicia or him are around.'

They said goodbye to Edoo and set off on their journey which would take two days at least. That night they camped in an open overgrown field near a stream.

CHAPTER 19

'We'll have fish tonight,' said Aaron to Johnathan, 'but first I'll play for you on my harpsichord a song called 'The Swallow'. I knew it as a young boy like yourself.' Jonathan observed Aaron's fingers plucking the strings with a quill. When darkness fell they went outside and sat on a form. Jonathan's short legs swung to and fro.

Aaron was star-struck, gazing at the heavens. 'So many stars, thousands upon thousands, far, far away and so small,' he marvelled.

'Like me,' Jonathan chuckled innocently.

'We're all minute in this vast universe.'

'What's a universe?' the boy asked.

'Everything around us and beyond; there is no end. Jonathan, you are small but wise; I'd like to think that every star is a note.'

'What's a note?' Jonathan knit his brow.

'A note is a sound and many sounds make a song, like the one I played for you.'

'Then all the stars will be songs.'

'Indeed, indeed. Have you ever seen a shooting star?' Aaron asked, stretching.

'Never.'

'When the shining star falls, it breaks into a beautiful melody.' Aaron started to hum. After the evening meal Aaron tucked sleepy Jonathan in the edge of the room on his favourite soft plantain leaf mattress.

꿏

Pinkus sailed into Kingston harbour at sunset and berthed the schooner alongside the shallops near the turtle pens. The fugitives trudged through the winding narrow lanes towards Aaron's plantation. The procession was headed by Pinkus, followed by Ezekiel and Shyloh supporting and assisting Moshebere. Alimba played nurse to him. Behind them came Bundere with Mahadana carrying Yabassi. It was a considerable distance from the wharf to walk. Moshebere's swollen legs ached. Pinkus propped him up for a while on his back, and then Shyloh and Ezekiel took turns before handing him back to Pinkus.

꿏

Jonathan heard noises outside and skipped across to Aaron's four-poster bed. 'Strange sounds like a bird, but I don't think it is,' Jonathan murmured. Aaron peeped out the window and listened.

He recollected the tune, a signal between him and Pinkus. Aaron acknowledged, whistling back.

'Jonathan, it's my friend.' Aaron dressed in his silk embroidered gown, opened the door and stepped outside. Between the cedar trees Pinkus and several other silhouettes emerged.

'Pinkus, how wonderful to see you after such a long absence.' Aaron led everyone inside the opulent lounge room. An oil lamp hung over the wide front door beam.

'What a surprise at this incredible hour.' He observed with

gravity the exhausted people slumped on the floor. Mahadana crouched in the dark corner, holding Yabassi. Bundere sat beside her. Aaron noticed Moshobere's condition. Ezekiel and Shyloh propped him against the davenport. Jonathan wriggled his button nose and gawked at Pinkus who smiled at him. A second small oil lamp was hung by the windowsill. Pinkus quickly explained who the exhausted people were and why he had brought them along.

'Jonathan, please go and wake up the cook Adjaba and ask her to bring a large jug of hot chocolate for my guests.' The boy swung around, threaded and skipped along the porch. Mahadana was already fast asleep, totally fatigued holding Yabassi.

Adjaba and Jonathan returned with the sweet hot beverage. Pinkus's sharp eyes followed Jonathan's movements with fascination.

He towered over the boy. Peering down he asked, 'What's your name?'

'Jonathan, Aaron's best friend,' he said, sending a warm smile of which only children are truly capable. 'I work in the stables, clean and brush the horses' tails, and also help with household chores.'

'From next week he'll get his very own piebald pony, and I'll start giving him lessons in reading and writing.' Aaron glanced at the youngster. His cherub's mouth was wide open and the whites of his eyes swam from side to side. Jonathan shot across the room, wrapped his hands around Aaron's neck, crying with joy.

Pinkus felt a lump in his throat. 'What an exceptional reunion this is,' he said.

'Adjaba, fetch some salted beef, cassava and kenki cakes you baked yesterday,' Aaron said, clapping his hands.

'Yes'm.' Adjaba ran off.

'I'll help her.' Jonathan skipped behind.

Aaron sized up Ezekiel and Shyloh. 'You're as tall as I am, young blades.'

'It's Pinkus's cooking; his speciality, the baked belly of the Cayman Islands turtle,' Shyloh giggled.

'What adventures did you encounter these past months?' Aaron asked.

'We stayed in Barbados for several weeks. Big ships sail from Benin and Old Calabar with brass, copper, timber, ivory, spices. In the Bight of Benin the captains haggle with merchants and middlemen and pay a niggardly price for the goods. Once they arrive in the West Indies the ships' agents and factors double the fees. We sold a substantial amount of copper and brass.'

'Would you excuse me for a moment; I must check how Moshebere feels. He's not well at all. I think he should be seen by a doctor.' Pinkus was deeply concerned.

'Doctor Fairchild is my physician as well as Joshua's,' said Aaron. 'I'll be glad to take Moshebere to him. Remember Captain Joshua Quaile?'

'Yes, we met on several occasions. I saw him over a year ago. Remarkable fellow.'

'His brigantine, the Hurricane, was scuttled. She was not seaworthy anymore. Joshua bought a thousand acres, a plantation in Dickson South, above my place. He grows several crops and raises cattle.' Aaron paused. 'A twist of fate circumscribed Joshua's life. A woman, native of the Cameroons accompanied him from Africa. Her name is Nagamba, a sculptured tableau, walks on clouds. I'm sure Joshua will be interested in your brass. He has a fabulous collection. In fact, he kept the big brass bell of the Hurricane.'

Bundere looked up sharply at the mention of Nagamba. He remained silent, unsure of himself.

'I shall be most eager to meet with him again, and his lady,' said Pinkus.

The oil lamp glowed on the walls and on Mahadana's young tired face. Her lips were slightly opened as she breast-fed Yabassi. Aaron felt dizzy, and reeled.

'What is it, Aaron—anything wrong?'

'No, no, just the excitement.'

It was beyond the bounds of possibility. Contrary to all reasonable expectations, Aaron traced inch by inch Mahadana's profile, eyes, high forehead and—most conspicuous—her mouth and chin. She was an effigy; a striking image of Marufa and Bundere, a walking portrait of Ebouko.

Aaron, the milk of human kindness, stood and said, 'You're safe in my sanctuary; there are no slaves here. I have several stables, and breed horses. Everyone gets paid.' Aaron turned to the women. 'You can, if you wish, work in the fields for a few hours, or help with the cooking in the large house and attend the beautiful gardens. I am sure, Bundere, it will be interesting for you to work with horses. Jonathan will show you around. Near your hut you'll have a small plot. Pinkus, you still did not tell me the ladies' names.'

'My apologies,' Pinkus said, clearing his throat. 'Holding Yabassi on her lap is Mahadana, and Alimba is the mother of the twins.' Pinkus brushed his beard which was flecked with grey.

The following day Pinkus revealed to Aaron in detail the ordeal of the couples in Nevis and St Kitts. Aaron listened at the unparalleled miracle of events that had occurred. He still reserved his silence and did not disclose information about Marufa and Ebouko, deciding instead to let Nagamba do so.

'Tomorrow I'll take Moshebere to the doctor; then we will all pay a surprise visit to my friend Joshua.'

'Thank you.' Pinkus's eyes swam with tears. He pressed his lips to his Bible.

৵৶

Morning slipped into her gown of indigo. Aaron hitched his two horses to the curricle. Moshebere sat beside him. They galloped with the wind towards town. Aaron hopped from the curicle and ran towards Doctor Fairchild who was about to leave.

'Good morning, Doctor. I do apologise most sincerely, but I have with me a sick man who is in pain. It's rather urgent.'

'Yes, yes of course, do come in.' Moshebere leaned against Aaron and entered the dispensary. 'Sit here in this chair.' Fairchild wiped his pince-nez and examined the patient, noticing that, after pressing several parts of Moshebere's bloated body, the mark of his finger remained for a few seconds. The eyelids were almost shut, and he viewed the swollen testicles with great concern.

Moshebere stated that he had difficulty urinating and was parched with thirst and constipated. The doctor recognised the severity of the morbid disease and wrung his hands.

'I have seen many cases of dropsy but none so advanced as this one. May I suggest a treatment that might help the poor man's misery?'

'Please yes, do.'

'I have performed subcutaneous drainage, and can do so on him, extracting excessive fluids from his belly, legs and arms. It will somewhat restore his condition. I've noticed some exudation from two sores on his foot. I'll give you healing balm. He must put it on daily.'

The doctor busied himself with the extraction of excessive fluids, talking as he worked. 'I'm conservative and believe in herbs and their therapeutic properties. Twice a year, I receive from Virginia a shipment of significant cardinal herbs which are sassafras, ginseng and the Seneca snakeroot.'

'Fascinating,' Aaron remarked. 'I import and export several goods to New England, but have never dealt in pharmaceuticals. In 1603 the first cargo of sassafras left America for England. It was the outstanding, paramount export.'

'American Indians have used sassafras for generations to treat rheumatism and veneral diseases.' The physician wiped his pince-nez again. It was warm in the room. 'The Indians also introduced the Seneca snakeroot to the Europeans in Virginia who used it for dropsy, rattlesnake bites, bronchitis, typhoid, and others. I have here in my dispensary a tincture of the snakeroot.'

He opened a glazed cupboard and administered a small quantity of the bitter root to Moshebere. 'There you are, young man, drink it down. Bring him back in two days' time.'

'We are going to visit Joshua and Nagamba this morning.' Aaron took out a pouch with gold sovereigns. 'Thank you dearly, Doctor.'

The physician gaped at Aaron. 'You're too kind and generous.'

'No, not at all, I am sure we all need your propitious services in the future. See you in two days.'

Aaron raised his plumed hat and left with Moshebere.

CHAPTER 20

Nagamba moved like a swallow as soon as she saw Aaron's Berlin coach. Joshua ambled towards it. Aaron alighted, handing Jonathan down who skipped towards Nagamba. She lifted the boy and swung him in circles several times.

'You're a treasure and an inspiration,' she said and nuzzled him.

Joshua and Gashaka stood a few feet away when Aaron took Nagamba aside and whispered, 'I bring a rainbow.'

'Aaron, you're so unpredictable at times.'

Two major unparalleled events hit like thunderclaps. First was when Mahadana and Alimba emerged from the coach. The second occurred as their husbands appeared from within. It was more than flesh and blood could bear.

Jonathan stood behind Aaron tugging at his breeches. Gashaka leaped forward, his body taut with suspense. He gripped the stunned Nagamba and pulled her towards them. All broke into convulsive and hysterical weeping. The drama was soul stirring. Pinkus was mesmerised, seeing Nagamba with Gashaka for the first time.

A chant started as they broke into an impromptu dance. The six Cameroons moved in a shaped dome and opened like a fan swaying with a rhythm of the song. The afternoon was filled with joy reminiscing. Moshebere almost forgot the pains in his legs. An enchanted Nagamba pirouetted around.

'Joshua, it's good to see you again,' said Pinkus. 'Nasty weather.'

'Yes, the last time we met was during the hurricane season on the wharf. Remarkable how destiny winds and weaves us through the years. Here we are, the three together once more during the most significant time of my life: my wedding. I have already arranged the ceremony in a small Spanish Chapel.' Joshua could not suppress his elation.

'When?'

'In two weeks. Life's a paradox. I dealt in slavery for years, and met Nagamba in Benin, the cesspool of human corruption. Gashaka saved her from a tyrant captain, and brought her to my ship. I have tossed and turned for many sleepless nights feeling guilty over the blood of the slaves on which I built my empire of wealth. Now I will share my life with Nagamba, if I can, through our love for each other. Erase the putrified violations of my past.'

Pinkus gazed up at the trees. 'We are steered by an unfathomable great divine.'

'Aaron told me you had brass and copper on your schooner.'

'Indeed, yes. Joshua, I have a wide variety of goods to trade, and do enjoy sailing the waters of the Caribbean in my trusty schooner. Perhaps you could come with me on a trip occasionally, so that you do not lose complete touch with the sea.'

'I'd love that. Tell me, you sail the waters of the West Indies, but these waters are infested with pirates. How do you survive their depredations?'

Pinkus laughed. 'Many people ask me that. The answer is simple. My crew of fourteen are more than I really need, but they are highly trained and skilled gunners. We can easily outgun any ship smaller than us, but if they are bigger and more powerful vessels we can usually outsail them. I sail under many flags, using whichever one suits the occasion.

'My ship has been designed specifically with speed in mind. I have sacrificed some cargo space to make the schooner slimmer and more streamlined; the bow is flared and steeply raked for ease of passage through the water.'

'Yes,' said Joshua. 'As soon as I can I must have a closer look at this paragon of ships.'

'The pleasure would be mine,' said Pinkus. 'Don't wait too long. But you haven't heard the crowning jewel of my schooner. The keel is forty per cent larger than that of the normal schooner. This enables me to spread more sail than any pursuing vessels. Therefore we can outrun them. Clever, eh?'

'Well, yes, but if you are chased in waters where reefs are present, the odds are that you'll hit the reef, while they are still afloat.'

'Under normal circumstances, yes, but my keel is not a normal one. It is retractable, and can be cranked up inside the ship if we are entering shallow waters. Mind you, it takes ten of my well-muscled crew to pull it up and down, but it works. This means that we can go into shallower waters than any pursuers with fixed ones.'

Joshua looked at him in amazement. 'Well. I'm speechless. That is truly amazing. You are a most resourceful man Pinkus.'

Pinkus grinned. 'No, just a person who believes in survival. Keep that information about my keel to yourself as I don't want the pirates to start copying it. Anyway I'll take you to my Pandora whenever it is convenient to you.'

'Splendid. It would give me a chance to be on board a ship

again. I must admit I do miss the Hurricane, the oceans, the pounding of the waves and the winds.'

❧

The wedding took place in a small quaint chapel in Spanish Town. Joshua wore his white naval uniform and hat. Nagamba looked radiant with her burnished skin against the white flowing dress and a golden bandana around her forehead. A pendant hung from her neck. She was barefoot.

All the guests were in white. The bright rays of the sun streamed through the small windows. The pastor took the Holy Bible and placed his hands upon it. For the reverend this was a unique wedding. He lifted his head and closed his eyes for a few minutes.

'You will pledge now your vows before God. You may do so in Bantu,' he said to Nagamba.

'I, Nagamba, will stand by your side as a rock through the years, Joshua. I will be your lantern in the dark. Our spirits will fly together. We are one, inseparable. I love you, Joshua.'

'I Joshua Quail, with every step and breath I take, I will love you, Nagamba, for the rest of my days. I will protect you, Nagamba, for as long as I shall live. We will walk together into the sunset.'

The pastor placed his hands on their heads. Joshua slipped the ring on Nagamba's finger.

'May God bless this union. You are now husband and wife.' Gashaka wiped his eyes. Aaron stood and sang 'The Swallow'. His resonant voice veiled the little chapel.

The jubilation and celebrations continued throughout the long day and night on the plantation. Even the dogs joined in, baying. The slaves were invited to partake in the feast with food and drinks. Near their quarters, under the blue mahoe trees they clapped their hands, sang and danced to the rhythm of the hollow log drums. On their legs hung small bells, rattles and shells, strumming the calabash gourds with horsehair strings.

'My wife and I will retreat to the mountains for two weeks,' said Joshua with pride. He then turned to Gashaka, gripping his hand. 'You're in charge; it's your plantation now.'

On Friday, Aaron rode his curricle to town with Jonathan. 'We'll have the same as last week,' Aaron grinned to the vendor behind the counter. 'Your patisserie is exceptional. Jonathan loves your cheesecakes and tarts, but most of all, your puffs.' Coming out of the shop in haste, Aaron almost collided with Felicia.

'I do beg your pardon; it's all those cakes in boxes. I couldn't see you very well. My sincere apologies, Felicia.'

'Always so elegant,' she admired. 'Your colours match the wonderful scenery; the blues, yellows and greens. You're truly from a gentle breed, charming.. We seem to shop at the same time on Fridays. I discovered a new establishment in the bazaar which imports a variety of food from England and the New World. I'm sure you'll be interested to know.'

'Yes, I certainly do. Anything culinary or dealing with contents of the larder is important to me.'

'They stock sauces of every conceivable kind, bottles of oil, casks of anchovies, capers, sweet meats and other things. Follow me.'

'Have you heard the latest news?' queried Aaron.

'Oh yes, I read it in the morning gazette the other day.

The headlines were *Captain Joshua Quail married his African mistress, Nagamba. Guests included Aaron Pardess, philanthropist,'* Felicia said.

'A rather vitriolic comment,' Aaron said. 'Actually it was very simple but moving when Nagamba pledged her vows in Bantu. She translated it to me beforehand in English. One phrase of hers touched me. I *Nagamba will stand by your side as a rock.* Emotionally, I'm a strong person and do not break on the wheel, but when I heard their vows it pierced my heart. Can you understand that Felicia?' He looked deep in her eyes.

'Yes, Aaron, I can. It was long, long ago when I first met Francis in Sussex, but now my heart is dark and empty.' She sighed heavily.

'Nagamba and Joshua will reach great heights. Do you still ride to the bluff?'

'Absolutely, at least once a week, leaving early and return-ing in the afternoon. I tether my horse near the silk cotton tree and walk towards the steep escarpment. I stand there, feeling the wind rising from below the precipice, and listen to the crashing waves. Far out I see the tall ships.' Felicia touched Jonathan's mass of curls.

'You do have a heart after all Felicia.'

'I'm happy on the bluff away from Francis. There I breathe.' Felicia shuddered. 'I loathe the man. Francis rides out there on occasions but not on the days I do. He prefers to rub shoul-ders with the nobility, the gentry,' she smirked. 'They gallop on their fine steeds in the forest beyond.'

'Richard, my son, is in St Kitts at present, during the Christmas school vacation. He stays with friends of mine; they also have a teenager, and the two ride horses together. I'm planning to send Richard to England. He is adamant that he wants to become a doctor. Very proficient, and knows full well what I might quote in French: *connaitre le dessus des cartes.*'

'You speak French?'

'Yes I do.'

'Enchanting,' Aaron smiled. 'Well, Felicia, I'll see you next Friday near the pastry shop, au revoir.'

᠁

'Would you like to hold the reins, Jonathan?'

'Oh yes please,' the boy gushed.

'Don't pull them too hard, otherwise the horses will bolt and we shall, oops, overturn.'

Jonathan wriggled his button nose. Aaron loved the lad. He started to whistle and the horses trotted up the hill.

In the evening Gashaka paid a visit to Nagamba and Joshua. Gashaka cleared his throat.

'I think we should reveal to Bundere and Mahadana where their children are. May I bring them tomorrow afternoon?'

'Yes of course,' Nagamba said.

The following day Gashaka watched the intimate group sitting around him.

'No-one must utter a word about this meeting. Its secret must remain sealed. Our lives could depend upon it.' They solemnly agreed. 'My heart and soul goes out to our true heroes.'

'Pinkus, Ezekiel and Shyloh, I shall never forget your courage,' Gashaka said, his voice beginning to break. Nagamba walked towards the group and rested her head on Mahadana's lap. She touched Mahadana's bewildered face with trembling hands. Pinkus was perplexed. The tension was high.

'I know where Marufa and Ebouko are,' Nagamba trembled with emotion.

Aaron sighed. Mahadana swooned.

Gentle and silent Bundere hammered his fists against his temples. Aaron brought a carafe and sprinkled water on Mahadana. Pinkus' mind flashed back to where he first met the women in the market. The ailing Moshebere and Bundere fleeing from the belching fire in St Kitts. There was a death-like silence.

'Pay attention. I have a plan. Marufa and Ebouko are slaves in the service of Gableshaw.' He paused. 'This may come as a surprise to you, but the first person in the plot is Felicia Gableshaw.'

'Felicia?' mumbled Aaron, taken by surprise.

'Yes, Aaron, she is the opening page in this hunting game of mine. Please trust me. No harm will come to her.' Gashaka stood still like a young stallion.

'Pinkus, I need some rigging, ropes, an old canvas or sail, and some hessian sacks from your schooner.'

'Certainly, my dear boy,'

They listened as he explained the details of his plan. When he had finished, they were stunned, staring at him, amazed at his audactity and grandeur of scope.

'Gashaka, you're a genius. It is a plot that might succeed, but there is much danger,' said Joshua.

'See you next Thursday,' said Pinkus.

CHAPTER 21

On Sunday, Gableshaw arrived home at daybreak and fell on to the bed in a drunken stupor. Under normal circumstances slaves were not permitted to leave the plantation but Edoo seized the opportunity and promptly departed to the market in search of Gashaka.

'I have most important information about Gableshaw. I think we should see Joshua and Nagamba at once.'

'Today, this early?'

'Yes, it is urgent.'

✥

'Gableshaw assembled all the slaves in the compound yesterday. They stood in the heat for two hours. He weeded out the infirm and weak, and intends to sell them at a candle auction.' Beads of perspiration appeared around his eye patch.

'How many did that monster pick for the sale?' Nagamba raised her voice.

'Sixteen.'

Joshua paced up and down and clasped his hands behind his back. 'We have five days to execute our scheme before Friday morning. Edoo, I want you to select fifty strong men. It is imperative I have the names of each one. As soon as it gets dark on Thursday evening, Gashaka, you will arrive at Gableshaw's plantation and meet Edoo. Edoo, you gather the fifty, plus the sixteen sick behind the curing house, a distance from Gableshaw's house.' Joshua paused. 'Therefore timing is essential.'

'The fifty men will carry on their backs the ones in terrible health and bring them to my plantation, where they can be hidden, and given nursing care by Nagamba.'

'You, Edoo, with the strength of an ox, will support one as well,' interrupted Gashaka.

'Meanwhile I shall arrange for a certain captain on a shallop I know who sails to Virginia and will take them. They will be free men. That's why I need their names for manumissions and other documents,' stipulated Joshua

'We can follow the short route across the shallow part of the river,' Gashaka pointed out.

'Once the sixteen slaves are safe here, we will transport the fifty others to the ship in carts. I must ensure that everything is finalised. The captain will be paid. It will give us time to return to my plantation. Edoo can ride back to his plantation on one of my horses and Gasahaka will go to Aaron's place. All this must be completed before Friday morning.'

Felicia won't notice the missing numbers,' said Edoo. 'She never interferes and has no interest in plantation matters.'

⚓

Thursday evening was a peaceful one. Edoo assembled the slaves and with the aid of Gashaka sent them to Joshua. The sick were handed over to Nagamba, while the fifty others went aboard the ship.

⚓

On Friday morning Gableshaw emerged from the house, attired in flamboyant colours, flipping his small leather whip across his breeches.

He glared at Gashaka. 'Is anything wrong with the cattle?' he asked in a raucous manner.

'No, no, Joshua asked me to introduce you to Captain Pinkus, of the schooner Pandora. He is a close friend of the family.'

'How do you do?' Pinkus nodded and doffed his plume hat.

'Captain.'

'Captain Pinkus will be in Kingston for only one week,' Gashaka remarked politely.

'I thought you might be interested to visit my magnificent two-masted schooner and see the various merchandise I import from Europe and Africa, and sell throughout the Carribbean, and the Americas. Norfolk in Virginia will be my next port of call.'

Gableshaw gave a supercilious look to Ezekiel and Shyloh standing behind Pinkus. He wasn't sure whether they were mulattos or quadroons.

'Thank you for your invitation, I shall be delighted, Captain ...' he hesitated. 'I do beg your pardon, I clean forgot your name'. Gableshaw pursed his lips.

'Pinkus, just Pinkus'.

'Ah yes, Pinkus.' Gableshaw accentuated his name observing the man's distinguished chiselled features of the Orient. He also noticed his extravagant and ostentatious clothes. A golden fob watch chain hung from Pinkus's embroidered green waistcoat pocket. A *wealthy erudite Jewish merchant, astute, and affluent in money matters*, thought Gableshaw.

Pinkus was disgusted as the insolent lofty-minded lord

sized him up. He felt like a clown, wearing such absurd ridiculous garments, but today, humble Pinkus had to hide and sacrifice his true identity and asked God for forgiveness. The clothing he had borrowed from Aaron as part of Gashaka's grand plan.

'What is your output of sugar per annum?' Pinkus asked.

'Last year was an exceptional one, most profitable—a hundred and fifty tonnes—but a year prior to that was a disaster. The ship was caught in a gale, and was smashed to pieces, sinking with all the crew and tons of sugar into the deep.' Gableshaw took out his snuff box and inserted the powder in each nostril, then sneezed. 'Clears the head,' he added.

'I ship, barrels, tiers and casks of sugar and muscovado from Barbados, St Kitts and Nevis to the New World. In Virginia, slaves crave molasses with voracity, using it as a sweetener. The white Virginians relish the stuff as well.' With graceful manners Pinkus picked up his fob watch and looked at the time. Ezekiel glanced sideways at Shyloh trying not to laugh.

'I do know several plantation owners in Virginia, and can mention you to them if you wish.'

'By all means. In fact I acquired more land and bought 150 slaves from Joshua to expand my plantation,' Gableshaw smirked.

'I deal on a regular basis with transactions of sugar, but I must confess I know very little about the practical formulation and process of sugar making. I'll be most grateful if you'll be so kind to demonstrate and show me the boiling house.'

'Certainly.' Gableshaw led the way. Pinkus walked beside him. Upon entering Gashaka spotted Edoo. He braced his hands behind his back and indicated with his finger for the

Coromante to approach. There were several slaves near the kettles.

'There are different sizes of coppers. The purpose is to purify and skim the accumulative unwanted residue of each kettle by extreme heat and finally crystallise the sugar.' Gableshaw loosened his lace neckerchief.

'How do the slaves endure such extreme heat and repugnant stench?' Pinkus asked.

'The strong Nigger bucks tolerate it. The weaker ones are transferred to the curing house, and those unfit and maimed—we sell them at candle auctions for two pounds each,' laughed Gableshaw. Bundere started to shake. Flashes of hell were imprinted on his mind, of him standing for hours over the stifling coppers with ailing Moshebere in St Kitts. Shyloh held him close.

'It will soon be over,' Gashaka whispered.

Gableshaw, oblivious to the men at the back approached the third kettle. 'The sugar is browner in texture and gets even darker as we reach the last one.' He leaned forward.

'Interesting, most interesting. Let me see,' said Pinkus. He peered myopically into the molten vat. 'Oh look, what's this below?' he said, pointing inside. For a split second Gableshaw was distracted and bent even further, looking down into the bubbling sugar. Gashaka and Pinkus pounced, lifting Gableshaw up and pushing his head down. He kicked wildly, struggling for his life.

The stalwart Edoo sprang with lightning speed and grabbed the quivering Gableshaw by his feet, bunching his legs like a chicken, and dipped his body into the lava flow of liquid sugar.

'Bring a pitch fork!' Eddoo shouted. A slave ran to the corner and handed one to him. Edoo dug the sharp steel prongs into Gableshaw's abdomen and pulled him out. His features were unrecognisable. Chunks of flesh, like blubber, fell from his arms.

'He won't harm slaves any more!' Edoo yelled.

Ezekiel and Shyloh rushed outside and brought in the equipment from the Pandora. Edoo slung Gableshaw on to the canvas, and Gashaka and Bundere sleeved the mangled body in a large hessian sack. Shyloh picked the gory pieces from the floor and dumped them on the corpse. With ropes they tied Gableshaw's mortal remains and bundled him into the carriage.

Edoo followed Gashaka's two implicit cardinal instructions. The first was to leave Gableshaw's gelding on the Bluff; and second, the slaves had to scrub the floor of the boiling house with vinegar and leave no trace evidence of the butchery. Edoo struck fear into their hearts.

'The bad spirits will hunt and burn you in the underworld. No-one must know what happened here this morning. When the soldiers come you must say you haven't seen Gableshaw for many days.' The slaves trembled in fear.

Nagamba and Joshua were waiting outside when they arrived. Bundere was whisked indoors, feeling ill.

'It's done,' said Gashaka. 'I must take Pinkus immediately to the wharf and get rid of Gableshaw.'

'We'll be back in a few months,' Pinkus said and hugged Nagamba.

The three men heaving the cumbersome sack were inconspicuous, milling with the porters carting barrels from the sloops. The Pandora sailed into the blushing sun. Gableshaw's body was flung overboard miles out at sea.

Late in the morning Felicia entered the boiling house. 'Have you seen Francis?' she asked quite puzzled.

'No, I was wondering myself. If you remember several months ago he disappeared for two days,' the overseer said. She knew what he was implying.

'He could have ridden to Tumbridge's plantation and stayed overnight, which he often does, and got drunk,' she said.

'Is there anything I can do for you?' asked Edoo.

'No thank you; I'll wait until tomorrow.'

On the second day the gelding appeared through the fine drizzle and stopped near the stable waiting. Edoo was alerted by a slave. He knocked on Felicia's door; she came out drowsy, her gown unbuttoned. Edoo felt uncomfortable.

'Good morning, Edoo.'

'Lord Gableshaw's gelding trotted back without him.' The Coromante was nervous and fidgety, looking at her breast. He was amazed how white her skin was. Felicia covered herself.

'Could you saddle my horse at once,' she snapped. She watched Edoo dash off, and slammed the door behind her.

Aaron was walking with Jonathan around his beautiful garden when he saw Felicia riding on her chestnut mare.

'An early visitor,' he said, pretending to be surprised.

'It's Francis; haven't seen him for two days. I thought he might have spent some nights at the brothels or with Tumbridge endulging in orgies, but this morning his horse turned up without him. Do you mind if we head to the Bluff and check?'

'No, not at all. Would you like a drink first?'

'I'd rather go there now; it's a long ride, thank you.' Felicia's lips were pursed.

'I think we should take my Berlin coach,' said Aaron. 'It's far more comfortable. Leave your horse here.'

'Oh, I do love the Bluff.' Felicia skipped off the carriage and ran like a young girl towards the edge of the cliff. Her blonde hair and brilliant scarf billowed in the wind. Aaron watched her with delight and suspense as she reached the precipice.

She put her fingers on her mouth and screamed, 'Francis's crop and bag are here.'

Aaron raced towards her. It wasn't in his nature to put on a mask and play the feigned and spurious act *affaire de velours,* and yet he felt that Felicia was far better off without that immoral heinous husband of hers. Now she would be a free and wealthy woman.

'I think I'd better inform Colonel O'Reilly about this; I've dealt with him before on matters of the law,' Aaron remarked, looking at the raging sea below. 'If he's fallen down there, no-one will ever find him. He'd be smashed to a pulp against the jutting rocks and washed away with the monster waves.' Aaron was convincing knitting his brow.

'He did love the Bluff, this at least we had in common,' Felicia murmured.

Aaron placed a heavy stone to mark where the riding crop was found. 'We'll head back now; it's getting too late for you to ride in the dark. Please stay in my house for the night.'

'Thank you for your hospitality. I never had the chance to be your guest,' Felicia said, blushing.

The horses galloped past an avenue of blue mahoe, clustered with bright yellow flowers, flecked with deep red.

'The scent is intoxicating like wine,' Felicia said. They arrived at the semi-circled, sprawling house with spacious porches and louvres.

Felicia slept on an embellished-oak engraved and carved bed. The soft flock mattress was covered with blue silk sheets and above the canopy hung a light-blue mosquito net. 'You may borrow my nightgown,' Aaron said.

'I'll sleep in the nude, more comfortable,' Felicia sang out. 'But I must go home soon after dawn.'

She left early. Aaron, in his Berlin coach, followed.

Colonel O'Reilly, with ten red coats on horseback, arrived at Felicia's plantation before noon. O'Reilly was an odd figure, plump with a long thin moustache curled upwards above his lips, a reddish Edwardian beard, red pointed nose, and two large protruding rabbit teeth. His gait was somewhat awkward and vulgar. He walked with straddled legs.

Edoo, seeing the militia, sped to warn the slaves.

'May I introduce my friend Lady Felicia Gableshaw.' Aaron took off his hat with aristocratic bearing. O'Reilly smiled and kissed her gloved hand.

'It is an honour, my lady. Mr Pardess has explained to me the events and circumstances of your husband's disappearance. I suggest we ride to the Bluff with my soldiers for the investigation into the case, but before we do so I wish to question the slaves and overseer in the boiling house, with your consent please.' O'Reilly bowed.

'Follow me.' Felicia took off her pink straw hat. 'Edoo, come here, call the others.' The giant figure of Edoo towered over Colonel O'Reilly. He summoned the frightened slaves.

'When was the last time you saw Lord Gableshaw?'

O'Reilly reddened.

'Five days ago,' Edoo spoke up. 'We were discussing sugar casks and barrels to be shipped.'

Drops of perspiration ran down O'Reilly's face to his

double chin. He cast his eyes on the slaves. They looked tired and melancholic. O'Reilly snarled interrogating the first one.

'I no see him long time, I no see him long time,' the slave stammered.

'And you?' O'Reilly stamped his boots as he approached the second.

'He come morning, go away, no more see master.'

'I don't think any of them recollect exactly, they get confused,' Edoo remarked. 'Every day seems to be the same for them.'

'The overseer is quite right,' Felicia put forth. 'He's been with us for several years; most loyal. I trust his judgement.'

O'Reilly observed Edoo's black patch. He grinned and turned to Lady Gableshaw.

'Very well, I think we should presently make our way to the Bluff.'

'I've ridden to Tumbridge's plantation. My husband used to visit him, but he was not there.'

'I know Phillip, we meet on occasions in the tavern for a drink.'

Heavy squalls of rain the night before washed away all clues along the promon tory ridge. The militia scouted for days, combing the Bluff and miles beyond in the dense forest. After a fortnight of futile tracking and searching O'Reilly paid a visit to Lady Gableshaw.

'There's no trace of Lord Gableshaw. The rising wind from below the escarpment can be strong and the jagged crowning cliffs are slippery. I can only assume your husband tripped, lost his balance, staggered and fell several hundred feet down the ridge to the Caribbean. I'm so sorry to bring you such dreadful news, very sorry indeed.'

'His horse came home and waited for him near the stable.'
Felicia, half-dazed, looked across the window.

'If there's any way I can help you, please do not hesitate
to call upon me.'

'Thank you,' Felicia uttered. She led him to the door; he
kissed her hand again and rode out with his militia.

CHAPTER 22

A fortnight after Gableshaw's disappearance Aaron invited Felicia for lunch.

'I would have done so sooner but my better judgement compelled me to do otherwise. I thought you might need a friend. Have you made plans?' Aaron studied Felicia, who was wrapped in thought.

'Yes, Aaron, I have decided to sell and go back to England with Richard and buy a small cottage. It is ironic: I have resided in Jamaica for several years, not far from the ocean and never bathed even once.' She shrugged. 'I might find it strange at first to settle back home, but financially I'll be comfortable, and Richard can pursue his studies in medicine.' On a sudden impulse Felicia touched Aaron's hand. For a few seconds he was speechless.

'I've been unhappy with Francis for a long time and swallowed his insults and humiliations, but I was never unfaithful to him.' She pursed her lips. 'This unforeseen future appeals to me. I can spread my wings.'

'We're two opposites,' said Aaron. 'Throughout your life, Felicia, you lived and mingled with the aristocracy and nobility, whereas I conversed with ordinary people, the needy and the outcasts. On occasion I go to social gatherings but I find them an utter bore and, if I may add, they are a lot of humbugs.' Felicia doubled up laughing.

'Oh you are hilarious,' she said. 'What a good sense of humor, witty; I'll miss you.'

'Don't miss me too much, I might convert you to my level of thinking.'

'You have already in some ways. You must have had an impressive and varied childhood. Pray do tell me,' she said with burning curiousity. 'Were you born in Barbados?'

'Yes, my family's history will fascinate you, rather impressive. Jews were being persecuted in Portugal and fled to South America. In Recife, Brazil, the Jewish people were oppressed and trampled by the Dutch as well. My father, a brilliant man owned a large sugar plantation near Recife. The exodus of three hundred Jews began in the 1660s, including my father. Several Indians from a remote Dutch outpost in Surinam were brought to Barbados on English ships. They carried plants, seeds ands sugar cane. The Indians were ignorant of how to make sugar, but they planted the crops and extracted the juice from the thick stalks to make a sweet beverage.' Aaron studied Felicia's face, her eyes wide open.

'Father had already the acquisition of sugar knowledge and he, with other Jewish people, was the first to introduce the Barbados landowners to the skills of the sugar industry I am proud to say.'

'Most interesting.' Felicia was intrigued.

'Now I shall mix you pawpaw with pineapple and a dash of rum.' She tasted it and licked her lips.

'Let's go to the garden,' said Aaron. 'Look, Felicia, up there. A flock of large frigate birds perched on the swaying branches. They inflate their pendulous bright red wattle against their black feathers.'

'This island is bathed in colours,' she smiled.

'I must show you a fascinating plant. You may wonder why it is fenced so high. It is a Wax Rose with pink blossoms, and if we touch it with our fingers, the oil from our skin will soon cause it to wilt and die. Most incredible and inexplicable.'

'Aaron, you are familiar and excel in business enterprises, bonds, shares, stocks and properties. Please sell my plantation for me, as soon as possible,' Felicia emphasised with eagerness.

'Of course. In fact, a pebble fell into my lap. Sir Henry Darlington, a magnate sugar plantation owner, arrived two months ago from Barbados after having sold his vast estates. He was spared the yellow fever epidemic known as the bleeding fever, but his wife died. Hundreds of corpses littered the streets, slaves and whites alike.'

'How tragic, I read about it in the gazette.'

'It is his mistress who is the real reason for him coming to Kingston. His wife was aware of the liaison. Gossip is rife here: *cela va sans dire*. I was told this mysterious woman is elusive, cultured and attractive. What is most striking too, she comes from a wealthy Jewish family in Barbados.'

'Engaging combination,' smiled Felicia.

'Coming back to Sir Henry Darlington, potential buyer and a man well known to be extravagant with money; I shall pay him a visit tomorrow. First though, I have two favours to ask of you, Felicia. They are of great significance. I am sure you'll understand. Edoo, your overseer, visits Joshua's plantation regularly. He had befriended Gashaka. Do you remember him, Nagamba's brother?'

'Oh yes, I do,' she said with a twinkle in her eyes. 'Handsome man; the way he moves.'

'The first favour is: Edoo explained to Gashaka that the men in the boiling house are on the brink of total exhaustion, standing for hours over the suffocating coppers. He asked Gashaka to plead with you if he and the slaves could work for

Joshua. Of course all this depends on the sale of your plantation, which I shall attend to promptly. Henry Darlington is
eager to purchase acres of good land such as yours.'

They approached the stables. Jonathan led his pony
forward, slightly taller than himself. His small feet and the
pony's hooves wrung Aaron's heart.

'I'm going to take him for a short ride,' said Jonathan.

'Will he grow a bit more in height?' Felicia asked

'I doubt it, he's nearly ten,' Aaron sighed.

'You love the lad?'

'Yes, very much so. Incidentally Edoo has a great admiration for you,' Aaron smiled. 'He told Gashaka you walk, talk
and behave like a lady. He trusts you, a rare quality in a slave
for his white master.'

Felicia was amazed, lost for words, not believing her ears.
'Do I deserve such compliments?'

'Maybe Edoo felt your loneliness and humiliating years
with Francis. Slaves do have feelings. So, Lady Felicia Gableshaw,' Aaron chuckled. 'If I'm successful in selling your
plantation for the best offer, would you grant me these
wishes?'

'How could I ever refuse a gallant cavalier such as you,
Aaron?'

'My second request is for Jonathan's sake. I have melted
your heart once for the little fellow. He's often lonely and it
would be wonderful if Marufa and Ebouko could reside in
my house. He will have friends. The girl could assist in the
gardens and house, Ebouko will follow Jonathan's footsteps.'

'So be it, so be it.' Felicia wrapped her yellow scarf around
her neck.

'I'll see you as soon as I've spoken to Henry Darlington.'

He helped her climb into the coach. 'Thank you, Felicia.'

He kissed her gloved hand. The horses galloped and soon receded in the hazy afternoon.

A fortnight later, a few days before Felicia's estate was sold, Aaron bought her gelding and two mares, and Joshua purchased a substantial amount of molasses and cane stalks. They were hauled on the long carts with twenty slaves from Felicia's boiling house. Gashaka held the reins and Edoo sat beside him. The grateful Coromante touched his black eye patch with melancholy. The Berlin coach trailed behind with Aaron and Joshua sitting above the big wheels.

Aaron walked along the ship's deck and entered Felicia's cabin.

'Your mother told me you wish to become a doctor.' He observed the youth standing before him.

'Yes, and I am looking forward to seeing England.'

'Good sailing, Richard.' Aaron shook his hand.

'I'm going outside for a few minutes,' said Felicia. 'Can I have a word with you, Aaron, please?'

'Of course,' said Aaron. They stepped out on to the deck. 'Does he miss his father?'

'Francis never had time for his son. All he lusted for was his trollops, indulging in drinking and building his sugar empire.'

'Pleasant weather isn't it,' Aaron stated, changing the subject. 'The voyage should take six weeks, probably less with favourable trade winds.'

'I dislike *adieu*, so let's part with *au revoir*, otherwise I shall start crying, and that I dislike even more.' She gazed across the water and beyond at the Blue Mountains. Like a flash she cupped Aaron's face with her hands and brushed her lips upon his. She wanted him but she was sailing in two hours. How could destiny interfere at such a time?

'Write to me, Aaron.' Felicia tore away from him and ran into her cabin.

The Ark cruised out to the open sea.

CHAPTER 23

Mahadana was bathing Yabassi outside in a white tub when she heard the horses. The Berlin coach came to a halt. She held her breath seeing Jonathan step down holding Marufa's hand like a gentleman, and then Ebouko emerged, walking beside Aaron. Shocked, Mahadana's tongue cleaved to the roof of her mouth. She stood up leaving soap suds covering Yabassi's face. He squealed. Mahadana raced towards them. Two years had elapsed since they were separated.

'Mamma, Mamma,' sobbed Marufa. Ebouko, overcome by emotion, staggered, raising his hands high and reaching for his mother. Jonathan approached the distressed Yabassi and hugged him, wiping the soap from his face.

'Go and call Bundere from the stables,' said Aaron.

The children noticed how frail their mother was and how she had aged. The dramatic reunion was heart-wrenching as the four prostrated themselves on the ground in reverence to the spirits, and scattered earth upon themselves. Mahadana wiped the dirt from her lips and whimpered a faint cry.

'Will we ever be free from the white man?'

❧

The following morning Aaron decided to take the young-sters to his emporium. An easterly breeze rippled upon the waters and whisps of cirrus cloud fringed the grey sky.

The melancholic pule of the kite was heard in the distance. Marufa, Ebouko, Jonathan and Bundere strolled beside Aaron. The wharf was busy. Aaron bought a large basket filled with fresh buns. Ebouko suddenly tucked and pulled at his father's shirt with great agitation.

'It's him! It's him! The white dog!' he yelled.

'Who? Who? Bundere asked, taken aback at the sudden outburst.

'That captain, I recognise him. He was the one in Bonny in the slave market. He paid the caboceer and guard who snatched Marufa and me, and then brought us here on his ship.'

Captain Montague walked with his first mate, factor and shipping agent, oblivious to the spying eyes.

'I want you children to stay in the warehouse,' said Aaron. 'This could be dangerous. We'll be back soon.' Marufa, Ebouko and Jonathan huddled in a corner, and Aaron secured the door.

Pussyfooting, they slid among the casks and barrels, following Captain Montague and his companions, enabling them to eavesdrop on their conversation. The Captain approached the Nightingale and stopped.

'The inventory please, and list of slaves,' he snapped to the first mate.

'Sir.' The nervous officer handed him the long sheet. Captain Montague turned to the factor.

'You can start the scramble sale. I sail tomorrow.' He walked up on to the deck and entered his cabin. At the extreme end of the long quay the slaves' harrowing screams made the flesh creep.

Aaron did not wish to frighten the three youngsters, so on returning to the warehouse, being a good raconteur, he said, 'That captain is evil and should be punished. Let's go home and plan this.'

When darkness fell, he and Bundere rode back in the curricle towards the quay. Aaron tethered the horses behind the big trees and waited. Whores roamed in the darkness. Caterwauling cats prowled around the dirty bins.

'Fun for sixpence?' A prostitute approached Bundere. She could not see his face, only the silhouette reflected from the dim light.

'Sorry, madam, my wife expects me back soon. It is frightfully late,' he mimicked in polished English as he gave her a courtly bow.

'Your wife is at home and you are here. I am here to please. Which would you prefer?'

'I shall return next week at the same time to this precise spot. As a gentleman I shall pay you a shilling.' Bundere could not believe his own ears and he chuckled at the astonished look on the whore's face. He then turned and proceeded to the ship, scaling the thick ropes of the Nightingale below Captain Montague's cabin. Inside, Montague conversed with an officer.

'Well I had better get some sleep. Tomorrow will be a busy day.' Montague yawned loudly.

'Good night, Captain,' said the officer.

Bundere waited a few minutes before he knocked. Montague assumed it was one of the crew and opened the door. Like a whirlwind Bundere flew in, sprang and clawed him with a vice-like grip, and slashed his throat with his knife. Montague's clutched the ripped jugular, his eyes widening and blood spurting across his chest. Then he collapsed. Bundere, swift as a hawk, cleaved and decapitated the head, before placing it on the small table. He opened the door and looked out. Not a soul stirred. Bundere ran to the ship's side and slid down the scabrous hemp that passed as moorings.

The ladies of the night had disappeared. With nimble feet he sprinted through the narrow alleys and found Aaron. Both left in the curricle.

᪥

The next day Aaron arrived at the emporium. The quay bustled and droned like a swarm of bees in a bottle, with militia on horses. Colonel O'Reilly cantered up and down driving his gelding hard with his crop. The animal snorted and kicked, sending whiffs of steam from its nostrils.

'I want the whole area scoured, combed and sieved: every nook and cranny.' O'Reilly's raucous voice rent the air. Aaron stepped outside. O'Reilly dismounted.

'What's all the commotion?' Aaron asked in a cold tone.

'Hideous, a grisly sight. The first mate found Captain Montague's head propped on the table as a trophy. Such impertinent audacity. I'll get the swine,' O'Reilly shouted.

'Any clues?'

'No, not so far. It happened late last night, cunning invisible bastards. It was dark, except for the ships lanterns reflecting on the water.'There's plenty of room to hide between the timbers, bales and ropes.'

'I questioned one prostitute. An obscure man offered to pay her a shilling the following week. Apparently he was charming but in a hurry. She could not see his face. Silly bugger, a comedian as well.'

'You want my personal opinion? Aaron asked.

'Yes of course.'

'It's all to do with yesterday's scramble auction.'

'Maybe, and yet … somehow...' O'Reilly never finished the sentence; instead he just wiped his sweaty brow. 'Africans believe in witchcraft and voodoo, bloody savages.' He paused. 'I heard Lady Gableshaw left for England.'

'She decided to go back after her husband's mysterious death.'

'Pray do convey my regards when you write to her.' OReilly sniffed the air like an animal. 'I'll hunt them in every corner of this island. They most probably escaped and joined the Maroons in the Blue Mountains.'

⁊

'I hear two hearts beating. You carry twins Nagamba, congratulations,' Doctor Fairchild said happily.

'Two?' Joshua stared first at Nagamba and then at the doctor.

'Yes, Joshua. I shall give you two sons.' The physician laughed, putting his hat and coat on. 'I will visit you again next month.'

Joshua bent over, rested his head on Nagamba's stomach and cupped it with his hands. He then slumped on the mastic floor leaning against the cool stone wall and peered at his wife.

'Two?' he repeated, flabbergasted. Nagamba laughed.

⁊

The hurricane season arrived in August. The wind howled like a banshee and in the far distance streaks of lightning flashed across the threatening, dark sky. Joshua watched the birth of the twins with breathtaking awe. They mewled and whined as they were expelled into the world.

Doctor Fairchild cut the umbilical cord and said, 'Healthy, fine boys.'

The plump midwife wrapped them with linen swaddlings. Joshua wept with joy. He placed the first baby on Nagamba's right side and the second on her left.

'Thank you, Nagamba, for giving me two sons.'

'I love you, my albatross.' She stroked Joshua's wavy red hair. Gashaka brought two wooden cribs he had made with their names engraved above. Enoch and Amos. They were identical twins except for their eyes: Enoch's were greenish-blue and Amos's dark brown. Nagamba was fatigued after a long labour.

'I think we had better let her sleep,' said Fairchild. 'She needs to rest. Make sure she consumes ample goat's milk and cheese, legumes, especially the Acacia Villosa (very nutritious with pounded garlic). I also recommend calf's liver.'

'A friend of the family gave us bottles of the pistle of turtles,' Joshua remarked. 'He prepared it himself.''Oh yes, turtles are excellent: turtle soup, baked turtle—delicious and cheap in the market. I'll visit Nagamba tomorrow, see how everyone is faring.'

The wind increased outside. Nagamba was sound asleep. Joshua took gurgling Amos and laid him in the soft crib, and Gashaka nursed Enoch. Both men stood transfixed, gazing at the newborns.

Nagamba and Joshua celebrated the birth of their twins. They set free all their slaves, who were given the choice of staying on and being paid wages or, for those few who left for other islands, a sum of money was provided to start a new life as free men with manumission declarations. For every man, woman and child, Joshua pledged and executed an attested certificate that decalared that all slaves on his plantations were released from bondage—sealed, stamped, dated and signed. Aaron witnessed the deed. Gossip raged like a prairie fire across the country about Joshua's decree to free his slaves, and the belle of Africa giving birth to twins.

Young beautiful Quasha worked in the kitchen as a cook at Tumbridge's plantation. For several months she went with Gashaka on Sundays to the markets. They always met on Aaron's estate and were joined there by Edoo and Marufa. The four young blades were *boon* friends. Gashaka was enraptured, captivated by Quasha.

'I love her,' said Gashaka to Joshua, sitting on the porch one evening.

'Why don't you propose to her, and when you do I'll call upon Tumbridge.'

A couple of days after the birth of the twins Aaron took Jonathan to see them. The four camarades rode in the Berlin coach as well.

'They are so little,' Jonathan commented.

Nagamba placed Enoch on Jonathan's lap. 'Make sure you hold him securely and you, Aaron, can nurse Amos.'

'I have a surprise for you, Nagamba.' Gashaka ran outside and soon wheeled in a wicker double pram which he had constructed. The base was made of light obesh wood. The end of each axle was sleeved with a copper sheath and greased with animal fat for a smooth and quiet ride. At the top of the pram, for coolness and protection from the hot sun, Gashaka had affixed a pair of circumvoluted canvas shades, adorned and fringed on the four edges with red pompoms.

'My hero, Gashaka, thank you, thank you.' Nagamba hugged him.

'Quite an ingenious piece of art,' Joshua remarked.

'We're going for a short walk with the twins on the verandah,' said Gashaka as he walked outside with Quasha.

'I like your dress,' Gashaka whispered. They looked at each other in silence. He wanted to say so much but decided on the spur of the moment to postpone it for a later occasion. He suddenly held her close to him.

'I love you, Quasha.' He sought her parted lips and pressed against her, leaning on the stone wall. He then touched her young firm breasts. Amos start to whine, followed by Enoch. Quasha laughed.

'They get fed every three hours, and they're hungry. I might give you a son one day,' she teased and clung to him in rapture. 'We'd better take them back to Nagamba's milk.'

For several weeks it was a busy period on the plantation. Cocoa, indigo and cotton were harvested in large bales and stored to be shipped. The men in the tannery piled stocks of goat and cattle hide for export. Goat's cheese, milk, and beef cattle were sold at the market.

From the seeds of the Ackee fruit trees, which Moustapha gave Joshua in Benin, thirty saplings sprouted and grew. Later in the year Aaron received a letter from Pinkus.

'Dear Aaron, we shall be coming to Jamaica in the spring when the casuarina trees are in full bloom. Regards to Nagamba and Joshua, and a big hug for Jonathan, bless him. Your friends: Pinkus, Ezekiel and Shyloh.'

Moshebere's condition deteriorated. He was unable to walk, his joints ached. He had difficulty grasping anything with his hands due to the enormity of the swelling. Pains shot at his private parts and water was passed with great difficulty. He also developed weeping bed ulcers.

'Moshebere is dying,' Doctor Fairchild said with great anguish. 'Alas, it is beyond my medical expertise to help him. Moshebere's body is imbued with toxins. I cannot save him.'

The orifices in Moshebere's entire body burst, and he died with a morbid, corrupt stench.

CHAPTER 24

Several months had elapsed sinced Felicia departed for England. Aaron decided to write to her.

Good morning, Felicia.

The years are flying past so quickly. It seems like only yesterday that you sailed away. This year of 1705 is disappearing fast. Nagamba gave birth to twin boys. On the occasion all Joshua's slaves were granted manumission and are now free. Jonathan often rides with me to the bluff. He has become and accomplished rider. Gashaka is in love with Quasha, a ravishing maiden. She works on Tumbridge's estate. James, his son, is loathsome like his father. Both are perverts. Henry Darlington paid me a visit regarding horses. He bought four of my fine thoroughbreds. He goes riding with his bourgeois circle.

Am I being sarcastic? Are you smiling? So far, far away across the ocean. The illustrious aristocrat Haute Monde leaves a hollowness and emptiness inside me. They are disguised by false colouring. I never liked them. I am a product of a different world. How could you understand that, Felicia? Remember when you first saw Jonathan, he seemed like a freak to you but I think you like him. The little urchin. He is warm, intelligent and a delight.

On occasions I sail to Boston and Virginia where I meet the prospective gentry who are interested in buying horses from my stud farm. I am building more stables because the breeding season commences soon. I know how much you like horses. At present I have ten black Arabian stallions: five white ones and several mares in foal. Also, rather unique Barbary horses from Morocco, excellent trackers and fast. Twenty Jennets, a smaller Spanish breed, ideal for the young; and palfreys for women. What a menagerie with colts and fillies. I do so love those classic creatures. Jonathan brushes your gelding's tail, such an animal lover he is.

How do you fare in bleak England? (I shiver to think.)
Au revoir,
Aaron

On Sunday the Pandora cruised into Kingston Harbour and berthed alongside the tall sloops. A flock of honking geese flew past in V formation. Jonathan spotted the schooner, and ran towards Pinkus. He hugged the little fellow, as Nagamba and Joshua waved.

Pinkus embraced Nagamba. 'What a blessing,' he said, watching the twins.

'This is Enoch,' smiled Nagamba. The infant drooled over Pinkus shirt. 'And Amos, his brother.'

'What a happy reunion,' cried Pinkus.

'And a special one.' Nagamba rubbed her abdomen with both hands. 'An addition to Captain Joshua Quaile's family,' she laughed. They all stared at her blankly.

'Another one?' said Joshua, incredulous, almost tripping while holding Amos.

'Yes, they will grow together, fight together and run together,' Nagamba said, welling up.

'My beautiful albatross.' Joshua clasped her, squeezing grumpy Amos between them.

'Ezekiel and Shyloh loaded a crate from the schooner into the Berlin coach. Everybody climbed aboard and they headed towards Aaron's home.

For lunch Adjaba and Affra, the two cooks, brought several large salad bowls garnished and sprinkled with scented begonia blossoms, also known as bread and cheese.

After they had eaten, Bundere arrived. Ezekiel and Shyloh prised the top off the crate.

'The blunderbusses and flintlock muskets are a necessity against O'Reilly and his henchman,' said Pinkus. 'I am not convinced that he believed the manner of Gasbleshaw's death, but he has no proof. However, his militia can be dangerous.'

Aaron scrutinised the arms. 'Most destructive. The blunderbuss is an effective weapon, has a large bore, capable of spraying many slugs at close range.'

Pinkus held a musket rifle in his hand. 'Interesting to know the flintlock musket has the same lock as the original wheel lock or firelock gun sparks the priming. They were first used in 1547.'

'I think I shall leave some blunderbusses and muskets here in Aaron's cellar in case he is surprised by the militia and O'Reilly,' said Joshua. 'Bundere, you do the same, and take one of each up to the stables. Make sure you have plenty of powder and ammunition. The rest we will take home.'

'Joshua and Nagamba, would you like to go on board the Pandora tomorrow?'

'Indeed, Pinkus, thank you, we would love that.'

'We will have lunch on the schooner.'

'The little ones are tired,' said Nagamba, smothering a yawn herself.

'Yes of course.' Joshua picked up Amos and Nagamba

carried a sleepy Enoch. Birds screeched below the gathering dark clouds.

'I smell rain,' said Joshua as they rode home.

CHAPTER 25

The months flew past. Finally, Aaron received mail from Felicia.

'Dear Aaron,

There's a gale outside, piercing winds are blowing, and the snow drifts are high. To keep myself warm in bed I have two quilts, a copper hot water bottle, woolly garments and socks. At present I'm sitting by a blazing wood fire. There are several logs in a large copper bucket beside the hearth. A field mouse has scampered in and is sitting on the wood shivering, ignoring me as he cleans his tiny ears, and peers at me as if to say 'It's nice and warm here.' He just curled himself into a ball and dozed, adorable creature.

I'm going to Scotland in spring for several months to visit friends I have known since childhood. I'm looking forward to walking amongst the heather, seeing the long-haired shaggy Highland cattle, and visiting the quaint inns with their fine Scottish cuisine. English birds are another splendour of this beautiful countryside.

I read with interest in your letter about Henry Darling-ton and his elusive mistress. I only met him twice. I recall he was a good listener, man of few words, observant and staid. I like those qualities in a man. Aaron, not all aristocrats and gentry are conceited. Are you smiling? Of course you are.

I bought a small thatched cottage. Richard excels in

his studies. He is the centre of attraction to the pale rose-complexioned English ladies. On occasion he goes boar and stag hunting with friends, but I dislike blood sports. I must admit, I love the forests here, especially the oak trees when the leaves turn russet gold and the red squirrels hoard acorns for the approaching winter. The cog wheel whirls around, the rich and poor, they live and fuse together in perpetual motion.

I'm off to bed, I shall continue tomorrow evening. I feel miserable tonight.

Au revoir,

Felicia.

'I'm going to see Tumbridge tomorrow about Quasha.' Joshua tapped Gashaka on the back. 'Marriage is wonderful.' He grinned, stretched and raised his hands above his head.

'Thank you.'

Early next morning Joshua rode his sorrel gelding to Tumbridge's plantation, tethered the horse below the brilliant red, parasol-like flaming tree and walked towards the white mansion. A black servant opened the door. Next to her stood a piccaninny.

'Master Tumbridge at home?' Joshua asked with a smile, looking at the little boy.

'Yesum, I call boss.' She spun around, the child following her. In the hall there was a long billiard table and in the corner a spinet. Tumbridge stomped in.

'Oh, it's you, Joshua.'

Near the window a cage swung on a thick locust bean stand and inside two scarlet macaws screeched: 'Bloody hell, bloody hell.' The walls of the sumptious room were covered with animal skins, framed paintings and maps. In the centre there was a large cedar table with trenches of pipes, brass lamps and two looking glasses. James Tumbridge, his son, sat on an elbow chair, all puffed out and arrogant, smirking at the piccaninny kneeling below him, polishing his boots. Joshua ignored him.

'I'll thrash your black behind, you little bugger,' James shouted at the frightened urchin. 'Shine, shine and polish them well.' 'I won't detain you any longer, and come to the point,' said Joshua, biting his lip.

'Yes, we're going hunting shortly.' James smirked and followed his father with the corner of his eye.

'I'd like to buy Quasha from you. Name your price please,' Joshua asked in a diplomatic manner.

'You want that one in the kitchen so bad? Must be a good reason,' Tumbridge quipped, and glanced at James.

'Yes, that one.'

'A hundred pounds? She's a damn good cook. In fact, won't get another one like her. On the other hand, let's say a hundred and twenty pounds.'

'Agreed. I'll pick her up in my coach Sunday morning, and pay you then.' Joshua stepped outside. It was warm and humid. He turned and faced James who stood in the hallway.

'Is there a trough of water? The horse is thirsty.'

'By the first shed,' He slammed the door.

On Tuesday morning Joshua, Nagamba and the children came to visit Aaron for lunch. They decided to stay overnight. Gashaka, Edoo and Pinkus intended to haul mastic timbers on Wednesday morning from Aaron's warehouse on the quay to assist him erect and extend more stables. They drove two bullocks and carts to his estate.

In the kitchen on Tumbridge's plantation Quasha sliced the hogs' meat on the table with a carving knife. It was

Tumbridge's favourite meal. There were several female slaves cutting, peeling and plucking fowls, and straining vegetables, salads and fruit, when James entered the kitchen. Quasha trembled. At night he used to come to the slave quarters, drag her out and rape her repeatedly in the bushes.

She never mentioned this to Gashaka because she was afraid and wanted to protect him from the evil planter and his son. James frothed at the corner of his mouth thinking Quasha would be sold on Sunday. The thought made him angry. He approached Quasha from behind, dug his hands around her waist, lifted her skirt and ripped it. Everyone watched aghast. He opened his breeches. The long-suffering gentle Quasha wanted revenge. She shrieked like a frenzied trapped animal, swung back and with a sharp serrated knife in her hand struck with force across James' face, slitting his nose in half. He reeled back in shock. Quasha dropped the weapon and fled from the kitchen. The rest of the female slaves disappeared. Screaming and holding his pulpy nose he groped and stumbled his way towards the house.

'The bitch did it!' James bellowed as blood spurted everywhere, blinding him. Tumbridge sponged and bandaged James' face with linament and cotton. He administered a small vial of laudanum in a tumbler of water to ease the pain. Tumbridge used to give it to his bedridden, ailing wife of many years. After a while the blood subsided, but the swelling increased. The raw gap where one nostril was missing looked angry and inflamed.

'Aren't the prostitutes in the brothels enough for you?' Tumbridge shouted. 'You had to go and rape Quasha? Joshua is coming on Sunday to pay the 120 pounds. Numbskull, your poor mother should have drowned you at birth.'

'She'll pay with her life, that caterwauling cat,' James

screamed. 'Get the bloodhounds; they will flush her out. She couldn't have gone far.'

Quasha stumbled through the mastic and fiddlewood forest, trudging among the low branches and bleeding from the spiky thorns of bracken and bushes. She eluded capture by wading along the shallow purling streams to conceal her scent from the bloodhounds. Her navigation was muddled and confused by fear. She zigzagged desperately, in an attempt to reach the sanctuary of Aaron's plantation. Her head was spinning. Sharp pains seized her lower abdomen. In the distance she could hear the baying of the hounds pursuing her.

At last, exhausted, she spotted Aaron's stables on the brow of the hill. Her pains grew stronger but Quasha accelerated her pace. The dogs closed in as Tumbridge and James galloped towards her. The hooves of the horses thundered on the ground. Past the stables and down the hill she ran. Bundere, standing outside the stables, was alarmed when he saw Quasha fleeing, chased by the two men on horseback and four large hounds.

Quasha collapsed in front of Aaron's house clutching her stomach, in excruciating pain. The six-week old foetus was expelled. Bundere mounted a mare and galloped in pursuit.

'Get, get,' James squealed. The smell of blood drove the dogs mad. With their sharp canine teeth they tore, and clawed with savagery at Quasha's frail body.

'Stay indoors,' Joshua screamed to Nagamba and Jonathan. 'Take the twins and hide in the cellar.' Hearing the turmoil of the hounds barking he raced outside, pistol in his hand, followed by Aaron clutching a primed musket. Behind him came Pinkus holding his family bible. Gashaka and Edoo carrying blunderbusses rushed to Quasha. They looked at the dogs in horror, and fired their weapons.

James took aim at Gashaka. Within a split second Joshua fired and smashed his face with lead shot. James fell dead on the ground and his horse bolted.

In panic Tumbridge squeezed his trigger and fired at Aaron. The good-hearted Pinkus leapt in front of his friend raising the Holy Bible in mid-air, and the ball was deflected by the metal casing of the Book. The pandemonium frightened Tumbridge's horse and it reared its front legs, kicked and threw him off with a thud. Mighty Edoo pounced, falling upon him with full force. His powerful biceps coiled around Tumbridge's neck. It snapped like a twig.

'Gashaka, Gashaka,' Quasha groaned and then lay still. It was sinister and macabre. Gashaka knelt between her splayed legs and the tiny foetus. In the Cameroons he had observed miscarriages when animals aborted.

He had never touched Quasha: he realised it was James who had molested her. She would have felt ashamed and tried to conceal it from him. Gashaka rested his face against Quasha's soft belly.

'Quasha, Quasha, why did you not tell me?' His wrecked body shook with spasms of crying, and tears mingled with her blood. In inconsolable grief, with the blood of his beloved Quasha covering his face, he howled like a wounded animal.

Aaron had not cried for years, but seeing the broken-hearted young Gashaka, whom he had come to love, made him sob openly. He approached the trembling Gashaka and raised him.

'Let's go inside. I'll bury Quasha among my beautiful flowers. Jonathan will water them and take utmost care of her resting place.'

Gashaka picked up Quasha in his arms, laid her on the rocking chair and hummed. The women cleaned her body, wrapping it in white silk. The men dug a grave which Gashaka descended into, and stretched his hands as Quasha was lowered to him. He kissed and bade her farewell.

'Sleep, Quasha, sleep til I join you.' The men hoisted him up and shovelled the red earth upon her. The bees droned in the begonias.

Jonathan clung to Gashaka and wrapped his chubby hands around the tall man's legs.

'My dear Jonathan.'

A distraught Aaron shouted, 'We must act quickly and dispose of the bodies.' He watched Gashaka's dazed face shrouded with grief.

'You stay here with Quasha.' Aaron, Edoo and Bundere took the cart to the bluff and slung the two corpses and the dead hounds over the escarpment. They returned within a few hours.

'Thank you, Pinkus, for saving my life with your Holy Bible,' said Aaron.

'It was God's will; you are meant to linger a few more years in this world.' Pinkus showed Aaron the large family Bible in its copper sheath.

Gashaka stood and spoke in a tremulous voice as the others sat cross-legged on the floor and listened.

'I have no more tears to shed, but my heart pounds. Tomorrow I shall ride to Tumbridge's place and ask the slaves to join me. We will destroy the entire plantation before heading to the remote wilderness of the Blue Mountains where the Maroons are. I would deem it a paramount honour if any of you wish to follow me.'

Edoo was the first to speak.

'My shadow will follow your shadow.' His Adam's apple moved up and down.

'Aaron, the scholar, told me the word 'Maroon' comes from the Spanish, 'Cimarron', meaning untamed wild savage, like you Edoo.' Gashaka raised a smile.

Marufa, beside the Coromante, said, 'You are my life; I shall never leave you.'

Ebouko glanced at his parents and approached Gashaka.

'For years I have been plagued by nightmares in Bonny. Certain events cannot be eradicated. As from today I shall pledge my life to fight against slavery. We shall be outlaws but free men.' Ebouko's voice rang out across the room.

Gashaka tapped young Ebouko on the shoulder. The compassionate Aaron addressed the three braves.

'Please accept my help. Gashaka, I wish to give you a white stallion and you, Edoo and Ebouko, magnificent Barbary horses, and of course for the beautiful Marufa a palfrey. If the slaves join you, Gashaka, I know that Tumbridge had ten horses and a bullock, plus a collective assortment of arms. I went to his place years ago and watched him gloat over them.'

Gashaka clasped Pinkus's hands.

'When you see an eagle fly I shall be on its wings.'

Pinkus's eyes swam with tears.

'We will carry the torch of freedom for the future of all slaves,' Gashaka declared.

Yabassi was perplexed as he looked at his tall brother.

Ebouko kissed the frightened child, and whispered, 'Yabassi, I promise you that one day we shall meet in the mountains.'

It was still dark when they said goodbye to Joshua, Nagamba and the others. There was a hush in the forest. The farewell was emotional.

With loftiness of purpose, they waved and rode out through the screened refuge of the tall trees. The yard was deserted when they arrived at the plantation, apart from a few cackling ducks.

'The slaves are nervous and hiding. They expect Tumbridge and his son to confront them with a reign of terror,' said Gashaka. 'I'll call out to reassure them.' He dismounted and walked forward.

'I am Gashaka and these are my friends. Do not be afraid. The two white planters are dead. Do you hear me? They are dead.' Gashaka's voice was penetrating. The other three dismounted, and watched as, one by one with faltering steps, the slaves emerged. More appeared from the boiling house, distillery and sugar mills.

'Come follow us to the Blue Mountains,' said Edoo. 'We will join the Maroons and fight alongside them.' The slaves were completely taken by surprise, stunned by the four who had descended on them like a thunderbolt.

'I want each one of you to open the hogs' crawl and let them wander back to the forest. Break the gateposts around the cattle and goats' pens. Make sure you keep two nanny goats, the bullock, cart and horses.' Gashaka wiped his weary features, dripping with perspiration.

'Put some chickens and turkeys in crates. We will need food for the first few days before we go hunting.' Most important, we must gain distance between us and the militia who will follow.

'Demolish the sugar mills and the sugar pots in the curing house and distillery. Smash casks, kegs, barrels, and spill out the stinking molasses.'

The slaves ran pell-mell with machetes, hammers and iron bars, destroying the buildings and sheds.

The four entered Tumbridge's house. In the corner of the lavish front room, the two macaws screeched: 'Bloody hell, bloody hell.' Gashaka placed the bird's cage on the windowsill and pulled the door open. They flew out.

'Bloody hell, bloody hell,' mimicked Edoo.

'Let's go down to the cellar.' Gashaka walked along the narrow passage followed by the other three.

'They prepared themselves for any rebellion,' noted Gashaka. His eyes flashed across the hall of weapons, swords, bludgeons, bayonets, blunderbusses, muskets, knives, two barrels of gunpowder, two barrels of lead shot, and a cask of brimstone sulphur. In the kitchen they broke the pipes of wine, rum and brandy and took the salted beef, gammon, roundlets of oil and hogsheads of flour.

They went up to Tumbridge's bedroom.

'The blankets and quilts will be useful,' remarked Gashaka.

'What luxury the planters enjoyed from the blood of slaves.' He ran his fingers along the smooth cabinet, inlaid with ivory and tortoiseshell. 'Poor animals, they roamed free in the oceans and were hunted by slavers in the forests of Africa—before ending up as trophies to the planters,' Gashaka spat with bitterness. He held his axe high in the air and brought it down on the cabinet.

The four reached James's parlour. Gashaka found two trunks full of silver, gold and jewellery. 'This controls men.' Gashaka slipped several golden coins through his fingers and flung them in the air. 'We'll give the treasure to the Maroons. They can use it to barter for food and ammunition.'

'Now to the roof,' said Edoo, holding Marufa's hand. They clambered on top of the house, knocking tiles out. They axed and chopped asunder the mastic and cedar beams, all except two that remained standing.

'Those must be demolished,' said Edoo. Marufa, Gashaka and Ebouko slid to the ground watching him intently. As

Samson had destroyed the pillars and temple in the ancient city of Gaza, Edoo heaved his body, taut with rippling muscles against the pillars. They tottered and he sprang sideways as they toppled over.

Along the verandah the group spread out and trampled the jalousies. The mansion and plantation were now effaced.

The slaves assembled in the compound, goods were loaded; suckling mothers, babies and piccaninnies settled on the long cart. The two nanny goats were tethered by a rope and the ten horses from the stables were mounted by slaves, each holding a musket.

The exodus followed Gashaka, the partisan, astride his white stallion. He longed for all those he had loved and left behind.

'Maybe the Jamaican oriole will sing for Quasha in the dark.' He wiped his eyes with the back of his hand. The others rode beside him in the brilliant sun.

CHAPTER 26

Nagamba was devastated after Gashaka left, but she accepted why he had to go. Time was of the essence for the four to escape leaving no trace behind. She also knew that Gashaka wished to protect her and Joshua in case the militia arrived. Now that he was gone, all she could hope for was that Gashaka would someday ride back upon his white stallion.

Every single morning Nagamba walked with the children through the corridors of the Jamaican silk-thatched palms. The green-rumped parrotlet and the Jamaican pauraque flew between the trees and disappeared behind the hills.

'Aaron is coming with Jonathan today,' she said to Joshua, as he approached her. He knew why she was there and felt her sadness, for he too missed and loved Gashaka.

A fortnight had elapsed since that tragic day. Joshua hated Tumbridge and his son, more in death than in life. He tried to conceal his bitter feelings but Nagamba knew her man.

'My darling Joshua,' she said, clinging to him. 'He'll come back to us.'

Aaron arrived for lunch. Jonathan ran straight to Nagamba and stretched his little arms.

'I love you, Nagamba.' This was too much for her to bear on that particular day. She burst into tears.

'Oh, Jonathan, you bring so much joy into our lives.'

'Lunch please,' called Nagamba.

In the afternoon, they all wandered to the orchard.

'Nagamba, this is a slice of heaven,' praised Aaron. 'Paw paws, fig trees, soursop, and that glorious tamarind. I think those unique crab claws in the corner are fascinating.'

She pointed. 'The leaves are paddle-shaped with dangling flowers; humming birds pollinate them.' The Jamaican oriole perched high above the ackee tree.

'Gashaka used to spend much time here. Maybe he was speaking to Moustapha who gave him the seeds so long ago in Benin.'

Nagamba leaned against the large hanging branch and raised her head.

'Gashaka never left, he is with us,' said Joshua, hugging Nagamba. 'We shall follow his burning legacy. Come, let us sit on the porch.'

'You have been my rock and my light for all these years, Nagamba. Through you I have seen the truth and the light. My heart grieves for the Maroons in their struggle. In all humility I hope to be privileged to assist them one day soon.' Joshua kissed Nagamba's hand.

Pinkus sailed out to St Kitts in March, before the wet season.

ᘓᔑ

Once a fortnight Colonel O'Reilly used to meet with Tumbridge in the tavern over a glass or two of Madeira. Since he had not seen him for three weeks he wondered if he was ill.

I'll pay him an unofficial visit, he thought.

Not a soul stirred. A black hawk-eagle circled above and

two king vultures feasted on carrion. Chicken feathers were
scattered around the compound. A few goats de-barked
young saplings. Tumbridge and his son were not to be seen.
The mansion and all the buildings were in ruins. The place
was eerie. The plaintive shrill of the eagle echoed amid the
low clouds. A cold shiver ran down Colonel O'Reilly's spine.

*A slave revolt, an insurrection. They must have killed Tumbridge
and his son and fled.* He gazed once more at the black hawk-
eagle spreading its wide wings in triumph. O'Reilly breathed
fire, mounted his horse and galloped to the militia barracks
in Spanish Town.

Within an hour a troop of cavalry in scarlet red and navy
blue sat saddled on their restless horses waiting for orders.
O'Reilly sat on his sorrel mare with his head in the air. He
raised his right hand to his contingent of cavalry, signal-
ling the advance. They trotted towards Joshua's plantation.
O'Reilly rang the bell on the front cedar door.

Nagamba opened. She wore a light-blue muslin blouse,
almost transparent. O'Reilly observed her slight bulging
belly. *Another mulatto in the world,* he observed indignantly.

Nagamba followed his beady eyes with repugnance,
noting his priggish, erect stance.

'Is Joshua in?' he asked, his cold, piercing eyes stabbing
her. She knew he was a threat in her life. Her primitive
African instincts woke in her like a wild animal ready to
attack her young.

'I'll get him.' She stepped indoors.

'Good morning, O'Reilly,' Joshua greeted. 'How do you
do? This is a pleasant surprise.' Joshua glanced fleetingly at
the troopers.

'As a matter of fact I have come to ask if you have heard
or seen Tumbridge and his son of late.' O'Reilly twisted his

upturned thin moustache. He looked rather comical with his two front protruding teeth, red nose and red face.

'Last time I saw him was a year ago when he purchased material on the wharf,' said Joshua, quite nonchalant, lighting his pipe.

'I just came from his plantation. He and his son have disappeared. The place is pillaged and destroyed, all stock vanished. This disturbs me: I must solve the riddle.' O'Reilly's right eye twitched.

'First, there was Gableshaw's death, presumably an accident on the Bluff. Second, the decapitation of Captain Montague on his ship, the Nightingale; and third, Tumbridge and his son missing.' O'Reilly's voice was as hoarse as a raven's. His eyes darted from Nagamba to Joshua. Nagamba was as seductive as ever. She bloomed in pregnancy and looked at O'Reilly with defiance.

'We never associated with *that* lot,' she emphasised

'Ever since Tumbridge's wife died some years ago he sank into heavy drinking,' O'Reilly remarked. 'By the way, can I speak to that one-eyed nigger slave and your overseer?'

'I have no slaves on my plantation,' Joshua said, sending spiral whiffs of smoke from his pipe at his opponents face. O'Reilly jerked back and stiffened but did not move a muscle.

'As far as those two fine men are concerned,' Joshua remarked, 'well, they left yesterday.'

'It was the weekend, so they probably went frollicking with their lady friends,' Nagamba was quite convincing, but an ominous suspicion hung in the air like a dark cloud.

'I shall pursue the slaves, tread on their heels, hunt them in the forests and mountains.' O'Reilly gnashed his teeth. 'Whoever killed Tumbridge and his son will hang and be garrotted.' He lashed his whip.

'No doubt we shall meet again,' O'Reilly scowled.

'No doubt,' Joshua nodded.

O'Reilly strutted with a swaggering gait towards his horse. He turned around and watched Nagamba. In her eyes she carved across to him a message of doom. He tossed his head and rode. A flock of Jamaican crows flew above and cawed.

Nagamba gave birth four months later to a nine-pound daughter. After two exhausting days the baby was delivered. Doctor Fairchild remained in the house making sure complications did not occur.

'What a big girl,' Joshua exclaimed. 'She's your replica; your eyes, those large brown eyes I love so much.' Joshua's warm laugh echoed throughout the house.

Aaron held the infant and said, 'Lotus would be a lovely name; the beautiful flower.'

'What do you think, Joshua?' Nagamba glanced at him.

'Yes, yes, Lotus ...'

'Then so it is.'

Nagamba used the pram built by Gashaka. Every day without fail, she ambled up to the crest of the hill with the three children. She thought of her firstborn buried among the trees in dark Africa. He was tiny and hungry but she had had no milk to save him. Nagamba sighed and strolled home.

Aaron was busy on his stud farm extending his stables with Bundere's help. He was also teaching Jonathan to read and write in English.

'I think Bundere is prey to melancholy since Marufa and Ebouko left with Gashaka. I am concerned about him,' said Aaron to Nagamba. 'He grieves for them in silence.' He seemed to think for a moment.

'Why don't I bring Bundere, Mahadana and Yabassi to live here? Bundere is bright, young and healthy. His knowledge of animals is extensive. With my assistance he would soon learn about the crops for export.'

'It would be wonderful to have them near me,' agreed Nagamba. 'Bundere will be preoccupied, trying to cure his broken heart.'

'I'll fetch them tomorrow,' said Aaron. 'By the way I had an offensive visitor in my emporium last week.' He pursed his lips. 'A scrawny, wizened, ugly ass; a government tax official who came before noon just as I was about to close. I could have choked him with my bare hands.' Aaron tried to control his frustration.

'I dislike discrimination. The man's attitude towards me was insulting and spiteful. Did you know the Jews in Barbados are listed separately in the census?' he asked.

'No, I had no idea whatsoever,' said Joshua, astonished.

'Furthermore, Jews in Jamaica are now forced to pay a special Jew tax and a substantial one at that: abominable and infuriating,' Aaron raged. 'Jews are only grudgingly tolerated.'

'My dear Aaron, we love you,' Nagamba smiled. 'Charitable yet humble, to be a Jew with such qualities.'

'Jews stand on a pedestal with disparity,' Joshua said. People fear them because they are different. They are heaven-born geniuses, astute in commercial enterprises, stocks and share transactions.'

'Don't forget bartering, dealings, speculations.' Aaron wrung his hands and chuckled. 'My veins run deep with red Jewish blood,' he added, tossing his head with pride.

'Above all, Aaron, I envy your gentility and kindness for

those who seek help,' said Joshua. Don't despair; I too have enemies. After all I am most unpopular on this island since I married Nagamba and have three children. Gossip spread like wildfire throughout Jamaica the day my slaves were set free. Yes, Aaron, I am disliked but I stand unshaken and recognise the plight of the slaves.'

The following day Bundere, his wife and son were brought to Joshua's plantation.

'Now, young lad, let us ride to the Bluff,' smiled Aaron to Jonathan. 'You missed your lessons but we will catch up tomorrow with your studies. I'll make a scholar of you yet one day.' Jonathan looked up and brushed his face against Aaron's breeches, just above his knees.

Aaron thought he saw a mirage; the day was hazy, sultry and hot. The horses then cantered and the silhouette became more visible.

'A lady riding a black horse,' Jonathan cried out with excitement. The woman turned her head as they approached, and stopped. The piebald was nervous, flicking the flies away. The woman's face was as white as marble, surrounded by jet-black wavy hair. Her gaze was so remote and mirrored; a span of well over a thousand years echoing through centuries of diaspora. Aaron, with a palpitating heart, knew she was Jewish.

'I'm Rebecca,' she stated.

'I'm Jonathan and this is Aaron.' The boy was charming. Aaron was numb.

Who is this woman, all by herself on the Bluff? he wondered.

She sat on the horse side-saddle and wore a wide yellow hat laced with ribbon. A silk white blouse, semi buttoned, showed the top of alabaster breasts, and her attire was completed by a black waistcoat with golden buttons and a flared black pleated skirt.

'I only come here on occasion; the bluff, the ocean, what splendours of creation,' she exclaimed.

Suddenly a white hawk rose from the cliffs below.

'That's a rare sight. I've never seen a white hawk before.' She followed the bird in flight with wonder.

'Where do you usually ride?' Aaron asked.

'The other side, where it is heavily forested. I prefer galloping along the beaches. The horses love it as well; keeps them cool. Alas, my friend, Henry Darlington, does not.' Suddenly Aaron's memory sparked.

Henry Darlington, the gentleman who bought Felicia's property. His mind ran wild. *Henry Darlington; then this lady facing me must be his …*

The word charged at him. He felt instantly uncomfortable.

'You are brave to ride all by yourself.' Aaron scrutinised her sensuous lips.

'Henry went away for three weeks to Barbados; sugar matters which I find boring.' She took her hat off. 'It's frightfully warm.'

'I have some cool water in my saddle bag, would you like some?' Jonathan asked.

'You are a gentleman; yes please, it will quench my thirst.' Rebecca dismounted and they walked towards the precipice.

'You see those runners between the tall grass?' she pointed out to Aaron and Jonathan. 'The Bahamian Hutia rodents dig burrows and tunnel themselves during the day. They're nocturnal and only come out at night to feed, but the Jamaican owls, swift in flight, catch them.'

'They have another enemy: the Antillean nighthawks, who venture from other islands in squadrons.' Rebecca smiled at Jonathan, and then looked up at Aaron.

'You must be Aaron Pardess, the one who suggested Henry

buy Lady Felicia Gableshaw's property. He often mentions you and your stud farm. I must have been out the day you came to the house.' Rebecca studied Aaron's serious countenance.

'I saw Felicia several times after Gableshaw's death. Such a keen rider. She sailed back to England with her son Richard and bought a small cottage, hates the cold weather but will adjust to it eventually.'

'On your way home you pass close to my house. Why don't you come in for some refreshments? The day is still young.' She looked at Jonathan and winked. Aaron watched Jonathan's face.

'Lovely, thank you.' Aaron adjusted his ruffled neckerchief.

Rebecca entered the house and went straight out to the shady porch. Within a few minutes she returned with a large cake topped with mango and cream.

'Jonathan loves cakes, all kinds.'

'In that case, when you come next time we shall both bake one.' Rebecca was a world apart from Felicia; the complete antithesis.

'Now, a special drink I prepared: watermelon with pomegranate juice.' Rebecca swung back to the kitchen and returned with a slave carrying the drinks.

Jonathan gulped his drink down.

Rebecca chuckled. 'Had enough cake, Jonathan?'

'Oh yes, thank you.'

'You can take the rest home. Have it this evening with Aaron on the verandah when it is cool. Make sure the insects don't get to it. The flycatchers will swarm and the long lizards will attack and land on the cake. Then it will be a merry, merry evening with the merrywings.'

'You're funny,' Jonathan giggled.

'What a great sense of humour you have.' Aaron couldn't stop laughing.

'I must show you my study before you leave.' She led them through the house to a large spacious study. It was filled with numerous rows of books in English and French.

'You speak French?' asked Aaron, surprised.

'Oh yes, my mother is French, and taught us from early childhood. My father resides in Barbados. He is a physician and scholar, and reads voraciously. And for you, Jonathan, I have a delightful gift.' Rebecca stood on a short ladder and picked up a leather-bound book. 'It is a fascinating story about a warrior in ancient times.'

'I like reading.' Jonathan knit his brows.

Rebecca said with an amused twinkle in her eyes, 'I have a proposal to make.' She paused and rummaged through a maze of books.

'With your approval,' she said, glancing at Aaron, 'it would give me great pleasure to teach Jonathan French once a week. Shall we say Wednesday mornings? I tutor other students, plantation owners' children, and prepare them for higher education before they sail to England.' Rebecca observed the boy's beaming cherub face.

'We accept, thank you.'

'Would you like to come to my house this Sunday?' asked Aaron. 'Friends of mine I have known for years are invited for lunch with their children.'

'I would be delighted,' said Rebecca, standing close to him. 'Goodbye, Aaron. We had a lovely day.'

'Goodbye, Rebecca. I shall pick you up early.' Aaron mounted his horse. He watched her standing near the flame tree. A saffron finch sang on a branch. *Where have you been, Rebecca, threading across the opaque foggy years?* She had stepped into his life. He had only known her for a few hours. Aaron felt wretched thinking of Henry Darlington with Rebecca as his mistress. I *shall beard the lion in his den.* The word Mistress jarred and grated on him.

On Sunday, during lunch, Nagamba saw that Aaron was following Rebecca's every move, entranced by her. Rebecca was eccentric, intelligent, and gloved well into Aaron's life.

'You were born in Barbados?' asked Joshua.

'Yes,' replied Rebecca in a bright bubbly voice. 'I often went with my father to assist him on various plantations. He used to administer the Peruvian bark or Jesuit's powder to the slaves against the debilitating malaria. Is the sickness prevalent in Jamaica?'

'As well as other tropical maladies,' Joshua responded.

Rebecca nodded. 'Father is religious and a strict disciplinarian. I used to sneak to the beach and bathe in the sea when he wasn't around. He would never tolerate such behaviour, being rather prudish.' She stood up impulsively. 'Oh I do love Jamaica. It is exciting, sensuous. I quote, in French: 'piquant'. Aaron was intrigued listening to her.

'The Island has a fascinating history. The Spanish colonised the island for a hundred and fifty years years until 1655, when English soldiers invaded the island under the command of General Robert Venables and Admiral William Penn. Do not forget the Maroons whom I admire. They fight in packs like wolves against the white man's oppression. Governors, militia, tyrants, notorious buccaneers, bandidos—' She glanced at Aaron and smiled. '—the invincible architects of Jamaica. What a powerful breed of men, plus the aristrocratic humbugs.' She clutched her sides laughing. Aaron stared at Joshua who turned to Nagamba and the three broke into a fit of hysterics. Lotus started to cry. Rebecca walked around the room, picked up the baby and nursed her.

'I think she has settled,' said Rebecca, laying the baby in the pram. Lotus was drooling and turning up her toes. Nagamba's eye lit up with astonishment.

'I used to help Mother with my younger brother. Nagamba you have a lovely family with outstanding Biblical names.'

'Do come and visit us. We could go for long walks or visit the markets on Sundays.'

'That would be delightful,' said Rebecca.

'Come, Rebecca, I'll take you home,' said Aaron. As they rode through the forests Rebecca marvelled at the brilliant orchids twining around the giants towards the light.

'I met Henry Darlington on his plantation when my father attended the sick. Henry was kind to the slaves. Life became intolerable at home. Father clipped my wings, so to speak. Henry and I met secretly for weeks in the most bizarre places. He intended to purchase a house in Kingston and asked me to live with him. By nature I am impulsive. I agreed and we soon sailed out.'

'Was Henry married at the time?' asked Aaron.

'Yes, but childless. He often came to stay with me for a period. He is a wealthy man. On occasion we visited the mineral springs in the Cayman Islands and hot springs in Nevis. I love bathing there.'

'Was your family spared the yellow fever?'

'Yes, but Henry's wife was a victim. He stayed with her til the end. Six months later he sold his property. With him I was unbound, unchained, unrestricted and unbridled.' She laughed, her voice pulsating above the virgin forest.

'Rebecca would you like to take the reins please? I must stretch.'

'Yes, certainly,' she agreed, smiling. 'This is wonderful.'

In the house the room was cool. The louvres were down. Her breast brushed against him.

'Aaron,' she murmured with bated breath.

'Yes, Rebecca.'

The call of the diaspora echoed across the centuries and God in His infinite wisdom smiled on that unparalleled day of their lives.

CHAPTER 27

O' Reilly paced the hot red brick compound towards the regimental parade ground. He carried a swagger stick under his arm and had a sword on his side.

'Attention,' Sergeant Major Sinclair bellowed. He turned around and saluted O'Reilly. The soldiers looked magnificent in their red coats lined with blue.

'Splendid, splendid performance.' O'Reilly, after inspecting the soldiers, gave a slight cough. Major Beaconsfield, Sergeant Major Sinclair, Captain Stovold and two lieutenants approached him.

'The heat, so muggy, most uncomfortable,' O'Reilly grumbled.

'Indeed it is, indeed; not the slightest breeze nor a cloud, but sun, sun, sun, and those wretched flies.' Major Beaconsfield swiped and crushed one on his hand.

'We leave the day after tomorrow to track the rebels, and by golly, I'll slice and burn them at the stake.' O'Reilly wiped his sweaty forehead. 'Have you got the list of all the provisions we're taking on horseback?' he addressed Sinclair. 'Go and check every item on the inventory with Sergeant Horsham on the double.'

'Yes, sir, right away,' he saluted.

O'Reilly watched as Sinclair crossed the parade ground with rapid strides to where two Lance Corporals were chatting with Sergeant Horsham. Sinclair raised his hand to draw their attention as he approached. O'Reilly saw the list being handed over.

Horsham, holding a truncheon, perused the contents. He brushed his goatee, saluted and dashed off. Sinclair hurried back to the group.

'I suggest we have thirty militia on horseback, plus ten packhorses with all the provisions,' said O'Reilly. 'Detach two of the troopers to look after the horses. Lieutenant Marriott, you'll be in command of ten troopers, and Lieutenant Belvedere will be in charge of another ten. The last division of ten soldiers and three officers will follow my instructions.

'Five packhorses will carry cooking utensils, blankets, water, surgical and medical dressings, and food. The other five with arms, ammunition, muskets, and in separate pouches, musket balls, powder and slow match, machetes, axes and long knives. Two days later in the early dawn the troopers assembled. Each one had a musket in a scabbard by the side of their horses, and their swords were carried low on the hip, held by a sash from the shoulder. O'Reilly and his officers had in their holsters single and double barrel pistols primed with powder and shot. Both were placed in a belt. On this occasion, shot was also put in a bag on a leather sash, similar to a Sam Brown but wider. All the soldiers were provided a hard pack with field rations.

'By Gideon, let's get the bastards,' O'Reilly shouted, and with a whip and spur trotted away with the redcoats.

✺

The fugitive slaves covered miles upon miles of winding trails through the dense forest. With machetes they cut through tall bamboo and ferns. It was several weeks since they had started trekking. There were isolated plantations which they avoided to gain distance from the pursuing soldiers. Gashaka decided to abandon the ox and cart in the thick scrub with the goats, as both hindered their marches. The slaves bore the most essential items on their shoulders. Gashaka carried one small chest of gold on the back of his horse, and Edoo had the second with silver. There was an abundance of game in the forest, which could be roasted on open fires. Both were excellent hunters, stalking their prey with great skill.

'I think it's safe to camp here for the night.'

Beside small fires slaves huddled for warmth. A rippling stream purled nearby. Two furry bushy tailed racoons with sharp long snouts were sniffling between the trees looking with curiosity at the glowing embers. Suddenly a slave screamed, as a large boa constrictor entwined the man's chest, twisting and sliding upwards, coiled around his neck. The patterned muddy-brown serpent hissed and raised its head. Gashaka sprang with a cutlass and cleaved its head with one blow. The headless monster's body remained wriggling for several seconds.

Edoo and Gashaka grappled, slashing and hacking it. The beast swelled his bright red prehensile tail and with its powerful muscles crushed the slave's neck. The boa's grip slackened and lay still. The young unknown slave, his eyes wide open, lay dead on the jungle floor. The irony of his fate was to be transported from Africa wearing an iron collar, and to meet his death a from a boa constrictor collar in the jungles of the West Indies. Gashaka sat beside the lifeless body sobbing and stroked his forehead with tenderness. The image of Quasha stole through the dark shadows. I *might give you a son one day.* She could have been his wife.

A few feet away, Marufa clung to Edoo. Gashaka curled

himself on the warm earth and fell asleep. The slaves were on the move at dawn.

'We should reach the mountains soon,' said Gashaka. Nimbostratus clouds gathered. A fine drizzle began to fall.

'I wonder how many Maroons are out here hiding.'

Edoo surveyed the horizon. 'Hundreds. They have scouts and lookouts in these hostile regions.'

'They spotted us miles before,' said Gashaka. 'For years the militia have been hounding them in hot pursuit, but the rebels escaped with their brilliant jungle warfare. The mountains are well suited to wearing camouflage. The soldiers are not familiar with this terrain, inaccessible by horses. Furthermore, the Maroons are disciplined and organised. Many runaway slaves confederate with them. We will camp here and give the men and horses a rest.'

CHAPTER 28

The first rays of the sun percolated through the heavy mist with a chorus of the Blue Mountain vireos. At noon the group reached the base of the spectacular mountains. They dismounted and held their breath. The Maroons rushed down like gushing waters. They made the ground shake, howling and circling the alarmed fugitives.

Gashaka knew he was amongst friends. He sighed with relief and smiled when the tall Atlas leaped like a cheetah in front of him.

'I'm Quao, leader of the Maroons across the Blue and John Crow Mountains.' He turned to the man standing beside him. 'He is Cuffee, a great Chief.' Quao observed the physical strength of the mighty Goliath Edoo and assumed him to be the ring leader. Quao was impulsive, wrought with excitement and enthusiasm, extending both his hands to Edoo.

'It is he who is the brave, the power behind us all, none like him.' Edoo pointed to Gashaka.

'What an honour to be among such warriors like yourselves,' said Gashaka.

'We spied and followed you from a great distance,' Cuffee exclaimed, holding the abeng in his hand. 'With this cow's horn we communicate in groups spread across many miles. We also have our special code to track the militia movements. Another effective method is the cry of the ridgeway and sharp-shinned hawk: that means danger.' Quao imitated the birds.

'The second is the shrill of the bald-headed black vulture.' Quao whistled the high pitch. 'That sound means it is safe.

'The militia burn with indignation and frustration. We cover the mountains like a glove and worm ourselves from cave to lair, burrowing across the cliffs, detouring and attacking from all sides.'

'Genius, genius.' Gashaka clapped his hands.

'There is our haven in the splendour of the high mountains. In spite of their soldiers, arms, horses and tracker dogs, they are outfought and beaten each time.' He stamped his bare feet for emphasis.

The mist lifted and the warm sun cloaked the valley. Gashaka informed the Maroon chiefs about what had transpired with Tumbridge, his son and the plantation.

Three weeks later the Maroon scouts, with the abeng, signalled their code and warned Quao, Cuffee and Gashaka of the approaching militia posse. Gashaka had so impressed the Maroons that they showed him much respect, considering him to be a mighty warrior and strong leader. The troat urging the bloodhounds grated, and the horses gained momentum. Quao again imitated the ridgeway and sharp-shinned hawk.

'It's too bloody quiet,' said Major Beaconsfield. 'They're cunning and elusive, so let us divide into three groups in a semi-circle facing the mountains. Lieutenant Marriott will command the contingent on the left and Lieutenant Belvedere to the right with ten troopers.'

O'Reilly twisted his long thin moustache and said sternly, 'Major Beaconsfield, your thinking is sound, but would you kindly allow me to issue the orders.' He turned to address the other officers.

'At day break, at the sound of the bugle, the officer and my ten men will advance with the track dogs from the centre. On hearing the bugle call, the left flank, commanded by Lieutenant Marriot, and the right flank, under Lieutenant Belvedere, will attack at the same time. By jove, I'll get them,' O'Reilly shouted. 'The packhorses will remain secure in the forest.' He took out his fob watch. 'It's precisely two of the clock in the afternoon.'

Early the following morning at the base of the mountain Quao and Cuffee hid behind a huge boulder. A narrow trail wound up to the 1,000-foot ridge. The rebels dispersed above and around the steep slope laying a strong ambuscade.

On the soldiers' left flank the lithe figure of Gashaka, accompanied by Edoo, Marufa and Ebouko, hid behind the silk cotton tree and tall tussocky grass, watching and waiting. Each held a long knife.

'The officer is veering the horse away from his men to check the terrain. I'll take a short cut through the forest and surprise him on the other side,' Gashaka whispered. Unaware of the Maroon's proximity, Marriott rode his horse with caution between the gnarled thickets, and thought he heard a noise.

'I had better return, although it could probably be a small animal on the prowl.'

Every time the horse stopped, Gashaka froze and stood

still. He then crept forward, crouched and was soon only a few feet away when he saw the man's back.

Gashaka lunged with his knife which pierced and lodged in Marriot's shoulder blade. For a split second Marriot turned and gaped at his assailant. The officer kicked the horse's flank with his sharp spur and it bolted. As Gashaka watched, Marriot leaned across the animal, in excruciating pain, and his left foot slipped from the stirrup. He let go of the reins and his whole body reeled sideways. The spur became entangled in the stirrup. Marriot slumped, head down as the sorrel raced through the needle briar hanging branches and out to the open plain on the far side, hidden from the militia. He fell backwards with his foot still hooked in the stirrup. The spiny stones and gravel flayed his skin, and his flesh was shaved to the bone leaving a trail of raw bloody flesh. The horse then gave a mighty kick and Marriot was thrown clear. Not long after, two bald-headed black vultures swept down and started tearing at the corpse. Gashaka ran back and was greeted by Edoo.

'See the soldiers, they're waiting for him to return,' said Edoo.

'We'll get each and every one. We'll play a lethal game. I haven't got a knife, it's in the officer's back'. Gashaka glanced at Edoo.

'You can break their necks.' Edoo handed him another knife.

In silence, the four circled the ten soldiers who they could hear arguing: 'I always seem to have stomach cramps before battle; it's my nerves, my poor bowels … I must go.' The trooper went behind a clump of bushes. Edoo waited for a few moments. The man grunted and heaved as the Goliath twisted the trooper's neck with his muscular arms. The neck snapped. Edoo snatched the man's sword, musket and shot, and then joined the others.

'Marriott has been gone for quite a while. He said he would be back shortly. Where the devil is he?' the man growled. 'I'll take a look around.'

'He was adamant and gave orders to stay,' argued the second trooper.

'Steady the buffs. I am not going to be blamed for your bloody stupid actions,' a third soldier snapped. An argument escalated into a brouhaha.

'I am off.' Another trooper held his musket across his left shoulder and groped about in the trackless, thick forest, unaware of the imminent trap. Gashaka stalked and followed. Myriads of gnats and mosquitoes stung the trooper's face. He laid his musket down and scratched with great irritation. Gashaka pounced with the blade and perforated the man's skull, twisting and jerking the knife upwards. Within seconds the soldier was lifeless. Gashaka released the sword from his scabbard, took the musket and shot, and fled.

'The dogs are barking on the other side. Our horses are restless, the waiting is nerve-wracking,' the trooper scowled and pouted his lips. Ebouko lurked nearby.

'I can hear what sounds like treading steps. It could be Marriott; I'll check.' The soldier trudged on through the crackling brittle undergrowth and tripped over a snake which hissed and hooked its poisonous fangs into the soldier's neck. Ebouko stopped in his tracks. The snake slithered away across the poisoned man's face. Ebouko retreated.

'We're trapped,' declared another trooper. 'There were ten of us and now we are seven. The others have vanished. 'I have this terrible premonition: first they got Marriott, I should have known when he didn't return sooner. The Maroons know this endless maze; they even disguise themselves by covering themselves with branches and foliage. Our only chance to get help is for one of us to sneak over to O'Reilly in the centre.' The soldier blanched, his teeth chattering.

'I'll go,' he said finally. 'Meanwhile, prime your muskets.'

The massive cedar branches swelled and spread across like arms in supplication. The soldier took a few steps and stopped. Edoo, like a predatory cat, hid in the shadows and crawled along a thick lower branch. The soldier advanced and waited beside the tree. He paused, scanning the clearing, and then stepped forward. Edoo swung with full force and landed his powerful fists on the man's head, killing him instantly.

'There are six left, we'll eliminate them!' said Gashaka. He sniffed the breeze like an animal. Quasha's face rose through the empty void. He was not there to save her from Tumbridge, his son and the bloodhounds. Tonight he was exacting some revenge.

Led by Gashaka the four warriors flew like arrows and slew the troopers. Marufa looked at the sprawled bodies and the effusion of blood. She wanted to flee from all this, and ran towards Edoo, her man, her hopes and despair. She rubbed her face against his bare chest.

꧁꧂

At the sound of the bugle, Reilly's section advanced. To the right, under the command of Belvedere, ten men marched towards a narrow trail. The soldiers were agitated with fear.

'They could be anywhere on the slope,' fumed O'Reilly. 'We'll cordon them on three sides. They'll be trapped. I want to capture one special rat and hang him by his …'

The militia carried their muskets at shoulder length when nearing the enemy. They moved fast.

Sinclair shouted 'Port Arms', his voice hoarse as a raven's. The soldiers shifted the muskets across their bodies at an angle with the barrel pointing above the left shoulder.

'Halt!' O'Reilly shouted. He glanced to his left and put his hand above his ears. 'Where on earth are Marriott and his troopers? I can't hear a damned soul. Horsham, Stovold, patrol the forest towards Marriott and see what the hell he's doing.'

Gashaka warned his three friends. Moving swiftly and with a diligent use of cover they detoured through the gullies and joined the Maroons opposite, on the soldiers' right flank. In the semi-dark of the dim forest, Horsham and Stovold stumbled across the corpses of Marriot's command.

'They're all butchered,' screamed Horsham and vomited.

'The ten horses are still here,' said Stovold. 'But Marriot's horse isn't.' He looked around. 'Marriot isn't here either.' They galloped back to report to O'Reilly.

The right side of O'Reilly's face sagged at the news. The battle commenced with suspense and the sound of the bugle reverberated once more.

'Ye Gods and little fishes,' O'Reilly howled across the valley. 'Don't let them slip through the net.' He ordered Belvedere on his extreme right to attack. Belvedere, with his ten men, scaled and flanked the towering cliffs in single file while O'Reilly, his officers and troopers proceeded into quick march through the centre, ready to charge in open order.

In the centre with O'Reilly, Beaconsfield cried out. 'Fire at will!'

The Maroons met them with a barrage of musket shots. Quao with his lance skipped like a mountain goat, now joined by Gashaka, Edoo, Ebouko and Marufa hidden between rocks.

Gashaka said, 'I'm going to check on their movements. I'll see you later.' The sharp-shooting Maroons pounded the troopers from the cloud-capped mountain. Gashaka, with nimble feet, watched the last soldier of Belvedere's party. He followed and hid between some bushes. The soldier turned his head when Gashaka pounced and pushed him over the cliff edge. A chilling scream waned as the trooper fell to his death. Immediately, four soldiers raced away in the direction of O'Reilly's party, terrified. Belvedere scrambled up towards the crags with the remaining five.

'Unsheath your swords,' yelled Beaconsfield, leading the centre detachment forward. He clambered up the slippery rocks. Stovold and Sinclair followed behind. The ten militia men spread out. O'Reilly remained concealed in the gully.

Quao threw his knife with deadly accuracy. It zoomed through the air and lodged in Beaconsfield's skull. He rolled and tumbled down the slope, landing at O'Reilly's feet. Stovold, Sinclair, Horsham and the ten troopers dispersed among the clump of trees.

Dark clouds gathered. Soon after, lightning flashed through the forest; thunder rumbled like canons above the mountains. The gusting winds lashed the forest with fury. The frightened bloodhounds became disoriented by the powerful noise and scampered in all directions. One dog yelped when two rebels dug their knives into the miserable animal. Belvedere groped through the blinding rain with his five men, when, to their horror and dismay, the trail ended and in front of them was a sheer cliff that descended over one hunded feet. They were trapped, with only one exit. The Maroons stung like hornets. Belvedere was the first victim. The five remaining troopers fought bravely but were killed in a hail of bullets, as were several of the maroons. The carnage was horrifying. During the confusion and the deafening sound of musket shots, Quao, Cuffee and several maroons slipped below the escarpment and raced towards the forest.

'There is no-one here. A few white cowards escaped towards O'Reilly. The rest were killed,' said Quao. 'We will muster the eleven horses, veer to the middle and take the remainder belonging to the troopers. The rain and thunder will muffle the sound of hooves.' Cuffee loved the graceful animals and he approached them.

'You will ride with us now,' he said tenderly, and brushed his face against one. He remembered long ago when he raced with a fawn as a child in Africa and chased the rainbow down a hill, skipping faster and faster towards the colours lacing the horizon. But it vanished and he was saddened. Cuffee's gentleness poured out. He loved and hated with extremes. The dreams and aspirations of his life were shattered by the white man. Thus, the rebel swore to hunt and kill his predators for the rest of his life.

'It is a deluge,' cried Stovold. 'We will never make it in this dirty, foul weather. The muskets are futile, can't even prime the powder, too bloody wet.' He kept wiping the stinging rain from his eyes and nose.

'The devils will pluck us one by one,' screamed Sinclair at the top of his voice. 'We can't go on this wild goose chase!'

'Calm down at once,' ordered O'Reilly. 'The bastards have killed Belvedere and six of his men.' The officer and soldiers descended the slope in quick succession when a bright flash of lightning hit the musket held by a trooper. He sizzled like a burning torch.

The storm raged. Gashaka stood beside a massive rock. The rain eased slightly. He looked like an exquisite sculpture *Fáit a Peintre* with his chiselled profile. He gazed up at the angry, phenomenal elements in battle and heaved with the rhythm of the wind upon his chest. The contour of the tight breaches against his loins exposed a man with feats of strength and vigour. His physique rippled with taut muscles. Gashaka was screened by trees around the rock.

He stepped forward, leaning ahead, and primed his musket. The winds pounded the branches. Lightning flared upon the slope, exposing Gashaka, and the rays from his shiny steel musket beamed down the valley. He gazed down but it was too late. His instinct had failed him. Destiny, the age-old betrayer, had sealed his fate. O'Reilly glanced up: for a brief moment he saw and recognised him at once. He was awed by the magnificent physique, the almost ethereal sight of Gashaka illuminated by the lightning flashes. He took out his pistol from under the oilskin mackintosh and fired. The shots penetrated Gashaka's upper left thigh. He fell.

'I got him, I got him!' O'Reilly shouted. Shocked, Edoo and Ebouko carried Gashaka to a nearby cave and laid him down.

'The savages are swarming and shooting all around us,' Stovold screamed. 'Let us retreat; otherwise we'll be garrotted and done away with.'

'The English do not ever retreat,' O'Reilly bellowed. 'We will advance to the rear.' The bugles rang across the ravine and the hounds converged.

'Heaven's above,' Sinclair screamed with rage. 'They have

taken all our horses, including the pack horses.' He ordered several troopers to check the side where Belvedere was.

'They have gone as well,' shouted the private.

O'Reilly, angry but badly shaken at the calamity confronting him, yelled, 'They have executed twenty of my men, cleared out the horseback provisions and stolen thirty horses. What a disaster: a losing battle. At least I killed that nigger. We have only a few horses and men left.'

'Damn it, we can't even bury our dead,' Stovold called out bitterly. O'Reilly mounted his frisky horse and with his riding crop hit its rump. The contingent of defeated cavalry left in haste.

CHAPTER 29

'The lead shots have to come out,' said Edoo to Gashaka, lying on the ground in the cave. 'I'll go with a few men and fetch Quao and Cuffee. The packhorses must carry medicines intended for the soldiers. Marufa and Ebouko will stay with you.'

Like a whirlwind Edoo and the four Maroons raced off for help. Within an hour Cuffee and Quao galloped back with the militia's pack horses. They carried two chests: one with medicines, field dressings and a variety of surgical instruments; the second containing herbs, ground pepper in jars, elder, lemongrass and pound garlic for fevers and pains. Several bottles filled with vinegar, laudanum and rum were also included. Strapped on the horses were a stretcher, hammocks and blankets.

Edoo was familiar with the use of laudanum having seen it administered on many occasions, and sniffed it, recognising the strong acidic smell. He tipped a dose of the drug into a vial.

'Drink this, Gashaka. I must remove the lead and this will help to numb the pain. I'll try to be gentle.' Gashaka sipped the bitter drug.

'Hold his legs and hands tight.' Edoo lanced the scalpel deep into the aperture of the wound and extracted the lead balls. Gashaka's entire body was drenched with perspiration. He winced in pain.

'Sprinkle vinegar on the open wound and give him rum,'

said Edoo. Marufa lifted Gashaka's head, trickled the liquor into his mouth and then sponged him with cool water. Ebouko, Quao and Cuffee went outside, each carrying a calabash, and gathered lichen covered with morning dew and moss between the rocks, and also red soil near the gully. They brewed the ingredients in ground pepper, elder and lemongrass. Edoo packed the resulting poultice on the inflamed lesions and smeared a layer of mud over it for protection, covering the top with leaves. Every few hours he was given more laudanum and the dressing was renewed.

'We are going to bury our heroes before the vultures and eagles pick their bones,' declared Cuffee.

The slain Maroons were brought down from the ridge and interred deep in the forest. Carrion hawks screeched.

'It's peaceful here for our warriors,' Cuffee sighed. The soldiers' corpses were left for scavenging animals.

For three days Gashaka was treated with the African therapeutic balsam.

'The militia will return and attack with greater force,' said Quao, 'though not for a while. It will give us time to move the women, children and men further away where they are well sheltered from the harsh elements, and the troopers will not dare to ascend among the hidden endless caves camouflaged by trees. 'The cowardly yellow bellies.' 'We have plenty of food, arms, ammunition and horses.' Quao placed a soothing hand on Gashaka's forehead.

'I love you, Quao and Cuffee, my brothers. I have been thinking how to solve this unforseen crisis over the last few days.' Ears strained, everyone listened. Edoo reclined beside Gashaka. 'If I stay here I'll be a burden; your braves will have to cart me around from one summit to the next pass.

'Our traditional African healing practices are at times

curable but often fatal. This injury will take weeks to mend, if it ever does.' Gashaka paused. 'My upper thigh throbs and the swelling hasn't gone down. Complications may develop. We must act now.' Gashaka turned to Edoo.

'I want you, Ebouko and Marufa, to take me back. We will take refuge at Nagamba's house for as long as is necessary and safe from that poisonous viper O'Reilly. But most important is the help of the great physician Doctor Fairchild, whom I trust with my life.' Gashaka glanced at Quao and Cuffee.

'He has many potions and cures for various ailments and diseases. I saw him bleed slaves on the plantation with excellent results. Above all, he has respect and compassion for us. The doctor has had wide experience with musket shooting injuries. The poison in my body is spreading. You understand Quao why I must leave immediately to save my leg.' Gashaka's eyes pleaded. 'I must live to be able to return and fight alongside you.'

'I will draw you a map, a shorter route to go back, densely forested and concealed from the militia,' said Quao. Ebouko approached Gashaka and sat on the ground cross-legged.

'I belong here with the warriors, Quao, Cuffee and the Maroons. I shall never rest til we squash the tyranny of slavery and break the white man's oppression.' Ebouko's lips quivered. Saliva dripped upon his chin.

'One day, Ebouko, I shall take you to meet Cudjoe, our wise leader, chief of all the Leeward Maroons in the northwest remote Cockpit country, called 'Land of the Look Behind'. It is a wild isolated area with many jagged peaks. Under the command of Cudjoe and his two brothers, Accompong and Johnny, are hundreds of Maroons.' Quao raised both his hands above his head.

'The militia have Black Shot bounty traitors whom they

pay for each captured runaway slave,' fumed Cuffee. 'We snared a spy. He wore a silver-laced hat, had fifteen pounds in his blue coat and yards of Osnaburg. I cut his tongue out, gouged his eyes and left him in the forest.'

❦

Morning broke with a vermillion sky. Edoo removed the stretcher from the pack horse to transport Gashaka. He then secured the poles to the saddle straps on the horse. Between them they managed to heave Gashaka aboard. Marufa placed a pack covered with a saddle blanket beneath his head and gazed at his eyes. They both knew of the ordeal which was to follow. The five surrounded Gashaka.

'Take care of my stallion.' Gashaka touched Cuffee's face. 'We'll ride together someday.'

'The Abeng will be heard from afar by our warrior scouts upon your return,' said Quao with emotion. Ebouko kissed his sister. Quao and Cuffee clasped Edoo's hand and hugged Marufa. Two vultures lanced the rising sun and flapped their wings in farewell to the three receding figures.

Quao and Cuffee, chiefs of the Windward Maroons in the East, climbed higher and disappeared in the mist, where they were free.

After days of trekking, Gashaka developed a high temperature. The wound was weeping, discharging pus. Edoo drained the festered canker, daubing and sprinkling it with vinegar, and gave him more laudanum and pounded garlic mixed with water. The rugged terrain caused the stretcher to move up and down. Gashaka bit his lips in great pain.

Edoo abandoned the horse. He hid the litter and other effects in the undergrowth, and then whacked the horse's rump but the beast did not move, and turned to look at Edoo, snorting, almost saying 'What was that for?' So Edoo thumped it harder and it bolted. The essential items were hitched on Marufa's shoulder, and he carried Gashaka on his strong back.

They rested several times a day, leaning Gashaka against a tree.

'My leg is swollen. I don't like the shade of the skin,' said Gashaka. Edoo shook his head, he too was worried. 'We have no more laudanum. I have to change your dressings. Marufa, hold him tight.' Edoo discarded the putrid compress and, to his horror, maggots were crawling on the raw wound. He poured some vinegar and plastered it with salt to scorify the inflammation and kill the vermin, finally covering it with fresh clean bandages. Marufa held Gashaka, resting his head against her chest as he screamed with agony.

'We will reach Nagamba and Joshua's place in two days at the most, maybe before. We must keep going, day and night.' Edoo panted heavily bearing Gashaka.

It was almost dawn. Marufa pulled the brass chain and the bells chimed. Joshua opened the door, startled at a caller at this early hour. Behind him Nagamba stood numb.

'Gashaka is gravely ill,' said Edoo, lumbering forward with the invalid on his sore back.

'Here.' Nagamba whirled in front of Edoo who prostrated Gashaka on the four-poster bed. Gashaka's body pulsated with high fever and tremors.

'Nagamba, Nagamba,' he sobbed.

'You are home,' she whispered. 'Joshua, go and fetch Doctor Fairchild please.'

Nagamba brushed her lips on Gashaka's burning cheeks. Soon after, the doctor arrived and rushed to Gashaka.

From his black leather bag he pulled a pair of instruments to examine the wound. He lifted the compress, gasping at the putrid flesh, and swabbed and cleaned the wound. He then applied a fresh poultice.

'The odour, excessive swelling and the greenish grey colour is gangrenous,' said the physician. Joshua was stupefied and Nagamba felt faint.

'It has been infected far too long, and spread from the thigh upwards to near the groin,' the doctor warned. Gashaka turned to Nagamba.

'O'Reilly shot me; I want you to kill him. The man must not live. When Pinkus returns to Kingston, ask him to take Marufa and Edoo to Monserrat as free people.'

At noon everyone gathered in the room. Joshua stood next to the bed.

'Kind Joshua, liberator of slaves.' Gashaka was short of breath and coughed. He beckoned Edoo and Marufa to come near.

'If I was an eagle I would fly to the remote mountains and join the heroes. Soar higher, free … free.' Gashaka's voiced grew faint. Aaron and Jonathan approached. Gashaka lifted his weak hand and touched the boy.

'I love you, Jonathan.'

Aaron bent and pressed his ear against Gashaka's lips.

'Do you think eagles fly in Paradise?'

'Yes.' Aaron kissed him.

'Remember, Nagamba, a long time ago Moustapha said to us: our spirit will meet beyond. Maybe he is flying in our garden now.' Gashaka's condition deteriorated during the night. Fever plagued his wrecked body. He lingered til dawn.

'Let's catch the goats.' Gashaka, holding Nagamba's hand gasped his final breath.

CHAPTER 30

D ay after day Nagamba strolled up the hill. The blue warblers and the elfin wood warblers serenaded her. They were used to her presence and flew from tree to tree. The apparition of Gashaka riding his white stallion haunted and tormented her. With vengeance in her heart she schemed and plotted O'Reilly's death. To kill him all she needed was to squeeze half a pint of lethal pure Cassava juice and that required two Cassava roots. Nagamba often cooked the bamming Cassava cake the Arawak Indians used to make.

For generations the Africans knew that the bitter roots were extremely poisonous, and fatal if eaten raw. In the Cameroons Nagamba used to extract the toxic milky sap from the long brown tapered roots by crushing them in a Tipitipi. Another method she used was to triturate and pulverise the tubers with a pestle, and then press hard with a heavy stone and draw out and drain the volatile poison. Cassava also grew for cultivation in Bahia, Brazil for thousands of years. Wild cassava is still found in Brazil. It was staple food when the Portugese arrived there in 1500.

On Friday, Joshua rode with Nagamba and the children in their coach to town. To their surprise, Rebecca, Aaron and Jonathan appeared.

'I know a popular pastry shop, not far away,' said Aaron. 'They also have other confiture, bonbons, chocolate candy and much more.'

They sauntered towards the shop. Rebecca kept kissing Aaron. 'Je t'aime, Je t'aime, Aaron,' she whispered in his ear. Nagamba and Joshua watched them with amusement.

'By the way, did you see the public announcement in the morning press?' Aaron asked.

'No, I haven't. We just arrived. What exciting news prevails in Kingston?' Joshua remarked.

'Ah, here's the shop.'

'Public announcement: Governor Lord Archibald Hamilton will be in attendance at the formal gala ball on the 31st December, 1711, seven of the clock at Government House. Colonel O'Reilly will be present. The military regimental band will play under the conductor Patrick Clark.'

A cold shiver ran through Nagamba at the sound of O'Reilly's name. She clung to Joshua and trembled.

'Very interesting,' said Joshua.

'Are you going to the ball with the *hoi polloi*?' Aaron asked Rebecca.

'What do you think, *chérie*? I'd love to meet the present Governor, a fresh novelty in the tropics. I remember when Henry Darlington was invited to dinner by Thomas Handasyde, the former Governor of Port Royal, and took me with him. The opulent dignatories were present. I felt rather uncomfortable. I thought the Governor was a pompous ass,' Rebecca chuckled, 'stiff and starched.'

'Hilarious, indubitably hilarious,' Aaron laughed. Rebecca kissed Aaron on his cheek.

'A month from today,' Nagamba drawled. 'One month.' She glanced at Joshua. 'Yes, we shall go.' Joshua understood why she decided this once O'Reilly's name was mentioned. A dark cloud weighed upon him.

'I suppose you all wonder about Henry Darlington. I left a

brief note telling him I am getting married to Aaron.' Rebecca's face beamed with happiness. 'Life with Aaron is full of *joie de feu*. I do hope my parents will attend our wedding, set for the 15ᵗʰ of March. I have already written to them.'

'Yes, indeed, it's going to be an unforgettable wedding. All the Jewish citizens of Kingston will be invited. And you, my dear Nagamba, will be my archangel, Joshua my best man.' Aaron skipped around like a young boy.

'And now let's spoil the children and ourselves. I'm parched and ravenous.'

Upon departure in the afternoon, Aaron sang out, 'Please come on Sunday for lunch. Rebecca's preparing a special Jewish meal.'

A month later Pinkus sailed into Kingston.

'O'Reilly is prowling with his militia men on horses near the plantation,' said Nagamba. 'Take Edoo and Marufa to Monserrat. It's too dangerous for them to stay.'

Joshua said to Edoo, 'Here's Gashaka's share of gold that Moustapha gave him in Benin. You'll both need it.'

'In this small bag are important documents,' said Joshua, handing it over. 'Tickets of identity as free slaves, signed, sealed and attested by myself and Aaron. Also, indentures for both: keep them constantly on you.'

'I purchased some land there,' Pinkus remarked, brushing his long beard. 'I shall help Edoo and Marufa to find pastoral acres near me. I won't be sailing as often as I used to, but Ezekiel and Shyloh are skilled and competent to undertake for themselves our trade, and are experienced merchants.'

'Monserrat is peopled mainly by Catholic Irish, Triton

dark features. The English own the large plantations whereas the Irish are subservient.'

'There is an interesting story attached to Monserrat,' said Joshua. 'A prominent wealthy Dutchmen, Samual Wadd, lived in illustrious splendour, his stone house replete with servants and slaves. In 1654, in what was most probably a political conflict, Samuel Wadd smeared the governor in a defamatory and disparaging manner, calling him an Irish murderer and an Irish barbarian. He was found guilty and executed.'

'Mind you,' Pinkus gave his opinion, 'the Irish and English still disliked each other, although Wadd was a Dutchman. The English exceeded the Irish in number and they possessed the best sugar plantations.'

Anxiously listening, Nagamba interrupted. 'I dare not let Edoo and Marufa out of the house, ever since the day Gashaka was brought home. They stay in the cellar. O'Reilly has spies and watches us.'

Mahadana and Bundere came to see them before they sailed. Pinkus drifted out with the schooner late at night. Marufa and Edoo peeked through the porthole at the fading lights. Edoo's thoughts were on Gashaka flying with the eagles.

CHAPTER 31

31ˢᵗ December, 1711 – Government House, Kingston, Jamaica.

The aristrocratic Governor, Lord Archibald Hamilton, entered the sumptuous hall with pride in his carriage.

'The Governor, Lord Hamilton,' the head butler announced. All guests turned and watched the imposing figure enter. He was in an immaculate white suit, with a waistcoat underneath trimmed on the edges with gold buttons and stiff sleeves. His shirt was ruffled on the cuffs, and he wore a laced neckcloth, silk stockings, tight breeches, fawn kid shoes, and a wide-brimmed hat with flamingo plumes on it.

From the ceiling, scintillating brass and bronze candle chandeliers swung. Upon the walls copper lanterns were lit with whale oil. The merrywings attracted by the flickering glow swarmed. Plush velvet chaises and red divans embellished the glittering mansion.

On long wide oak tables, punch bowls were placed alongside a variety of decanters, flagons and carafes. Lord Hamilton clapped his hands and summoned the slaves, who commenced serving Madeira, wines and rum on a silver tray.

One plantation owner and two Lords of Trade stood beside him. Hamilton gazed at the magnificent oil painting of Sir Thomas Modyford, governor of Jamaica in 1664.

'Brilliant fellow was that doughty Modyford,' said the Governor sipping his wine. 'Prior to coming to Port Royal he owned several sugar plantations in Barbados. Land was cheap in Jamaica and being an opportunist he acquired several estates. He also lured the poor whites from Barbados to buy pristine land and grow indigo, cotton and cocoa walks. Modyford mediated and persuaded the debonair King Charles II to grant a credit, and distributed the first million acres of land in Jamaica, and lowered the taxes for the new settlers.

'If I may be so presumptuous, he was a fascinating character, yet a tyrant,' said the Lord of Trade, Nickleby Whitehead. 'He sent Henry Morgan with his henchmen to Cuba and Hispaniola between 1665 and 1675. With 1000 brigands they tramped the swamps of the isthmus and set the City of Panama ablaze. The wild bulldog returned to Port Royal a hero.' Whitehead laughed with sarcasm, nearly choking.

Hamilton filled his pipe.

'Now to the subject of sugar,' Sir Roger Middlebar said. 'The present bumper crop of sugar exported from Jamaica, Barbados, St Kitts and Nevis provides Europe with almost half of the sugar consumed there. It is of paramount importance.'

'Indeed, indeed, in spite of the plantation above Port Antonio which is prey to constant night raids by the Windward Maroon,' Lord of Trade Benjamim Rowland growled with ill-temper. 'Even the militia admit they are battling with invisible feral animals.'

'Cudjoe the hunchback dwarf is leader of the rebels filled with hate towards us,' said Hamilton. 'Now if you would excuse me there is someone I want to see.' He bowed and walked away.

Nagamba watched O'Reilly, her mind in turmoil.

O'Reilly did not believe in premonitions, but he noticed Nagamba staring at him with a disconcerting intensity in her gaze. With a snort he tossed his head and swilled some brandy.

'Spot the two militia officers laughing over there,' said Joshua. 'I do like the scarlet ribbons around their necks and the red garters showing when they bend over.' Aaron laughed. Rebecca smiled and touched the tip of his nose.

'Shall we blend with the distinguished nobility?'

'I'm thirsty,' replied Aaron. 'Do you mind if we have a drink first?'

'Not at all.' Joshua grasped Nagamba by her waist.

Holding the silver ladle Aaron poured the fruity beverage from the punch bowl into the four silver goblets.

'This is refreshing.' He wiped his lips with his silk embroidered handkerchief. 'What an extraordinary medley of hosts are here tonight. I recognise a few prosperous merchants and purveyors of food and drink as well as some *hoi polloi* imperious Government tax officials I detest.' Aaron continued sipping his drink.

'There's Lord Gaunt, a plantation magnate,' Joshua remarked. 'I met him on several occasions. He is flirting with Lady O'Shaunessy on the velvet chaise.'

'Lord O'Shaunessy is in England at present on business,' said Aaron with humour.

'Well, Lady O'Shaunessy seems vivacious and happy with Lord Gaunt.' Joshua glanced at Nagamba and winked.

'Darling, where did you learn all this *bavardage canard*?' Rebecca asked.

'Eavesdropping in town?' Aaron laughed. 'Smell the perfumes, so many women.' Beneath their luxurious brocade and embroidered dresses the ladies wore cane hoops, layers of petticoats and tassled girdles. Their white necks and hands were bejewelled with burnished diamonds, gold and pearls.

Nagamba's concentration was fixed on her seashell vanity bag firmly gripped in her hand. Inside, the small stone bottle was filled with the deadly bitter cassava juice.

She watched O'Reilly approaching.

'Nagamba, Joshua,' O'Reilly drawled, with a drink in his shaking hand. 'All is well on the plantation?' he asked with bleary eyes. It was his fourth pint of Madeira. His memory had become blurred. Nagamba looked at him with disdain and turned on her heel.

'Who is the woman with the extraordinary head gear?' asked Lord Gaunt, still billing and cooing with his coquette.

'She's Joshua Quaile's wife,' said Lady O'Shaunessy. 'He brought her from West Africa when he was Captain of the Hurricane brigantine. I think Joshua is a dashing cavalier, so handsome, but you are my beau.' She snuggled up to him.

Gaunt was dressed in a fawn coat lined with black sarcenet, a waistcoat underneath, trimmed with yellow ribbon, embroidered sleeves, flowing cravat, and white silk shirt.

'I've never met her,' the Lord remarked. It was Nagamba's gait that intrigued him. Equally fascinating was the garland of feathers coiled on her head.

'She's captivating,' he said. His life was circumscribed by prodigious drinking, consorting with harlots and discreet aimless rendezvous in high society, Again he observed Nagamba. She reminded him of England in autumn, the chestnut trees swaying in the breeze, the russet leaves blazing in the rising sun. He felt uneasy and stiffened.

'I have been too many years on this tropical island,' he

said in a muffled voice and swept Lady O'Shaunessy up in his arms. Nagamba's sad melancholy eyes caressed Joshua's face.

'To which island shall we fly, my albatross? Remember many years ago when we sailed on the Hurricane? You said that albatross mate for life. If one dies the other pines away. I love you so dearly, Joshua.' He brushed his short beard against her hair.

'Fairchild is waving to us. Come let us join him.'

'Good evening, Doctor,' said Nagamba

'How are the children?' He asked.

'They are different in character. Amos is often moody and grumpy, Enoch is a precocious child and Lotus is wild. Amos was the first of the twins to be born during the hurricane. He always crouches in a dark place with fear when the wild winds blow. Animals behave in the same way. They feel the drop in atmospheric pressure before the storm, then crawl into a ball and hide. The Caribbeans called it the Hurricano or whirlwind.'

'I always find the subject of the Arawak Indians shrouded with mystery,' the physician remarked. 'They lived in the Caribbean for 1,500 years and vanished into history.'

'They could predict and forecast hurricanes days before they struck,' commented Rebecca, 'and believed in sorcery and witchcraft—namely the infernal spirits who angered their Gods, inflicting the hurricanes as punishment.'

'What a lot of rot, complete fiddle faddle,' Aaron said.

The regimental band started to play.

'Why don't we indulge in some of the superb cuisine? I am ravenous.' Joshua tapped Aaron on the shoulder. Nagamba clutched her cowrie vanity bag, watching O'Reilly swaying drunkenly.

'I predict the death knoll will toll for O'Reilly,' said Fairchild. 'Like the doomed fate of the Duke of Albermarle, and Henry Morgan, the pirate who fought his own destiny and refused Doctor Hans Sloane's medication and chose with dogged resolution to consult a black doctor who, in a warped bizarre method, infused him with urine. Morgan's body was then plastered with clay. He was forty-five, and died in a savage way several months before the Duke of Albermarle. Both were patients of Doctor Sloane who resided in Jamaica for fifteen months.'

'Revolting,' scowled Joshua.

'My father often mentioned the intellectual Doctor Sloane who used to prescribe laudanum for dysentery which was rife at the time. He could discern between the notorious syphilis and yaws, and treated those cases so common amongst slaves by lavation in a hot house,' said Rebecca. 'I read in one of Doctor Sloane's reviews that seventeenth century physicians were partial and inclined to practice blood letting for every conceivable ailment. My father opposed this course, claiming that from his medical point of view most cases result in death,' Rebecca emphasised.

Fairchild said, 'Henry Morgan and his horde of pirates in Porto Bello, Panama were convinced, and their principal way of thinking was that in order to get rid of jaundice one should imbibe goose dung, diluted with water.'

Guests were milling around, dancing to the rhythm of the band.

'Good Lord, look who is flouncing on the dance floor,' Rebecca laughed.

'If it isn't Sir Henry Darlington himself with a wench,' Aaron noted.

Nagamba's eyes were focused on O'Reilly shuffling

towards her. 'I'm going to get some of the delicacies over there,' she pointed out to Joshua.

Voices and music seemed so remote. She walked to the extreme corner, making sure O'Reilly was following her. Most of the guests were dancing and drinking at the far end of the hall. She pressed her thumb against the cowrie vanity bag clip. O'Reilly swigged his glass of rum and staggered facing her.

'The ... lightning ... slave,' he babbled incoherently, saliva dribbled on his beard. The long and wide exquisite silk cloth flowed over the four sides of the table. O'Reilly swayed losing his balance, and fell to the ground coughing. Nagamba prised open the stone bottle and mixed the poisonous cassava juice into O'Reilly's almost empty glass. 'Have another drink, let us celebrate,' Nagamba whispered.

'It's all blurred,' he stammered, gulping the milky sap. 'Mm, strong drink.' He stumbled, raised himself up and drank some more. Nagamba with nimble feet slipped across unnoticed and joined Joshua.

'I must get some fresh air.' O'Reilly reeled and staggered towards the open door into the garden.

Joshua glanced at Nagamba, realising what was happening. Oblivious, the doctor was chatting to Rebecca, when he noticed O'Reilly.

'It's getting rather late, shall we go darling?' Nagamba asked.

'Yes, I think we should.'

Not a soul heard or saw O'Reilly collapse near the mimosa tree. He clawed his stomach with his fingers, and wretched with agonising pains. His body was attacked by muscle spasms and tremors.

He struggled to breathe; his screams were muffled by the

regimental band. Somewhere in the dark corridors of his mind he heard Nagamba's voice: *Have another drink, lightning?* Her face faded into darkness. O'Reilly paid his debt to nature.

At the inquest Fairchild, after examing O'Reilly's body, stated:'Alcohol poisoning, too many quarts of Madeira followed by several glasses of brandy and rum.' He was aware that this was not the case. From the symptoms, Doctor Fairchild understood what killed O'Reilly and he knew who committed it, but he would never betray them. Joshua and Nagamba were his patients and friends for many years, loyal and devoted. O'Reilly was a milita butcher, craving for power and greed like so many planters in Jamaica. The silent Hippocrates oath was sacred.

CHAPTER 32

Pinkus cruised on the Pandora into the magnificent harbour.

Every Jewish citizen of Kingston was invited to Rebecca and Aaron's grand wedding. Doctor Hillel, Rebecca's father, her mother and younger brother and sister sailed from Barbados for the occasion.

The major domo announced their arrival. After they had exchanged introductions, Dr Hillel said to Aaron, 'And you must be the cavalier and philanthropist Rebecca wrote so often about.'

'Welcome to Kingston,' Aaron smiled.

Mrs Hillel examined in detail her future son-in-law standing before her.

'You'll make a fine husband for Rebecca.' She nodded her head several times, a trait so characteristic and singular to Jewish mothers.

There was a hush in the synagogue except for the white-neck Jamaican crow screeching outside. The ceremony was conducted by the Rabbi and read in English and in Hebrew. At the end of the service the Hazan (cantor) chanted. His voice rose with sublimity.

'Shma Israel Adonai Elohaynou Adonai Ehad.' *Hear o Israel the Lord our God the Lord is one.*

When the traditional glasses were broken everyone cried out in jubilation.

'Lehaim, Lehaim!'

Soon afterwards, the guests strolled around the lovely garden.

'This is most cosmopolitan,' Doctor Hillel uttered, meeting Nagamba and Joshua.

The feast of reason and the flow of soul commenced with food, drinks and music. The Rabbi stood under the giant cedar.

'Let us toast once more to Rebecca and Aaron on their blessed seventh heaven,' he said, lifting his wine glass. 'Lehaim, Lehaim.' Everyone cheered and clapped their hands.

'Lehaim, Lehaim. To Life! To Life!'

The brass symbols rang and pulsated. The flute trilled like a bee in a bottle to the Jewish rhythm of the fiddle. Drums beat accompanied by peals of bells. The guests rejoiced, sliding, and bobbing up and down. Rebecca glided like a butterfly in her bright, flowing dress, crusted with colourful sequins. Aaron danced with his wife, and then with a hilarious Nagamba who was trying to follow Aaron's footsteps but treading on his toes. Rebecca swung Joshua to and fro as the tempo increased. The hauntive but mellow clarinet reverberated above all the other instruments.

Pinkus, Ezekiel and Shylo leapt in circles with the young girls.

Holding Rebecca close to him Aaron said to Doctor Hillel and his wife, 'We're going away for a while, to paradise, the mineral springs near Morant. Our house is at your disposal. Jonathan is a perfect host.'

The moon sneaked through the half-shut louvres in the room.

'Aaron.'

'Yes, Rebecca, my wife. Thoughts that breathe and thoughts that burn.' His young body seamed against hers.

'We are one before God. Inseparable.'
'Good night, Aaron.'
'Good night, my dear.'

ఴఄ

Aaron never heard from Felicia again. The following year
Rebecca gave birth to a son, Gideon. Aaron prayed fiercely.

'Almighty God, cloaked in your holy shroud of mystery.
How could I understand your exalted infinity? Mortal man
that I am. With every drop of blood in my veins I have loved
you all my life. Guide me for the rest of my days to be virtu-
ous to the needy and downtrodden.'

In God's palm they came by night with caution through
the forest to the portals of Aaron's haven for help. The crimi-
nals, runaway slaves, prostitutes, and destitutes, all under the
seal of secrecy—they pledged only to Aaron, Rebecca and
Jonathan.

Aaron was the manna in the wilderness. With the enduring help of faithful Ezekiel and Shyloh, many sailed out and
settled on other Caribbean islands. Through the rolling years,
Jonathan, fluent in French and English, was in charge, and
managed Aaron's business affairs. Pinkus took Alimba and
her sons to live with him on Monserrat. On occasion he
sailed the schooner, where Ezekiel, the new captain, was
proud to display his seamanship. Every year Joshua and
Nagamba stayed for several weeks with Pinkus on Monserrat.

ఴఄ

Amos watched his mother tending the bed of begonias
around Gashaka's and Quasha's graves. She hid in the silent

labyrinth of her secret world. Nagamba's mind spun back to her first born in Africa. Had he lived he would be twenty now.

'I still have both your pram and cribs in my bedroom,' Nagamba said, sifting the soil through her fingers.

'I recall since early childhood the fascinating stories you told us at bedtime about Moustapha, yourself and Gashaka.' Amos touched his mother's face with tenderness. Their resemblance was striking.

'Gashaka was as bold as a lion. He reminded me of Tony, a Coromante slave in 1675 who plotted a rebellion on a plantation. He was caught with other partisans and condemned to be burned at the stake. Facing the marshal Tony lifted his head in defiance and raised his inspiring voice.

'If you roast me today you cannot roast me tomorrow.'

Amos rode daily to the bluff and stayed there for long periods.

Seventeen years had passed since that day in August during the hurricane when Nagamba gave birth to the twins on a soft bed. A year before, during the same month in Nevis, Mahadana heavy with child, stooped with a hoe weeding in the fields under the broiling sun. She squatted and lay among the tall yellow sugar cane when Yabassi was expelled into the world. The finger of destiny had thus decreed years later Enoch, Amos and Yabassi like three impalas roamed the vast plantation as blood brothers. They attended the exclusive school in Kingston with Lotus, the twins' sister. Often Mahadana and Yabassi sat with Nagamba on the porch. Their conversation revolved around the Maroon wars.

'Is Ebouko alive? Is he in the Blue Mountains? Did he join the Leeward Maroons in the remote northwest? Mahadana's pinched face was etched with sadness. Yabassi watched the beautiful Jamaican spindalis fly in the orchard. He was thinking of his brother.

Nagamba loved Yabassi like her own son. He awakened in her the memory of Gashaka. Thoughts raced and shot at her like barbed arrows. Yabassi turned his head. Nagamba pleaded with her triste eyes.

CHAPTER 33

On Saturday afternoon Aaron paid a visit to Joshua and Nagamba.

'I'm glad you're here today,' said Joshua. 'I thought of a rather unusual subject which might be of interest to you. We export cattle and goat hides to Europe as well as different lucrative crops. Pinkus is the expert on certain exotic plants which grow in abundance on the island, and he taught us their therapeutic constituents for medicinal and culinary purposes. We could ship herbs and spices to New England.' Joshua's eyes were fixed on Nagamba.

'Excellent idea and should generate considerable revenue,' remarked Aaron.

'We can also sell turtle meat in salted barrels,' Nagamba added. 'Bostonians would relish this. The taste is similar to veal and chicken.'

'I like the idea of launching such a venture.' Joshua was getting excited.

'I know two planters in Carolina who would be interested. In fact, Joshua, you met them some time ago here on the wharf. They are presently residing in Charleston. I think we should engage them in correspondence and discuss this,' said Aaron. 'By the way, there was a short column in yesterday's paper as follows: "Lord Gaunt was found dead at his home." He hung himself. I wonder what happened to Lady O'Shaunessy.'

'I haven't the foggiest,' said Joshua. 'Now to more pleasant topics about Carolina. We will take our three young blades with us, and introduce them to the outside world.' In all the years since Benin, Joshua had never left Nagamba, not even for one day. She wrapped her arms around her man and kissed him.

'We will only stay for a short period,' he whispered.

᠊᠊

After two months they sailed out with the trade winds towards the American east coast. Nagamba was watering her plants on the windowsill when, to her dismay, she saw a young woman and her son running in desperation, chased by a white man on a horse. The mother's back bled profusely from lacerations. Her scanty lower cloth was torn, revealing on her buttocks a round mark where she was branded. She swooned and fell. The boy crouched beside her and whimpered. Alarmed, Nagamba ran outside. The rider dismounted and hastened towards the slaves.

'What are you doing on my property?' yelled Nagamba.

'The niggers escaped, not the first time,' scowled the angry white overseer. Nagamba's eyes grew wide in anger as the man held a thick rope, ready to coil it around the slaves. Memories began to stir in her mind of kidnapped women and children in Benin.

'Never, never again, as long as I shall live, no more collars of rope or chains. Now get out of my place, Brown Fow.'

'I do beg your pardon; and what is Brown Fow?'

'White face, like you!' spat Nagamba.

'African bitch, a slave like yourself defies a white man with impertinence and arrogance.' He approached her menacingly.

Nagamba started retreating nervously. Her legs felt weak. *This is dangerous,* she thought. I *must lure him.*

She screamed, turned and ran into the front room. He pursued her. Nagamba reached for the ornamental African assegai hanging low on the wall, and threw it with pinpoint accuracy. The razor sharp edges of the spear pierced the overseer's stomach and impaled the man to the door. His cry of agony echoed through the plantation.

Bundere came running towards the house having heard the turmoil. His eyes took in the situation and he turned to the shocked face of Nagamba.

'Come and sit down.' Deftly he removed the dead overseer from the door and took him outside.

'I must see to that poor slave and her child,' Nagamba said.

'Just wait there. I'll bring them inside.' Bundere arranged for Nagamba to provide medical assistance for the distressed mother and child.

'I'll throw the devil over the cliff on the bluff together with the saddle. We'll hide the horse in the woods.'

Plantation owners and merchants converged in the large garden. Amos, Enoch and Yabassi stood near Joshua. Aaron spoke behind them with an agent.

'I say, can we discuss the shipment of herbs? It's an important issue,' the arrogant planter said, facing Joshua, whom he had previously met.

'And who are those two mulatto outcasts, and the other negro?' he queried.

Joshua became pale and bit his upper lip.

'My sons.'

'I didn't know you were married to a black wench, and the negro is your son as well?' he said in a mocking tone.

'How dare you insult us!' lashed Joshua. 'You lousy swine, bourgeois nouveau riche.'

Aaron heard the heated discussion and spun around. Joshua's blood surged through his body. He was livid, ripping off his ruffled neckerchief and swiping it twice across the man's face.

'Apologise at once, or face me in a duel.'

'Damned if I apologise to a nigger lover.'

'Then you will hear from my second.'

❧

On Joshua's plantation the twins were shielded from the slurs of the outside world, but today in Carolina the shame and disgrace of being called outcasts and mulattos shocked Amos and Enoch. They were young but already their hearts were filled with bitter resentment and anger.

❧

At dawn the bell of the church rang out six of the clock. Amos trembled. He thought of Tony the Rebel.

If you roast me today, you cannot roast me tomorrow.

Aaron gritted his teeth, his mind racing. The exile of his people after the destruction of the second temple in 70 A.D., the persecution of the Spanish Inquisition, negroes, slaves and Gashaka ...

The second opened a wooden box with two smooth-bore flintlock pistols. He spoke to the two men about reconciliation, but was rebuffed from both sides.

'Choose your weapon please and take your places.'

The two men stood back to back. Joshua watched the hawk perched high on the tree. The autumn golden oak leaves spun from the top and with a rising breeze somer-saulted to the ground. The duellists started walking. A split second before turning round the large bird shrieked. Joshua aimed. The planter's hand was unsteady. The shot penetrated his chest with force. His knees gave way and he fell, mortally wounded.

&s

'Let's go home,' said Joshua. This humiliating stigma towards the ones he loved so well, and dear to him, was more than Joshua could bear. Pangs of regret and the irrevocable sins of his past as a slave trader and those implicated in slavery rose from the depths of his being and haunted him. Better if he severed all ties with Carolina. Freedom: so powerful a word.

Joshua detested the white planters and the militia who violently abused the slaves. Deep in the recess of his mind a lighthouse shone: the Maroons. He knew there and then what he must do.

&s

Nagamba had not been well of late. On Saturday morning Yabassi knocked on her door. Nagamba's face beamed when she saw him.

'Is Joshua in?' he asked.

'No, he's checking the cattle with the boys.' Yabassi hugged and held her fast before sitting on the cane chair.

'My dearest Nagamba. Some things cannot be explained.

They are beyond words, sealed inside.' He drew a long, deep breath. 'There is a constant battle within me. Where do I belong?' Yabassi then stood and approached the window. To his delight a humerus swallowtail butterfly was perched on a low branch.

'Are you aware it is the largest of its kind in the Western hemisphere? Come and see,' he told her. She watched it flutter its brilliant large wings.

'I must find my brother. It has been many years since I saw him leave with Gashaka. I have decided to join the Maroons. Here is a map Aaron gave me. Some areas are familiar. I'll trek by night past Spanish Town, veer left and climb up to Pedro's Cockpit. During the cool morning hours I shall cross the savannas and aim for the great river.' Yabassi touched Nagamba's trembling hands.

'I have studied the chart for weeks. I'll strap a canvas bag on my back, with a long knife on my side, most essential, and follow the great river towards Mantica Bay. Beyond the rolling mountings are the Maroons. Yabassi touched her right cheek with his index finger.

'You understand I cannot go on living not knowing the whereabouts of Ebouko; it grieves me to see you so sad.'

'There are four chambers in my heart,' Nagamba said in a sourdine tone. 'One died with Gashaka, the other perished when Ebouko left, and when you are gone the third chamber will pine. The last one will linger to the end with Joshua.'

'I love you both.' And he left.

வ

Mahadana and Bundere sat on the porch in the evening. Lines of sorrow stamped her gentle face. The merrywings circled around the candle. She was tired and watched her husband. Bundere pined for his sons. He would never see them again. If he only could erase the white man's insanity, stop that perpetual spinning, and flip through the pages of his life to a world of long ago in the Cameroon village.

All seemed futile at present, without hope. Bundere walked towards the stables and rode out to the bluff. He stood on the cliff above the precipice and felt the clean sea air rising from below, and then jumped.

Mahadana reclined on the cane chair. Maybe one day, she thought, she would sail to Monserrat and see her daughter Marufa.

CHAPTER 34

'We haven't been up the mountains since our wedding,' Joshua said. 'The small hut must still be there. Why don't we go for a visit and take Lotus with us?'

'Yes alright, I shall never forget those blissful weeks,' said Nagamba, walking arm in arm with her husband.

'Do the soldiers scour the forests around here hunting the Maroons?' asked Lotus.

'Fear not,' Joshua reassured her. 'I always carry my blunderbuss in case of any unpredicted situations.'

They duly departed and for several days scaled the pristine elevation. The log cabin, hidden among the giant trees and jagged cliffs, was camouflaged by hanging, creeping undergrowth.

'A few days' work ahead of us,' chuckled Joshua.

Lotus roamed off to pick wild berries when she heard crackling leaves and turned. A young Maroon with a machete stood in front of her.

'Young lady, I won't hurt you. Take me to your father. I'll follow from a distance. Make sure the militia are not in the vicinity.'

Lotus ran back panting.

'Father, there is a Maroon. He is hiding over there and wants to speak to you. He caught me unawares.'

Joshua and Nagamba scanned the area. Close to the mastic tree the man appeared.

'We watched you coming up the mountain.' said the Maroon. 'Our chiefs Quao and Cuffee wish to meet you.'

'We would be delighted.'

'Gashaka told us about you.'

'When and where do we meet?' asked Joshua.

'In two days' time before sunset, behind the massive silk cotton tree on the brow.' He pointed and left.

༄

The sun sank as four braves appeared in silence like phantoms through the bushes. Joshua was intrigued.

'How do you do? This is my wife Nagamba and daughter Lotus.' They shook hands.

'It's an honour to meet you,' said Cuffee, eyes on Lotus. Her dark sparkling eyes portrayed that cemented bond of brotherhood. Lotus' heart was with the Maroons. In recognition he bowed his head smiling.

'You are very pretty,' he said to Lotus and turned to Joshua.

'It is my wish to help you. I have access to a schooner which can supply you with weapons and provisions.' Joshua watched the warriors with admiration.

'Our gratitude goes beyond words for your offer. Thank you, but it is too risky to stay here any longer. We will talk further. My two men will escort you back to your hut. Hurry, the troopers patrol all around.'

༄

Cuffee, who loved and hated with extremes, thought of Gashaka. His loathing towards the milita churned inside him. Cuffee ultimately knew that his fate and end would be on the mountains he loved.

The magnificent eagles, hawks and vultures high off the ground greeted the familiar sight of the wild roaming Cuffee. They squawed in acrobatic flight and flapped their powereful wings. Cuffee looked at Lotus once more. His chest felt tight. He turned and waved. Quao followed. A barrage of shots was heard.

Joshua, Nagamba and Lotus swiftly retreated into the cabin.

'We will hide outside at the back,' said one of the Maroons. There was a gibbous moon.

'I think we should split in two divisions,' said Major Stovold to Sergeant Major Sinclair. 'Fifteen troopers will follow me and the other fifteen in your direction. The bastard rebels are invisible.' He snarled in anger. 'We must not be trapped this time. What a disaster it was under O'Reilly's command,' said the Major. 'Prime your muskets.'

Palpable shadows seemed to float to and fro. Two troopers crouched behind the large boulders studying the hut.

'I can smell their stinking bodies. We'll crawl a bit closer.'

Through the wooden slats Joshua aimed his blunderbuss and riddled both men with lead shots. Joshua ran outside. The two Maroons jumped in front and dragged the bodies deep inside a cave.

'Nobody will ever find them there,' said Joshua. 'Take their muskets. We had better leave this mountain.'

Lotus looked thoughtfully after Cuffee as he walked away.

Before dawn, Joshua, Lotus and Nagamba weaved between concealed caves with caution and descended the slope.

'I hear footsteps,' said Captain Stovold, waving his troopers to go to ground.

The three were confronted as the troopers stood up.

'Good morning,' Joshua greeted the soldiers. Captain Stovold looked at him in astonishment.

'Joshua, what are you doing up here?'

'I bring my family to the mountains every year. We love it and we do not quarrel with the Maroons. They fight you, not us. I have no slaves on my plantation.' Lotus smiled victoriously.

Something stirred in the Major's memories, but he suppressed it.

'Well, I bid you a very good morning and good hunting. Come on, Nagamba, lets go.'

'Darling, I think we should send the woman and boy to the Blue Mountains with our two loyal Mandingos. They have been here too long and there is much danger. The militia are searching for the missing overseer and the two slaves,' she added with concern.

'Yes, they must leave early tomorrow when it is still dark,' Joshua agreed.

The Maroon scouts blew on the abeng. It echoed across the narrow corridors of the Blue Mountains. Quao stood on a steep rock and scanned the rugged wilderness. Cuffee was below. The Mandingos and slaves accelerated towards the sound of the horn. Within half an hour Quao spotted them and imitated the safe shrill code of the bald black vulture.

'I see two males, one carrying a child on his back and the other running with a woman beside him,' said Quao. 'Let's greet them.' Other excited Maroons followed.

'We recently left Joshua's place. The mother and her son escaped from another plantation where the cruel owner treats his slaves like beasts.' The Mandingo panted.

'Joshua wanted you to know the doctor was not able to save Gashaka's life. His last thoughts were of you.'

For weeks Cuffee rode Gashaka's stallion after he left, through the valleys and forests. Cuffee's heart ached, his body and soul scorified by love, hate and vengeance. He shouted Gashaka's name. It rolled and roared above the peaks.

'Men like Gashaka never die. His spirit rose from the mist and carved the crowning loftiness.'

'Joshua has a friend, the captain of a schooner who knows where to purchase arms, for you with funds supplied by Joshua,' said the second Mandingo. 'We shall return in about a month and give you specific details.'

'Risky, a dangerous game,' Cuffee remarked. 'Joshua is a brave man to be admired and respected.'

Quao swept his hand across the inhospitable isolation, and then touched the boy's head.

'This is your home; you will fight with us.' Tears of gratitude trickled on the mother's gaunt cheeks. The tired youth rested his head upon Quao's shoulder. The following day the Mandingos departed.

※

Joshua paced the room, his hands clasped behind his back. 'I shall sacrifice my days giving aid to the Maroons to defend themselves: a cause I believe in implicitly.'

'Halleluiah,' cried out Aaron, smiling at Rebecca. Pinkus wasn't surprised as he held his bible. He knew Joshua's heart well.

'Not a word must seep through these walls,' Joshua paused and gave a muffled cough. 'I sent two of my most trusted men to the mountains. They have just returned having met Quao and Cuffee, their leaders whom Gashaka met. Pinkus, I need your help please. Will you be able to arrange a supply of arms?'

'Yes.' Without hesitation Joshua opened a bronze coffer and handed Pinkus a large amount of gold.

'I'll sail with you and help the crew to land the weapons in a deserted hidden cove. I suggest crates of muskets, blunderbusses, ball and shot, machetes and long knives. The Maroons willll load their packhorses and slip back to the refuge of the mountains.'

Pinkus nodded. 'You have a map?'.

'Here.' Joshua produced one.

'I must ensure there are no dangerous reefs,' Pinkus stated. Both of them examined the details of the chart.

'Ah, here is Basnets Cove, ideal beach.' Joshua pointed to it. 'The Maroons will need medicines as well. I shall arrange with Dr Fairchild who obtains his provisions from the apothecaries in Kingston. He never asks questions. A man of honour.'

'Also most essential: turtles and salted preserved meat,' said Nagamba.

Joshua turned to Pinkus. 'May I send the Mandingos to contact the Maroons of the arrival of the Pandora in the evening of the 15th June at Basnets Cove? This will give us two months for preparation.'

'Absolutely, good timing.'

'Splendid. I'll join you as well in this noble escapade,' cheered Aaron. 'The camaraderie of a lifetime.'

'Is your son in Barbados?' Joshua asked, turning to Rebecca.

'Yes, Gideon lives in the house of Aaron's father, who passed away.'

'Amazing, but the old building has had some alterations done to it but stands firm despite the hurricanes,' remarked Aaron. 'By the way, Sarah, my younger daughter is coming over this weekend to ride with Amos to the bluff. The other girl in fact, quite a woman, is totally different, helps Jonathan in the emporium. On the wharf she deals with ship captains, plantation owners and agents regarding merchandise. She loves mixing with nobility. Dammit, I'll never understand her. She's certainly a flirt. Her proud carriage, ostentatious clothes and coiffure remind me of Queen Anne.' Aaron squeezed Rebecca's fingers.

'I do hope she does not follow the Queen's ways. Poor Anne was impregnated time and time again by that animal husband of hers, Prince George of Denmark. No wonder she died in 1714 at the age of 49; totally exhausted from childbirths. I dare say he was a real ping pong.'

'Please, Aaron,' Rebecca laughed in hysterics.

Nagamba, with eyes wide opened, asked, 'What's a ping-pong?'

'It is a Chinese game with bouncing little balls. That Prince George was busy bouncing his little balls.'

Rebbeca clutched her aching sides, tears in her eyes.

'Though it is interesting to note she was the last queen to exercise the right of the monarch to cancel parliament's decisions,' said Joshua. 'Her sister married William the third. They never had any offspring, and Mary, young as she was, died of smallpox in 1694. William reigned alone until 1702 when Anne became Queen.

'I wonder who will pluck our beauties.'

Aaron watched Amos and Enoch with amusement. His glance conveyed the implication to Nagamba who breathed deeply and raised a smile.

The first time she met Aaron on the Hurricane he kissed her hand, uttering her name softly. Three men were central, influencing her life. Three men she loved: Joshua, Aaron (devoted friend, none like him) and Gashaka. How she ached daily for him. Nagamba's tormented past returned and she thought of Kumbo, her first husband, his body crawling with safari ants, and her dead infant in the dark forest.

She felt a strong premonition of impending doom, which to her despair she could not shake off. She feared death daily. However, as long as Joshua was beside her she could go on living.

Grey-faced Joshua approached his offspring. 'Should any calamity befall Aaron, Pinkus or myself, promise me to follow this pledge.' Joshua's Adam's apple fluttered. 'The Maroons are your brothers as are all slaves in bondage. Remember your mother's African blood flows deep in your veins. She stands on a pedestal. Slavery is a virulent pestilence that must be eradicated; it is corrupt and sinister.'

Through a mist of a foggy veil, the faces of Moustapha, Gashaka and his wife appeared. Joshua raised his voice like a trumpet blast.

'I believe in freedom and equality for all men. One cannot kill idealogy.' He watched Nagamba's large moist sad eyes. Aaron was moved. Sensitive Lotus reclined beside Nagamba.

'Cameroon blood,' she said with pride, caressing her mother's features, and turned, smiling, to Joshua. 'And English blood.'

CHAPTER 35

Pinkus liked to consider himself as a swashbuckling buccaneer, but in fact he was a cautious captain. In the early evening, under the minimum of sail, he steered his schooner into the isolated bay on the wild north coast of Jamaica. He had a date with the Maroons.

The bay was wide but narrowed at the entrance which was guarded by a small uninhabited island, covered in dense jungle. Pinkus eased his ship past the western channel and into the cove.

'Pinkus, this is excellent,' said Joshua, standing beside him. 'That island gives us perfect cover from the seaward side. It would be difficult for any ship on the open sea to spot us in here.'

'Joshua, my friend, that is precisely why this spot was selected for a rendezvous with the Maroons. The Royal Navy has stepped up patrols in recent months, and I don't want to meet up with one of their frigates.'

Pinkus scanned the shore through a telescope. 'I can't see the Maroons at all,' he said.

Joshua grinned. 'My dear, Pinkus, you're not supposed to see them. They'll appear when they are satisfied the coast is clear, and not before.'

'Yes, I know, but we are vulnerable here, like sitting ducks. I'll be glad when this transaction is over.'

'Relax, have faith,' said Joshua clapping Pinkus on the

back. He spotted movement on the shoreline. 'Look, there they are, right on time.'

A relieved Pinkus steered Pandora further into the bay and gave the order for the anchor to be dropped. The ship glided smoothly to a stop.

Joshua watched as the boats were lowered and the cargo swayed over the side and loaded into them. He left Pinkus nervously parading the quarterdeck, and went to the lead boat as they headed for the shore. As soon as they reached the shallows Joshua jumped out impulsively and reached the sandy beach to shake hands with Cuffee.

'It is good to see you again, Joshua. How is your family, especially the lovely Lotus?'

'They are well, thank you. Look, Pinkus out there on the ship is decidedly nervous so can we please get this cargo ashore and then away from the beach. He is so afraid of a Royal Navy ambush.'

'Of course, Joshua.' Cuffee shouted a series of orders, and swarms of Maroons emerged from the jungle and began to unload the boats. The crates were lifted, carried ashore, broken open and the contents distributed among the many Maroons. Pinkus arrived on the shore to hasten the unloading process. Once this was completed the cargo started to move off the beach. The packaging was also distributed and carted off as well. It could be useful for many purposes. The Maroons wasted nothing. Finally the Maroons started to move off the beach.

Pinkus stared towards the west and saw in the distance, to his horror, a white sail in the emerging twilight.

'Joshua, come here, quick!' he shouted.

Alarmed by the urgency in Pinkus's voice Joshua responded swiftly, his eyes fixed on the horizon.

'That's a frigate, probably Royal Navy,' groaned Pinkus.

'Would Pandora be able to outsail her?'

Pinkus considered this quickly. 'I think so; the frigate will be a square-rigged vessel. Now the wind is from the west, so if we sail across her bows and head north she would have difficulty following us. The secret is to stay out of range of her gun batteries. They are formidable.'

'Then fly, Pinkus, fly at once and head into the night. The night will be your friend. Go.'

'What about you, Joshua? Aren't you coming?'

'No, I'll stay here and help the Maroons to clear the beach. It's quite likely that the warship will send a landing party ashore. Go, Pinkus, I'll make my way back over the land.' Pinkus leapt into a boat and gave the order to return to Pandora.

Joshua and the Maroons started to head inland. On the hill he looked back and saw that the boats had reached the ship and the anchor had been pulled up. Pinkus was wasting no time.

On board Pandora, Pinkus had turned into a human dynamo. The boats were swayed aboard, the sails were being hoisted, and Pandora started to slowly glide towards the east end of the island in the bay. They could no longer see the frigate. As the ship's speed increased Pinkus began to relax. He knew that the warship would spot him as soon as Pandora cleared the small island but estimated that he was still out of gun range.

From a commanding height on the hill, Joshua saw that Pandora was now out on the open sea. Pinkus was running for his life.

'May God be with you, Pinkus,' murmured Joshua and turned to follow the Maroons.

On the sea Pinkus spotted the Royal Navy vessel coming

up fast from the west, with the wind filling her sails. Frigates were among the fastest ships on the high seas. He calculated distances and ordered a course to the *nor' nor' east* across the path of the other ship, while steering slightly away from it. The calculations were inspired guesswork, and Pinkus prayed that they were correct. The advent of the night would also be his ally. He watched as the enemy turned to intercept him, but he felt that such a course alteration would reduce their speed, and made a silent prayer. They were getting closer and closer.

At last Pandora was north of the approaching man-o-war which launched a ranging shot with its bow chasers. It was still out of range however, and the cannonballs dropped short.

'Right,' said Pinkus. 'Steer nor'west by north.' He looked at the frigate as it tried to follow his change of course, slowing perceptibly as it did so.

Pinkus laughed gleefully. 'That showed him!' In the western skies, still lit with the diminishing rays of the setting sun, Pinkus saw another sail. He studied it through the telescope. 'That's a ship of the line, a third rater by the looks of it. I'm glad we are well out of his way.' He watched the rapidly disappearing coast of Jamaica. 'I wonder how Joshua is coping. I hope he is safe.'

Ashore, Joshua and the Maroons had reached the high tops of the hills and were heading towards the mountains.

'Joshua, we are well on our way and I doubt that the Royal Navy will catch up with us now. We are too fast for them. I suspect they will land a shore party which can tramp around until it gets tired.'

'Yes, you're right, Cuffee. I was thinking the same, but now it is important I return to my wife and family.'

'Joshua, I will send you back with two of my trusty

Maroons on horseback. You will be home much quicker than if you were still on Pandora.'

Joshua smiled gratefully.

Three days later, tired and sore, the party arrived in the mountain stronghold of the Maroons. They were highly organised and Joshua was shown into a small hut where he was given a brief but satisfying meal and fell asleep almost immediately.

Later that day he was woken up by a genial Cuffee carrying two cups of the famous Blue Mountains coffee.

'Come, Joshua. You can't spend the rest of your life asleep.' Joshua opened a bleary eye and glanced wearily at him. 'Here, a drink of the best coffee in the world. Come on, try it while it's hot.' He handed over the cup, forcing Joshua to sit up.

Cautiously, Joshua sipped the fragrant brew. It was delicious. He felt refreshed almost immediately.

'This has truly a magnificent flavour, Cuffee. The best coffee I have tasted.'

'And it's grown locally,' smiled Cuffee. As soon as you're ready, we'll start you on your way home, with one small change to the plan.'

'A small change? What's that?'

'I have decided to be your escort. You and I will fly like the wind as soon as you've fully woken up.'

'This wouldn't have anything to do with my daughter would it?'

'Oh, would she be at home now?' asked Cuffee coyly.

Joshua laughed. 'Cuffee, you're a conniving rogue.'

One hour later, with suitably provisioned saddlebags, the pair set off, intending to travel as far as they could before nightfall.

Three more days passed. They crouched in a stand of trees on the edge of Joshua's plantation and surveyed the scene. Everything looked peaceful: the animals grazed as people tended to their duties. They even saw Lotus as she plucked some flowers for the house.

'Nagamba is expecting you, Joshua,' said Cuffee. 'We sent word ahead of our intentions, so no doubt you will get the fatted calf for dinner tonight.'

'Thank you for that, Cuffee, and don't forget: keep your cotton-picking hands off my daughter,' said Joshua with a laugh.

'Joshua, my intentions towards Lotus are strictly honourable.'

'Yes, I know you well enough now.' Together they mounted and rode into the plantation. Nagamba came running out followed by Lotus.

Joshua embraced Nagamba. She held him tightly and prayed they never be separated again. Together they went inside the luxurious house followed by Cuffee and Lotus.

Later that evening Joshua pleaded fatigue and retired with Nagamba. Lotus and Cuffee sat on the verandah and talked well into the night.

At breakfast the following morning, Cuffee said that he could only stay two days, and even that was taking a risk. To remain any longer would simply be too dangerous for him.

'I am a wanted man with a price on my head.'

Lotus bit her lip. 'Come on, Cuffee,' she said impetuously. 'Let's go for a ride over to the cliffs above the sea. It's a beautiful spot.'

'Cuffee, please be discreet and bring her home safely,' said Joshua. 'She is the light of our lives.'

'I will protect Lotus with my life if necessary.'

Joshua nodded. 'Well, let's hope that won't be necessary. Off you go then.'

⟨✦⟩

Two days later, an ominous premonition welled up inside Nagamba when she saw Lotus and Cuffee approaching.

'My very dear Joshua and Nagamba,' Cuffee said in a trembling voice. 'I love Lotus and want to spend the rest of my life with her. Long ago as a child I chased the arch of the brilliant rainbow down the hill and sobbed when I could not grasp it. Lotus is my rainbow. I shall never let her go.' Tears appeared in Joshua's eyes. Nagamba clenched her hands upon her bosom.

'Father,' said Lotus. 'Cuffee's blood mingled with mine will cover the mountains for generations to come in freedom. Cuffee cannot remain here so we will go and live with the Maroons.'

'Lotus, are you sure about this?'

'I want to enjoy freedom with Cuffee and to stay with him, just as Mother is sharing her life with you. You can't deny me this. Please father.'

'And what would you do if I say no?'

Lotus looked wild and pale; she had half-expected this reaction from her father, but she wasn't willing to accept it.

'Please don't do that, I beg of you. I would then have to choose between you and Cuffee, and that would break my heart.'

Joshua took his daughter's hands. 'Lotus, my beloved daughter, and you, my friend Cuffee: if Nagamba agrees I will not stand in your way, but there is one condition.'

'What is it, Father?'

'That you get married in the eyes of the church before you depart for the mountains.'

'To walk with Lotus beside me as my wife through all our days; that I do desire. But to arrange a wedding; surely that will take weeks.

'No, if you consent to this we'll find a priest today and you can be married. Do you agree?'

Cuffee hugged the sobbing Nagamba, and then Joshua. Lotus broke down in tears.

Joshua knew that Aaron had more than a passing acquaintance with many people and was a most persuasive person, so he rode off to Aaron's plantation to see about a priest.

He was away for a few hours, and upon his return he cried out: 'Aaron will be here with a priest by lunch-time. Come, Nagamba, we must prepare a wedding feast.'

Shortly after midday Aaron arrived with a big grin on his face, Rebecca in tow, and a stern-faced and sweaty priest in the coach.

'Greetings, lovely Nagamba. I have a gentleman of the cloth who is willing to perform the ceremony between Lotus and Cuffee. He was a trifle reluctant initially, but I managed to persuade him that it was a worthy cause. Hello, Lotus.' He jumped down from the coach and embraced her.

He turned to the priest and handed him an envelope containing his fee plus a handsome remuneration. The priest's face became more mellow and tolerant when he saw the amount.

At Cuffee's request the ceremony was simple and short. He was anxious to return to the safety of the mountains.

Aaron gave a moving and beautiful sermon on the sanctity of marriage and the noble ideals that the young couple strove to live up to.

In mid-afternoon, after a tearful farewell, the young couple rode off. Joshua and Nagamaba, arm in arm, waved until the couple were out of sight.

For years following this day, Joshua supplied arms and other provisions to the Maroons, which were distributed in different hidden locations along the coast. Joshua insisted on accompanying Pinkus on these potentially perilous journeys. He met Cuffee on the beach and occasionally ventured up into the mountains again to see his beloved Lotus. Several times Lotus accompanied him back to the plantation to visit her mother. It was dangerous but Lotus seemed to thrive on it.

CHAPTER 36

Yabassi trekked across the hot arid savannah dotted with exiguous acacia shrubs. On the far horizon he recognised the commanding range of mountains.

'Alone and young,' said Cudjoe.

'How can you tell from such a distance? You have the sharp eyes of a lynx.' Ebouko leaned against a rock.

'The way he moves; light and quick. Who dares to trail on his own?'

'We will soon know. Blow the abeng, he will hear us,' said Cudjoe.

Exhausted, Yabassi lay under the thorny bush. His feet were blistered. He leapt up at the sound of the horn and scanned the harsh land. He thought he saw something scrambling but the mirage soon rose with the heat and vanished. Yabassi pressed on. Not long after, the Maroons appeared.

Cudjoe resembled a small wild bear. Behind him Ebouko approached limping. Yabassi did not recognise him. Ebouko's eyes were glued on the young panther.

'How did you find your way to this isolated place?' asked Cudjoe. Yabassi opened his bag and took out the map.

'This is a treasure. I followed it though. I must confess it was difficult, but I relied on my instincts and followed the stars.' Ebouko kept staring at him. Yabassi smiled.

'I survived on the brown anole lizards, Bahamaian hutia

and green iguanas. I am quick with a knife.' Yabassi's eyes sparkled. Cudjoe was intrigued by his manners. He was educated, and displayed his trust in the people he had just met, but his innocence and enthusiasm were qualities which captured the leader.

Could he be? Ebouko shook his head and dismissed such thoughts with sadness. The flight of too many years ago melted and faded away. When had he last hugged little Yabassi?

Yabassi pointed his finger at St Catherine. Ebouko and Cudjoe leaned over with burning curiosity.

'My name is Yabassi.'

Ebouko reeled and almost fell.

'The pains in your leg again?' Cudjoe bent to help. Ebouko howled. His body shook.

'Yabassi, Yabassi, my brother.' Everyone held their breath. Cudjoe was struck like a thunder clap. Yabassi knelt and rested his weary head on his brother's shoulder.

'The troopers chased me on a steep ledge. I slipped, landing near a cave, with a broken ankle and crawled inside. It was agonising,' said Ebouko. 'The militia cowards searched what seemed for hours and then in frustration left.' Yabassi sat up.

'Cudjoe found me and strapped my foot. I hobbled for several weeks; the bone never healed properly. Often I get spasms of shooting pains, but I can still run, just not so fast.'

The two men wound their way through a maze of caves towards the small, hidden Maroon settlement.

'I love the wilderness,' Ebouko said in a hushed voice. 'We will fight the white man's river of blood wherever they tread.'

'We split into two divisions. Quao and his followers

raided the plantations inland of Fig Tree Bay and Dry River. I followed Cuffee.'

'Several expeditions landed at Port Antonio. They infiltrated the interior on their horses, carrying large supplies of ammunition. We slaughtered many and took their animals, provisions and arms. Months later I decided on the torch of war with Cudjoe in the far north-west.

'Come Yabassi, let's get some sleep.' Twisted lightning struck the distant mountainside.

CHAPTER 37

Ebouko and Yabassi fought side by side with the Maroons against the militia. In 1728 a new governor of Jamaica, General R.O. Hunter, frustrated by the striking wars crippling the development on the northeast of Port Antonio, wrote in the gazette as follows:

> The new settlement of Port Antonio is proceeding with good prospects. I am thoroughly convinced that a good settlement there will very much add to the strength and security of the island not only against a foreign enemy but also against the insults of the rebellious negroes.

Cudjoe, leader of the Leeward Maroons in the isolated northwest, watched the rare white hawk glide across the cockpit country. The cold wind stung his eyes and dried the tears on his cheek. The bird arched its chest. Cudjoe sighed, his thoughts swung to Sutton in Clarendon where he was born. His father had worked as a slave on a plantation. How his mother must have suffered during his childhood because of his deformities. She would have ached deeply when he left to the 'Land of the Look Behind', and pined for her dwarfish son whom she dearly loved. Through the years Cudjoe's sharp-shooting Maroons, having concealed themselves inside caves, aimed their muskets at the approaching Militia. The hooves of their horses drummed across the valley and deep gullies. Cudjoe gazed up at the magnificent high-soaring hawk.

'Fighting, white against black, is futile.' The wind howled. He wiped his face.

Late at night his loyal Maroons were assembled around him. Cudjoe had a broad neck with a prominent flash on his corpulent back. His fanatical look blazed across them.

'How dare the militia spend twenty pounds for every captured man, dead or alive. And ten pounds for every negress, and piccaninnies as well.' He stretched his sore arms with difficulty above his shoulders.

'I was informed by a spy,' said Yabassi. 'More expeditions will sail from Kingston to Port Antonio. The army are desperate to flush us out of the mountains to the northeast. We have defeated them time after time.' Yabassi rang his fingers through his hair in anger. He approached the crippled leader and sat beside him.

Cudjoe swelled with deep emotion. He appointed a strong ambuscade of rebels. He divided his Maroons into three divisions. 'Each will comprise 120 men, to attack St James's, St Catherine's and St Anne's plantations. All this must be executed by night.' Cudjoe roared like a lion, sitting cross-legged on the ground.

'Captain Mingo, with Ebouko and Yabassi, you will be the initial force to start above Kings Valley to the mountains, and follow the great river towards Javarine Cove before Mantica bay. There is a cotton plantation and livestock. Muster the cattle and hogs from the pens; use lances as well as muskets, herd them along the river.

'Second party, under Captain Accompong, detour and advance from Mantica Bay and below. Get arms and ammunition on the way.

'You, Johnny, swift on your legs, continue and set fire to the sheds and buildings, trample the cocoa walks and indigo on the coast to St Anne's to the isolated plantations. Shoot to kill when confronted and steal more horses and ammunition. The three squadrons will leave at first light. The white men shall never win.'

For years the Maroons were hunted without success. Somewhere, wandering the lofty wilderness of the 'Land of The Look Behind', the heroes Ebouko and Yabassi vanished into oblivion.

CHAPTER 38

The two-masted schooner sailed out of Jamaica at dawn and plowed through the billowing waters. Her sails shivered with the westerly winds. Tufts and filaments of clouds chased each other across the sky.

Nagamba sat on a bench at the stern. Joshua stood by the wheel smoking his pipe. This time he was given the great privilege of being honorary master of the Pandora by Ezekiel. He wore an embroidered stomacher against the morning chill and adjusted his captain's hat which he always wore when sailing on his annual trip to Monserrat.

Pinkus waited ashore for their visit. On board the ship Ezekiel, Shyloh and the crew attended to their sailing duties. Joshua loved to be back at sea. He looked at his wife and smiled. Wrapped around her frail body was a navy-blue flowing dress banded with white, and a shawl.

It had been over thirty-three years since he first met Nagamba in Benin. He was then captain of the Hurricane brigantine. He remembered Moustapha dying of leprosy, so long ago now, saying to him: 'Nagamba is the greatest gift in your life. She will stand by your side as a rock, a lamp to light your years.' Joshua's heart ached with the vale of years thinking of his dear friend. The salty ocean spray spattered Joshua's face.

'We will make good timing to Monserrat,' said Ezekiel. The schooner had been sailing for several days south of Haiti and Domingo, escorted by schools of dolphins and flying fish. Shyloh and Ezekiel were doing the climbing in the rigging, persuading Joshua not to ascend the mast by appealing to his ego, emphasising and telling him of his greater expertise in helsmanship and his keen weather eye.

Joshua had been secretly fearful of scaling the mast to the cross-trees, not for his life but for fear of ridicule at his slow stiff movements. He had no doubt that he could reach the crows nest, though not with the catlike agility of the sailors.

From a distance Nagamba saw the lonely albatross fly towards the Pandora; with trembling lips she uttered a faint cry. Joshua saw the bird. They had not seen another albatross since leaving Benin. Her large span of wings hardly moved, as she glided above the water. She followed the ship for several hours before arching her brilliant white chest and soaring up into the sky.

Nagamba grew cold.

'Ezekiel, can you take the helm for a while?' said Joshua. He approached Nagamba and put his arm around her.

On the sixth day, everybody on board was on deck staring apprehensively to the north, suspicious of the weather. The ship was becalmed, the sails limp, and there was not the slightest ripple on the shimmering waters. Throughout the day the sky was streaked with low clouds and it became muggy and humid.

'We must be close to the Antilles.' Ezekiel's latest reading had put them where they should be, in its lee. Joshua dismissed this at once, knowing full well the accuracy of his position.

'No, Ezekiel. The weather's getting worse and we could be in for a blow. I've seen these conditions before: they usually precede a storm, or worse.' Ezekiel threw him a frightened look. Joshua smiled reassuringly.

'Now Ezekiel, please don't be scared. You're too experienced a sailor, and you know how to treat the sea with respect. Come let's secure the ship, batten everything down, and reduce sail.'

Ezekiel was relieved at having tasks to perform and scurried about the ship with the crew. His seamanship was first class.

Despite his display of boundless, cheerful optimism, Joshua worried about the weather, which deteriorated by the hour. They were definitely in the calm before the storm due to the erratic sea patterns, dark cloud formations and the panicked flight of birds.

'A hurricane's heading towards us,' Joshua bellowed. 'We'll rig accordingly. Put enough sail on to run into her when she hits, but not enough to cause us damage. We can always alter one's rig. Batten down the hatches, and check the ballast in the lower hold. We have a few hours at best. A major hurricane, I feel it in the air. I've been through one many years ago.'

'Nagamba, don't leave my side. Stand near me all the time.' Joshua secured her to the mast with a rope for her own safety. Other lifelines were rigged along the decks.

Massive cumulus clouds towered in the sky, driven furiously by some malevolent force. It began to rain, gently at first, and then strengthening and becoming torrential. The wind howled, and the four were deeply afraid.

They eyed each other with concern, watching the ominous dark clouds now delivering frequent windy squalls. Joshua surmised that the hurricane had swept between Domingo and Porto Rico, side swiping both and was heading straight towards them.

As the fresh winds struck Pandora she veered southwest in the direction of the Lesser Antilles. They seemed to be weathering the storm well, when the sky turned black as night and the howl of the savage wind was like a shrieking banshee. The four roped themselves together to the main mast. Heavy rain came in sheets, lashing the schooner. The wrath of God, like in the days of Noah, was upon them. The main mast groaned under attack from the piercing, roaring winds and huge seas broke over, some sixty feet high, and threatened to swamp and overturn the schooner.

Awestruck, they looked on in fear and horror at the might of Nature at its most powerful, as she swept away all before her.

As quick as the hurricane had hit, she left. The raging storm eventually subsided. The deafening shrill eased and the calmer weather was palpable. Through the clouds a piece of blue sky appeared. The pressure of the air dropped. Soon after, on the extreme side of the eye wall, a brilliant white cloud rose like a phantom.

'We're in the eye,' said Joshua as he paced the deck and peered at the wreckage. The main mast was almost ripped from its base. The fore mast stood firm. Twisted and tangled broken spars, shrouds, canvas and rope lay strewn about. A complete devastation.

'We shan't make it. The Pandora can't withstand another such onslaught,' said a worried Joshua. 'We must act now before the storm returns. It will come with great force from the other direction. I will rope myself and Nagamba to the fore mast.' He gazed up at the sky.

'The helm is still intact. Ezekiel and I will lash ourselves to it. Maybe we'll be able to steer her through the storm.' Shyloh trembled, his eyes swimming with tears.

'It's getting dark again. The winds are whipping. Brace yourselves. God bless!' Joshua hailed. 'Hold my hand, Nagamba. We'll fly to the island where the albatrosses are. I love you.'

'I love you, Joshua.' Above the wind she cried out, 'How many years have we been married?' She reached out a desperate hand, the premonition of impending doom rising within her.

'This year is 1734, so we've been together for thirty-seven years. Hold on, my darling.'

The wind slew above the rising, gigantic swell. Ezekiel looked up, his face ashen, his teeth chattering in fear. With terror in his heart he watched the giant, leviathan wave bearing down on them with a large mantle of white foam. Within seconds he took his hands from the wheel and wrapped himself around Shyloh standing next to him as the mammoth wave slammed into the ship. The sixty-foot monster wall of water picked up the schooner and twisted it about violently. She dived vertically into the sea and broke her back, sank and rose, and then was dragged down and swallowed with the undercurrent. Nagamba and Joshua, tied to the mast, surged through the deep as though they were burning at the torch. Their searing lungs filled with water. Death was merciful in the jaws of their last sleep.

THE END

WEST INDIES SOCIAL CLASSIFICATION

Social classification in the West Indies in the 17th Century was based on shades of body colour.

1. Top were pure whites;
2. The musteefino, the hybrid of a white and a mustee;
3. The mustee, the offspring of a white and a quadroon;
4. A quadroon, that of a white man and a mulatto;
5. The mulatto, the original racial admixture of a white man and a negro;
6. A mulatto and a negro were sambos.

The first three stages of descent ranked as white. They were always free.

A mulatto might or might not be free; it depended on the attitude of the father when the child reached adolescence. Most of the children of such liaisons remained slaves.

DRAMATIS PERSONNAE

Aaron Pardess	Plantation owner
Adjaba	Aaron's housekeeper
Alimba	Wife of Moshebere
Amos & Enoch	Twin sons of Joshua and Nagamba
Atakanga (Chief)	Chief Slaver of Cape Coast Castle
Benjamin Doncaster	Company Factor
Billy Fidelity	Slave Trader
Bundere	Husband of Mahadana
Capt. Chris Lawrence	Master of Rainbow
Captain Montague	Master of 'Nightingale'
Captain Joshua Quaile	Master of 'Hurricane' and 2nd Husband of Nagamba
Captain Van Den Hoosten	Ship's Captain, and slaver at Douala
Captain Stovold	Jamaica Militia
Captain Tobias Ramsay	Master of Arabesque
Colonel O'Reilly	Militia Commandant, Jamaica
Cuffee	Maroon Leader
Cudjoe	Maroon Leaders
Daboona	Female cook in Benin
Dr. Fairchild	Physician in Port Royal
Eboua	Head Guard of the Slaves (Fang Tribe)
Ebouko, Marufa	Children of Bundere
Edoo	Overseer and slave to Lord Gableshaw
Ezekiel	Assistant to Pinkus

Gashaka	Slave, brother of Nagamba
James Tumbridge	Son of Philip Tumbridge
Jonathan	Dwarf and friend of Aaron
King Adebayo	Chief Slaver in Calabar
Kumbo	First husband of Nagamba
Lonegan	Company Agent
Lord Francis Gableshaw	Plantation Owner Port Royal
Lady Felicia Gableshaw	Wife of Lord Gableshaw
Lotus	Daughter of Joshua and Nagamba
Mahadana	Wife of Bundere
Marufa	Daughter of Mahadana and Bundere
Monneba	Headman of the Douala
Moshebere	Husband of Alimba
Moustapha	Slaver in Benin
Nagamba	Wife of Kumbo
Onana & Awana	Twins sons of Alimba and Moshebere
Philip Tumbridge	Plantation owner
Pinkus	Jewish trader in the Caribbean
Quao	Maroon Leader
Rebecca	Aaron's wife
Shyloh	Assistant to Pinkus
Sir James Farrel	London Financier
Sir Mortimer Jordan	General Agent
Yabassi	Son of Mahadana and Bundere

www.ingramcontent.com/pod-product-compliance
Lightning Source LLC
Chambersburg PA
CBHW062025170626
46813CB00001B/289